Soon, life would get back to normal....

Tyler would just have to be patient. Ruth loved him with all her heart, but she didn't have the strength right now to look after anybody else. And yet, Ruth knew with her conscious mind that her husband was right. It was necessary to leave the pain behind and get on with life. She just didn't know how to accomplish that goal, and she hated the way Tyler kept pushing her.

I'm not ready, Ruth thought stubbornly, as she crossed the ranch yard and climbed the steps to the veranda. Why couldn't he understand that she...

How long? a cold little voice demanded at the back of her mind. *How long will it take for you to be ready? And will he still be waiting?*

Margot Dalton is acknowledged as the author
of this work.

Special thanks and acknowledgment to
Sutton Press Inc. for its contribution to the concept for
the Crystal Creek series.

ISBN 0-373-82535-8

THE HEART WON'T LIE

Margot Dalton

THE HEART WON'T LIE

Harlequin Books

TORONTO • NEW YORK • LONDON
AMSTERDAM • PARIS • SYDNEY • HAMBURG
STOCKHOLM • ATHENS • TOKYO • MILAN
MADRID • WARSAW • BUDAPEST • AUCKLAND

Dear Reader,

In *Southern Nights,* as a counterpoint to Cynthia McKinney's ongoing struggle to find contentment at the Double C, Margot Dalton presented the riveting tale of Lisa Croft, a young girl who fortuitously landed in Crystal Creek after being buffeted by a disastrous encounter with the seamier side of Las Vegas. It was a wonderful story of "young love and love strengthened," according to the reviewers, with "something for everyone." Now, in the twenty-third volume of the Crystal Creek series, Ms. Dalton continues Lisa's story—her romance with Tony, the young veterinary assistant, and her moving conflict with her family. And those of you who have come to love Ruth and Tyler McKinney will have to wait no longer to see how they handle the blows life's dealt them. You won't be disappointed—but get out your hankies!

Next month, Bethany Campbell has devised a dramatic whirlwind of a conclusion to the Crystal Creek series. Her heroine is Beverly Townsend, her hero is a man the likes of which Crystal Creek has never seen, and readers visiting Crystal Creek for *Lone Star State of Mind* are advised to hang on to their hats!

Marsha Zinberg
Senior Editor and
Editorial Coordinator
Crystal Creek

A Note from the Author

It's not unusual for a writer to have an attack of the blues when a book is completed. After all, a story that may be read in a few hours takes many months to create, and during that time the characters become intensely real and vivid in the writer's mind. So you can imagine how I feel after completing *seven* books set in Crystal Creek! I've grown to love all these people. Their quirks and foibles, hopes and fears and dreams, are as real to me as my own. I can hardly bear to say goodbye to them all. In fact, I keep hoping that perhaps we'll check back on them a few years from now to see what's been happening in Crystal Creek. What do you think, readers? Maybe, with the bumper crop of babies that's recently arrived in town, we could do a whole new series of books exploring the lives and loves of the *next* generation.

Margot Dalton

Who's Who in Crystal Creek

Have you missed the story of one of your favorite Crystal Creek characters? Here's a quick guide to help you easily locate the titles and story lines:

Available at your local bookseller, or see the Crystal Creek back-page ad for reorder information.

CHAPTER ONE

THE BABY BEGAN to cry sometime after midnight, his plaintive sobs wailing and echoing in the wintry stillness. Ruth McKinney woke with a start and lay trembling in the darkness.

It wasn't her baby. The lonely sobbing wasn't a baby at all. It was just the wind, or some night bird screaming in the distant hills.

Ruth's baby was dead.

She clenched her fists and struggled to bring her breathing under control, forcing herself to deal with reality. Ruth had found that it was hardest to face the truth on nights like this, when she woke in the small hours of the morning and thought she heard a baby crying.

Those were the times when she longed to hold her child, when the emptiness of her body and her life seemed almost unendurable. In the daytime she could busy herself with endless work, and surround herself with people if she needed company. But in the darkness of the winter night, her hollow sense of loss was almost more than she could bear.

Sleep would be impossible now, she realized with a sigh. Ruth slipped from the bed, careful not to wake

Tyler who slept soundly next to her. She padded across the room, belted her housecoat around her waist and searched for her slippers, then let herself quietly out of the bedroom and hurried through the house to the kitchen.

Their new home was almost completed now, except for some ceramic tiles that still waited to be installed in one of the guest bathrooms, and Tyler's study on the lower floor, which wasn't yet paneled and floored with hardwood. They'd built the house into the hillside, so that both levels were flooded with light and commanded a sweeping view of the valley and the hills beyond.

Ruth had loved everything about their house, right from the start. She'd enjoyed the feeling of being perched high in the air like an eagle's nest, looking down over the rolling vineyards and the sprawl of buildings at the Double C. And she'd loved the sunny spacious rooms, decorated in the muted earth tones that she and Tyler preferred.

But that was before...

Ruth shook herself impatiently and crossed the room to make a cup of cocoa in the microwave.

There was no reason she shouldn't still love the house. Nothing had changed in her tastes or her lifestyle choices. They'd lost a child, that's all. It happened to all kinds of people. In fact, the doctor back home in the Napa Valley had given her a list of organizations that dealt with this kind of pain, where people shared the experience and gave comfort to one another.

But Ruth couldn't imagine herself joining a group like that. It was bad enough that she was still suffering so much. She couldn't bear the anguish of talking with others about her loss. It was just something that had to be endured, she told herself, and soon it would start to heal.

Everybody said that time was a great healer.

In the meantime, Ruth didn't speak of her feelings to anybody, not even close friends or the sympathetic family members who hovered around her, waiting for an invitation to pour out their love and comfort.

Not even Tyler... Ruth frowned and sipped her cocoa, standing near the counter and staring in brooding silence at the bleakness of the winter sky beyond the window. The wind was rising steadily now, howling and sobbing around the eaves of the house. Probably it was the sound that had awakened her.

She shivered, pulling her housecoat more snugly around her body. She'd always hated winter, though January wasn't as bad here in Texas as it was back home in California, with all that dreary rain.

If it weren't for the dark winter rains, Tyler probably couldn't have convinced Ruth to come back to the Hill Country so soon. She'd been so much more contented back there in her father's house, where there were no reminders of her married life and the child she'd lost. Here at the ranch, there were reminders at every turn.

Ruth rinsed her cocoa mug in the sink and went back through the silent house, pausing involuntarily outside one of the smaller bedrooms. At last, taking a deep breath, she pushed the door open and slipped cautiously inside.

Tyler had practically emptied the room while she was away, and Ruth never asked him where the contents were. All the little white cotton shirts, the clean stacks of flannelette diapers, the tiny socks and cuddly terry-cloth sleepers that had filled the bureau drawers were gone when they'd come back from California.

Probably Tyler and Cynthia had stored them over at the big house, where they wouldn't cause pain for Ruth. Everybody had been so kind to her. Ruth thought about their kindness as she sank down in the big rocking chair that still sat near the window. The chair and the bureau were the only pieces of furniture left in the room. Everything that looked like baby equipment had vanished along with the clothes—the changing table and crib and diaper pail, even the stuffed toys and whimsical mobiles that she and Tyler had selected.

Ruth appreciated the tact of the gesture, but sometimes she wished they'd left something behind. Maybe a couple of the big fuzzy rabbits in their denim overalls, or the lamp with its base shaped like a woolly lamb...

Of course, Ruth could ask for some of the baby things to be restored to the room, and then it wouldn't look so bare and desolate. Nobody would mind if she asked. But her request would initiate a dialogue, the kind of conversation that she dreaded, so she never spoke of the missing items. She didn't want anyone to know that whenever she came into this room, Ruth longed for it to be the way it was before, in the months when they were waiting with such eagerness for their baby to arrive.

Once, when Tyler was busy down in the vineyards and she was alone in the house, she'd even started a breathless, frightened search through the attic and the storage cupboards, looking frantically for the missing clothes and baby equipment, all the time wondering how she'd deal with the shock of seeing them again.

But she didn't find anything.

Ruth sighed and got up from the rocking chair. She paused by the window, looking down at the distant glow of lights in the big ranch yard below theirs, then let the curtain drop and wandered down the hall to the master bedroom.

Tyler still slept, worn out from the hard physical work he was doing every day. They were setting out additional vine stock, taking advantage of the cool weather to get thousands of dormant stalks safely transplanted, and every one had to be placed carefully by hand.

Normally Ruth would have loved the job, working beside Tyler on the windy hillside. These days, though, she rarely went down to the vineyard. She just felt so tired of everything.

The only activity she really enjoyed was going over to the Double C to help Lisa with her wedding preparations. There was little more than a month until the Valentine's Day wedding. They were making the bridesmaids' dresses now for Lynn and Ruth, and a little gown for Jennifer, who was too young to be flower girl but whom Lisa wanted in the wedding party just the same.

It was fun, sewing on the bright silky fabrics and chatting with Lisa and Virginia about everyday things that had nothing to do with pain and sorrow.

Tyler stirred when she edged into the bed beside him. He rolled over and put his arms around her, burrowing into her shoulder with a muffled, sleepy whisper.

Ruth pushed at him gently but he held on, moving against her with growing urgency. He wore just a T-shirt, and she could tell that although he was only partly awake, his body was fully aroused.

Probably he'd been dreaming, too, Ruth thought with a sad smile. But his dreams were clearly of a different sort than hers.

"Love you," he muttered against her throat, his face warm with passion. "Love you, love you. C'mere, honey. Come an' let me...."

"Tyler," she whispered, trying to edge away from him. "Tyler, please wake up. We can't do this. It's too soon since..."

"C'mon," he muttered, either ignoring her words or not hearing her at all. "Dying for you, girl. Please, please..."

Tyler climbed onto his wife and tried to thrust himself against her, his lean, muscular body heavy and powerful above hers. His mouth roamed hungrily over her face, her shoulders and breasts, while he continued to murmur broken endearments.

Ruth realized that he was still barely awake, and that the only way she could stop this was to wake him fully and tell him she wasn't interested.

She held herself rigid beneath him, her mind working rapidly as she struggled with her emotions.

No wonder he was so blindly passionate... Ruth couldn't remember the last time they'd made love. During the final months of her pregnancy she felt they had to be so careful, because of her instinct about possible problems. And, of course, she'd been too broken and hurt to contemplate a sexual relationship in the weeks since the accident.

But Nate Pundy had assured her at the last visit that it was safe to make love with her husband again. Probably he'd told Tyler, as well, Ruth thought with a grimace. It seemed that he and the doctor were always having cozy little private chats about her welfare and her state of mind, so Tyler was fully informed. Unless she yielded tonight, there'd likely be a fight.

He'd been the soul of consideration and gentleness at first, but Ruth sensed that Tyler had long since lost patience with their situation. If she rejected his sexual advances without good reason, he'd say something about her coldness and withdrawal, and then she'd accuse him of being unfeeling and selfish. Things would be said that neither of them would forget.

Maybe they should just have their fight and get it over with. After all, those words hung in the air between them all the time these days, unspoken but still powerfully real. Why not express their anger and put it behind them, the way they used to?

But Ruth knew that she wasn't ready to hear what Tyler might say to her, and was even more afraid of how she might answer him. She didn't want to get into that kind of conflict. She needed to maintain her silence and keep her pain to herself until she was stronger.

Finally, with a weary sigh, she yielded and let Tyler have his way, still not sure if he was fully aware of what he was doing. But he was certainly passionate. Of course, they'd always had a lusty, happy sexual relationship, right from the beginning.

"Folks would be amazed, wouldn't they?" Tyler had said to her once after lovemaking. "Everyone thinks we're such cold, button-down types, you and me, Ruthie. They probably wouldn't believe how much fun we have in bed."

"It's none of their business how much fun we have," Ruth had told him, smiling at his look of lazy contentment. "It's nobody's business but our own, darling."

And she'd reached for him again. In those days, there was no way to satisfy her hunger for him. She'd been shameless in her need, even following him out to the vineyard sometimes and making love under the whispering cedars.

The memory of that early passion made her feel sad, for some reason, even though her body was beginning to respond to her husband's urgency, opening softly and yielding to him.

No! Ruth thought in sudden alarm, clenching her jaw and trying to resist. *No, I don't want this! I'm not ready....*

But he was inside her now, moaning softly in pleasure, his eyes still closed as he moved slowly above her. She felt her body responding again, rising and pushing toward her own release, apparently independent of her rebellious thoughts.

At last she shuddered with climax, but there was none of the warmth and sweetness that she remembered, just a brief sense of physical relaxation and then a hollow sadness. Tyler lay above her, heavy and inert, his face buried in her throat.

Ruth shoved at him impatiently.

"Tyler!" she muttered. "Tyler, move over! You're suffocating me."

He grunted and rolled away from her, turning onto his side and falling immediately back into a deep sleep. Ruth knew that if she leaned up on her elbow and looked at him, his long thick eyelashes would be casting a shadow on his tanned cheek, and one of his fists would be tucked under his chin, giving him an appealing little-boy look.

She used to love watching him sleep after lovemaking. She could remember smiling at him, weak with tenderness, still feeling the richness of his love all through her being.

But now it was different. She felt nothing but coldness and self-pity and a strange, random anger that she couldn't understand. But she knew one thing, Ruth thought, as she lay with her hands behind her head and stared up at the ceiling. It was going to be a long time before she felt in the mood to make love again.

A long, long time.

TYLER WOKE in the dim morning light, feeling wonderful. He turned over to smile at his wife, who slept neatly on her side. Her face was turned away from him, her breathing shallow and almost soundless.

People always joked about the way women looked in the early morning, but they'd never lived with Ruth. There was something about her at this hour of the day when she lay sleeping, unaware of his gaze, that almost brought a lump to Tyler's throat. She was so touchingly vulnerable and childlike, her skin like cream dusted with rose petals, her hair tumbled casually around her face. It made him want to protect her and keep pain from ever touching her.

Then, abruptly, Tyler remembered all the pain she'd been through, and how little he'd been able to help. His face darkened with misery.

They'd never discussed the matter of fault and blame. But Tyler couldn't forgive himself for a lot of things . . . letting her walk off alone that night, having too much to drink when he should have been looking after her, his stubbornness in hanging on to that goddamn dog that she'd immediately hated.

If it hadn't been for the dog . . .

With an effort, Tyler forced his thoughts back out of that weary track. He sat up cautiously, taking care not to wake her, and tiptoed across the room to pick up his clothes.

Nate had assured both of them that nothing would have made any difference. It wasn't Ruth's accident and the trauma associated with her early labor that had caused the baby's death. The baby had only had a fifty-fifty chance of survival, no matter what they did.

Tyler needed to believe that. Even more, he needed to be assured that Ruth believed it, too, and that he wasn't to blame for her terrible suffering. Sometimes when he remembered the delicate, flowerlike face of his dead son, it was almost more than he could bear. Ruth hadn't been shown the baby, but Tyler had seen him.

He wished he could tell Ruth that he'd seen their child, that he'd been such a perfectly formed, beautiful little baby.

But they didn't talk much about anything these days. And they never discussed the baby or the bad time after Ruth's accident.

Tyler paused by the bed, wearing his jeans and carrying his boots and shirt. He looked down at Ruth's sleeping face, recalling the night before. No wonder he'd felt so good when he woke up this morning.

It was a pity that he'd been only partly awake through that little episode, Tyler thought with a fleeting grin. But if he hadn't been mostly sleepwalking, he'd probably never have had the nerve to approach her, even though Nate had assured him that it was all right.

"What you two need," Nate had said comfortably, "is to get back together and make another baby. She'll be fine once that happens, Tyler. A man and a woman need to stay real close in these tough times. That's what nature intended."

Tyler understood that the doctor's homely wisdom was probably right, but he didn't know how to deal with Ruth's silence and withdrawal. Even a good, riproaring fight would probably be a relief. It would clear the air, give her a chance to say the things she was thinking and get them out in the open. But they didn't fight, either. They just skated around the edges of the thin ice in their marriage, treated each other with a sort of distant courtesy and kept their feelings to themselves.

Maybe it would be different from now on, Tyler thought wistfully as he looked at his wife. Now that she'd finally allowed him to hold her again, maybe Ruth would start to warm up toward him, and let him back into her heart as well.

Lord, I hope so, he thought, creeping out of the bedroom toward his little dressing room. *I sure hope so, because I'm getting so goddamn lonesome, I hardly know what to do with myself....*

He ran down the stairs a few minutes later, fully dressed, and paused in the kitchen to make a cup of instant coffee and grab a couple of banana muffins from the tin in the cupboard.

He ate leaning against the counter, gulping his coffee and spreading the muffins liberally with butter before eating them. It might be hours before he ate again. Ruth used to get up and cook him a hot breakfast, calling him up from the vineyard about eight o'clock to eat with her. Often they'd go upstairs and make love before he went back outside.

But those days were long gone, Tyler thought grimly. Lately she'd been sleeping so little at night that she sometimes stayed in bed until nine or ten, then got up and picked at some fruit or a cracker or something. She seemed to have no appetite at all, and he was worried by her thin, fragile look.

The only thing she enjoyed was going over to the Double C to work on the preparations for that damned wedding.

Tyler grimaced. He hated fancy social occasions, because he always felt awkward about dressing up and standing around with a cocktail glass in his hand. In this case, though, he encouraged Ruth's interest because it was good to find something that occupied her mind, especially something that got her out with other people. The last thing she needed right now was to sit around by herself in the house.

His gloomy thoughts about his wife were interrupted suddenly when a small figure appeared down in the vineyards, moving briskly through the cold winter mists of early morning.

Tyler grinned cheerfully through the window, took a last hasty bite of muffin and bolted for the door, grabbing his jacket as he ran.

"Hey, Frankie!" he called, nearing the solitary figure among the trellised vines. "You're sure early. Don't you ever sleep, kid?"

"Not half the day, like *some* people," she rejoined with a teasing grin, her hands already dirt-smeared as she lifted a stalk into place.

Tyler smiled back at her, suddenly feeling much better. Frances Switzer was a college student from Austin, majoring in botany and specializing in vine culture. Tyler had hired her to help with the new plants when it became clear that Ruth was going to be either unable or unwilling to commit much of her time to the vineyard. Frankie, on the other hand, was delighted at the opportunity. She was using her semester break to work at the Double C winery and would probably miss the first couple of weeks of classes, as well. But, she assured Tyler, it was well worth her while. She was gaining more valuable experience than she'd ever get in a classroom, and earning good money at the same time.

Frankie Switzer's family had lived in the Hill Country for five generations, and she had the blond good looks of her German forebears. Her body was small and boyishly compact, much like Ruth's, but her coloring was different. Ruth had creamy skin and dark hair and eyes, while Frankie's eyes were cornflower blue, her short tousled hair as bright as spun gold.

If she'd been the dress-up type, Tyler often thought, the kid could probably have made herself into a real little Barbie doll. But there was nothing coquettish or artificial about Frankie Switzer. She was as straightforward and bluntly honest as a child, with an offhand tomboy nature that belied her feminine prettiness.

She lived in the guest house at the Double C, ate some of her meals at the big ranch house and some with Ruth and Tyler, and was treated like family at both places. She and Tyler worked together cheerfully at the backbreaking work of transplanting the vines, wrangling amiably over trivial things or talking about their lives, their various interests and, most of all, their shared passion for grapevines.

"Well, you're sure looking chipper this morning," Frankie observed, pausing to lift her baseball cap and scrub her denim jacket sleeve across her forehead before she moved off down the row of vines. "Must've had a real good sleep."

Tyler glanced at her, feeling awkward all at once. He knew why he looked chipper this morning. In fact, the warmth of sexual release still flooded his body, pulsing rich and strong through his veins and making him feel like a man again after all these lonely months.

But he and Frankie never talked about sexual matters, even in teasing. There was something quaintly old-fashioned about the girl, a kind of reserve and privacy that made men hesitate to be too free around her. Tyler, who spent his whole day in her company, had never approached any kind of familiarity with her. He didn't say anything to Frankie that he couldn't have said to his sister, Lynn, with equal comfort.

The truth was, Frankie felt like a sister to him, and Tyler probably found her comforting for that very reason. He realized that he must have been missing Lynn, too, these past couple of years when their lives were changing so rapidly. There'd been a time when he and his sister were good friends, with a close, confiding relationship. Now, he hardly saw Lynn anymore.

Everything in his world was so different....

"Yeah," he said at last, hauling a heavy wooden flat of little vine stalks into position. "I had a real good sleep, Frankie. How about you?"

She grimaced and bent to lift one of the dried plants, cradling the ball of soil around its roots. "I didn't get to bed as early as I usually do. I went to the movies with Joey Wall."

"The druggist's kid? I thought he was away at college."

"He is. He's going to A&M on a football scholarship."

"So what's he doing back here in Crystal Creek, keeping my right-hand man out too late at night?"

"It's *semester break,* Tyler," she told him with a pitying glance. "Remember? That's why I'm here."

He grinned. "Right. I keep forgetting. You look so at home here in the vineyard that it's like you were always here."

Her face clouded briefly and she bent to dig the little plant into the soil, plying her trowel busily. The peak of her baseball cap shadowed her expression, making Tyler wonder if he'd imagined that sudden look of tension.

"So, how was it?" he asked.

"How was what?"

"Your date with Joey Wall."

Frankie shrugged. "It was okay. The movie was really lame, though. It was one of those bang-bang-you're-dead things, with this incredibly macho guy fighting his way single-handedly through five continents and a couple of armies of bad guys. I wonder," Frankie added reflectively, leaning back on her heels, "why men like that crap. It has to be some strange kind of male fantasy."

"Women like those macho guys, too," Tyler argued. "They drool over their muscles."

"That's not true. Women hate that stuff," Frankie said with decision. "They recognize instinctively that it's a guy-type fantasy, and it worries them."

Tyler looked down at her as she worked, intrigued as he often was by the girl's observations. "Worries them? Why?"

"They don't like to think their men are dreaming about stuff like that. A woman would prefer to believe her man was dreaming about *her*."

Tyler chuckled. "You, too, Frankie?" he asked with a teasing grin. "Do you want your man to spend all his time dreaming about you?"

"I don't have a man," she said briskly, moving off along the row of trellises.

Tyler followed her in silence, staring thoughtfully at her slim, erect form.

The wind picked up again as they worked, howling down the rocky hillside, tugging at their clothes and chilling them as soon as they stopped moving. They were both covered with mud, damp from the sprays of water that were directed onto each row of vines after planting, and smelling pungently from the liquid manure that Tyler spread in the freshly dug trenches.

"This new hybrid should be great," he said with enthusiasm, examining a spindly vine in its ball of dirt while Frankie bent opposite him, raking the soil with her callused hands. "Shouldn't it, Frankie?"

"I hope so. The initial studies look good, anyhow." She grinned up at him, her blue eyes sparkling beneath the cap. "You've spent enough money on them, Tyler. What if they're not as great as you think, and you've already committed five whole acres to them?"

Tyler chuckled. "You sound just like my wife."

"Speaking of whom," Frankie said mildly, "here she is. Hi, Ruth."

"Hi, Frankie. How's it going?"

"Great," the girl said. "Tyler's not quite as lazy as usual. He says he had a good sleep last night."

Tyler exchanged a glance with Ruth, who stood nearby in jeans and a warm, down-filled jacket of bright cherry red that made her pale complexion glow and brought out the highlights in her dark hair.

He wondered as their eyes met if she, too, was thinking about last night, recalling those moments of blinding passion and sweetness that still made him shiver with pleasure when he looked at her.

But she glanced away after an awkward moment, turning back to Frankie, who had straightened and was smiling cheerfully at the boss's wife. Frankie was always pleasant to Ruth, treating her with a respect and gentle sympathy that she didn't show other people. It was one of the things that Tyler liked best about the girl, the way she behaved with Ruth.

And Ruth responded to their young employee with a warmth she often seemed unable to summon anymore. Frankie even made her laugh, made her eyes sparkle and glow sometimes with a welcome touch of her old humor.

"How many more do you have to plant?" Ruth asked finally, ignoring the girl's reference to the previous night.

"About a dozen more flats in this section," Tyler said. "See, Ruthie, this is the new hybrid stock I was telling you about. They look real good, don't they?"

Tyler held out the dried bit of vine with a hopeful feeling of expectancy, but Ruth merely glanced at it and nodded absently. "I guess they'll be all right. Will you two be coming up for lunch?"

"Lettie Mae said we should all come down to the big house for lunch," Frankie said. "She's serving left-over barbecue from last night, and she thought you'd probably be down there, too, Ruth."

"You're right, I think she mentioned something about that yesterday. As a matter of fact, I'm on my way down now."

"Still working on all that dumb wedding stuff?" Frankie asked.

"We have to keep working. The wedding's just a little more than five weeks away. There's so much to do, I don't know how we'll ever manage."

"That's easy," Frankie said with a wicked smile. "Give Tony a ladder and a hundred bucks, and let Lisa buy some new jeans. What more do they need?"

Ruth smiled at the girl's scornful tone. "Wait till it's your turn, Frankie. You'll have a whole different outlook when you're the one getting married."

"If I ever get married," Frankie said, "it'll be a wedding like Vern and Carolyn had. Just the two of us in the courthouse, and the janitor and the court clerk for witnesses."

"Did Carolyn have the janitor and the court clerk for witnesses?" Tyler asked with a grin.

"Of course not," Ruth told him. "She had Brock and Lori, remember? Brock was Vern's best man, and Lori was Carolyn's maid of honor."

"Maid of honor!" Frankie scoffed in derision, tugging at her cap and turning away to reach for another vine.

Tyler smiled at Ruth while the girl's back was turned. But there was no answering twinkle in his wife's eyes, as there would have been a few months ago. Her glance was calm and remote, chilling him more deeply than a look of outright anger.

"Well, I guess I'll see you at lunch," she said at last, hesitating near the row of trellises.

"Sure," Tyler said casually, aching with loneliness and disappointment. "Better get going, Ruth, before you catch a chill. That wind is pretty cool this morning."

He watched her face, longing for some kind of private sign that she recalled their lovemaking. Even if she'd say something about the job he was doing, about the new plants or the progress of the vineyard, Tyler would be happy.

But she lingered silently for a few moments longer, hands plunged deep in her jacket pockets, the wind lifting and tumbling her hair around her face. Finally she turned and hurried off down the hillside in the direction of the ranch buildings.

Tyler stood and watched her, keeping his eyes on her vanishing figure until she was nothing more than a bright splash of red against the sere brown of the hills.

CHAPTER TWO

"LOOK AT THIS DRESS! It's hopeless, girls. I'll never fit into this. It's like trying to squeeze a sow into a silk purse."

Cynthia McKinney chuckled at the despair in her stepdaughter's voice, then glanced over at the dainty sheath of blue silk that Lynn was holding up. She pushed her reading glasses up on her forehead, turning aside briefly from the pile of wedding invitations on the desk.

"Of course you will," she said. "It's almost six weeks until the wedding. You'll have your figure back before then. You've hardly lost it, actually. You look wonderful."

Lynn, whose face bloomed with the glow of early motherhood, smiled at the other women in the room. "Isn't she sweet? Thanks, Cynthia. But," she added glumly, "it's not true, you know. I feel as big as a house."

"Oh, for goodness' sake," Lettie Mae said. The cook bit off a length of thread and frowned at the strip of ribbon she was folding. "You just barely came home from the hospital, girl. When my niece Cora had her first, she gained eighty-seven pounds. Poor Cora, she had to wear her maternity clothes for another nine months. And by then, wouldn't you know the silly girl was pregnant again? She never did get out of those maternity clothes, as I recall."

Lisa and Virginia both giggled. Ruth smiled with them. "Cynthia's right, Lynn," she told her sister-in-law. "You really look terrific. My goodness, you're already wearing your jeans again."

"Yeah, but the top button's still undone," Lynn confessed. "I'd be in big trouble if I couldn't wear these baggy sweatshirts."

"Lynn's always been so tiny," Virginia said placidly. "After all, she was a jockey all those years. It's not easy for small women to have babies and keep their figures. You should see Brittany. That's my niece," she added for the benefit of Lisa, who hadn't met all of Virginia's extended family.

"The ballet dancer?" Lettie Mae asked.

Virginia sniffed. "I don't know what that girl's been doing lately, but it's sure not *ballet*."

Ruth smiled and returned to the piece of lace she was hemming, letting the talk and laughter flow comfortably around her.

The women were sitting in the sunroom at the Double C, which had been converted into a temporary workroom and overflowed with lace, silk, flowers, fabric samples and printed invitations.

Jennifer McKinney, aged fourteen months, sat on the floor near her mother's chair, wearing a pink T-shirt and denim overalls. The little girl played solemnly with a pile of fabric scraps and wooden spools, singing to herself under her breath as she lined up the spools on the floor.

It was amazing, Ruth thought, the way everybody had become caught up in the preparations for Lisa's wedding. Of course, Lisa Croft was a favorite with the family and the other staff members here at the ranch. Cynthia, especially, loved the shy, dark-haired girl who took such wonderful care of little Jennifer. To Cynthia's delight, Lisa had agreed to stay at her job after the wedding. She and her new husband, who was one of the veterinarians in Crystal Creek, would be living in a house on Double C property. Lisa would come up to the big house every day to help Cynthia, just as she did now.

"I'm not losing a baby-sitter," J.T. told everybody with a smug grin. "I'm gaining a vet."

"Did you try your dress on, Ruth?" Lisa asked. "Does the bodice fit better now?"

"It's perfect," Ruth assured the girl. "Those darts you put in really did the trick."

"I'll probably have to let mine out even more," Lynn said, examining the dress in her hands. "That's sure one good thing about motherhood," she added with satisfaction. "For the first time in my life, I actually have a bust."

The other women burst into laughter. Ruth bent her head over her work, thinking about the week following her own baby's birth. Her breasts had been so swollen that the pain was hard to endure, and she'd finally allowed Nate Purdy to give her something to take the milk away....

She felt Lynn's eyes resting on her and knew that Lynn was regretting her words, afraid that she might have hurt Ruth with her casual teasing.

This was hard for Lynn, too, Ruth thought with sympathy. Lynn was fully caught up in the excitement and pleasure of young motherhood, but she had to guard her tongue constantly and be careful what she said around Ruth and Tyler. It must be so uncomfortable for Lynn and her husband.

Ruth smiled at her, then held up her own dress for inspection. "I think they're beautiful, don't you, Lynn? We'll look pretty snazzy."

Lynn smiled back gratefully. "We sure will, Ruthie. We'll be knockouts."

Lynn and Ruth were going to be Lisa's attendants, with Manny Hernandez and Tyler as groomsmen. Most of the wedding party, including the bride and groom, had dark hair, and Lisa had chosen an unusual shade for the women's dresses, a soft gray-blue silk almost the color of wood smoke.

"Just because it's going to be on Valentine's Day," she'd told Cynthia, "I don't want everything to be all pink and white. We can have some pink in the bouquets, can't we? That's enough."

Lynn looked at the wisp of silk in Ruth's hands, her face suddenly gloomy. "But they're so *fitted*, Lisa. Can't we wear smocks?" she asked wistfully. "Something with some nice big pleats at the front? Maybe a sort of dressy caftan?''

Virginia glared sternly at Lynn, whom she'd cared for since babyhood. "Now, that's enough of *that* talk, missy. Cynthia's right, there's weeks and weeks till this wedding, and come Valentine's Day, you'll just slide into that dress as smooth as butter. You wait and see."

Lynn hugged the placid woman sitting next to her. "Bless you, Virginia. I wish I had as much faith in me as you always do. But even if I do lose all this flab," she added, patting the small bulge of her abdomen, "how am I going to try the dress on in the meantime? We're not going to have any idea if it fits properly when I can't even get myself into it."

"Let Frankie try it on," Lettie Mae suggested practically, squinting at a little basket she was decorating with flowers, her dark fingers quick and skilfull. "She's about your size, isn't she? I mean," the cook added with a teasing grin as she reached for her scissors, "the size you used to be, child, before you turned into such a mountain."

Lynn made a cheerful face at Lettie Mae, then nodded thoughtfully. "You're right, she is." She turned to her sister-in-law. "Ruthie, are they coming down here for lunch?"

Ruth nodded, frowning in concentration as she tried to thread her needle. "Yes, they are. Frankie says Lettie Mae invited them."

"I sure did," Lettie Mae said briskly. She set the basket aside and got to her feet. "And I'd better get into the kitchen and take that bread out of the oven, or there won't be a blessed thing to eat."

"Lettie Mae's fresh-baked bread," Lynn said with a sigh of bliss. "I can hardly wait."

"That's sure no way to lose weight," Virginia commented. "Eating fresh-baked bread all slathered with butter."

Lynn started to protest, but was interrupted by a muffled wail from the next room.

"Baby," Jennifer observed, lifting her head alertly, her hands full of bright silk ribbons. "Baby!"

"Oh, damn." Lynn sighed, starting to heave herself to her feet. "*Now* what? I just put him down a few minutes ago. He was full as a tick."

"Don't get up, Lynn. I'll go," Ruth said. She put her dress aside and hurried from the room, conscious of the other women's eyes resting on her with sympathy as she left. Sometimes Ruth didn't know what was hardest to bear, her own loss, or the heartbreaking kindness and understanding of others. Often it was enough to bring tears to her eyes, thinking about how loving and deeply concerned all of them were.

But there was nothing they could do. Nothing at all . . .

She slipped into the dining room and tiptoed over to the folding bed that stood under the windows. Lynn and Sam Russell's new baby lay on his stomach partially covered by a mound of blankets, his cheek flattened against the soft flannel sheet and his tiny rump lifted into the air. He wore a fluffy white terry-cloth sleeper with pale blue horses trimming the collar and cuffs.

Ruth bent over the baby, loving the warm, milky smell of him, the softness of his downy head, the look of his hands curled like pink flowers against the crib sheet. He screwed up his eyes and yelled, struggling to raise his head, his body writhing with agitation.

"Now, what's all this?" Ruth whispered, lifting the baby in her arms. She sat down on one of the dining room chairs, cradling him tenderly in her arms. "What's all this fuss? Your mama says you just had a big meal, little man. She says you're full, so why are you fussing?"

The baby's eyes widened when her heard Ruth's voice. He paused in the middle of another full-throated bellow to gaze at her solemnly, blinking in surprise.

"Well, hello there. How are you?" Ruth murmured, smiling down at him. "How's our little Mr. Russell? Did you know that you look just like your daddy? I think you're even going to have his gorgeous hair. Yes, you are. Oh, yes you are..."

She kissed his face, rocked and cuddled the warm little body, feeling soothed by the child. For a moment the aching void in her heart was filled and she was at peace. The baby, too, seemed comforted by her attentions, until suddenly he stiffened and went rigid in her arms, then opened his mouth to yell again.

"I think you've got gas pains, sweetheart," Ruth told him, setting him upright on her knee and rubbing his back with a gentle hand. "I think that's the problem. Let's see if we can help."

The baby's head lolled forward, his blue eyes bulged and his arms flailed as Ruth continued to caress his back. At last he belched, a surprisingly explosive sound to come from such a diminutive person.

Ruth chuckled and hugged him.

"There," she whispered. "That's better, isn't it? Now you can go to sleep. We'll tuck you in here and you can go right to sleep, and give your poor mama a little peace and quiet."

But she continued to hold him, kissing his soft head and cuddling him, reluctant to part with his warmth and sweetness.

Cynthia appeared in the doorway and stood smiling at them for a moment, then crossed the room and seated herself in a chair nearby, leaning forward to look at the baby's puckered face.

"He had gas pains, poor little fellow," Ruth murmured. "You should have heard him burp, Cynthia. It was practically earth-shaking."

Cynthia laughed softly, touching one of the small pink hands that lay against Ruth's shoulder. "Oh, he's a terrific burper, all right," she said. "I've heard him before."

Ruth smiled over the baby's head at the other woman. "So, do you feel like a grandma now, Cynthia? What relation are you to this baby, actually?"

"Well, I'm married to his grandfather," Cynthia said thoughtfully. "But it's hard to feel like a grandma when I have a little one almost the same age. I guess we're a really mixed-up group in this house."

Finally, reluctantly, Ruth lifted the baby into his bed and settled him on the flannelette sheet, pulling his blankets tenderly up around his shoulders and patting his back a few times.

She looked up to find Cynthia's eyes resting on her.

"Are you all right, Ruth?" Cynthia asked gently. "Is it getting a little better?"

"A little," Ruth murmured, looking down quickly at the baby again, fussing with his blankets so Cynthia couldn't see her face.

"I know it must be hard for you, coming over here and being surrounded by talk of babies and weddings," Cynthia said. "Sometimes I wish we'd all just disappear and quit hurting you."

"If you all disappeared," Ruth said with a shaky laugh, "I'd probably never make it, Cynthia. Since I've been back, it's all that's held me together, the family and the happy things going on over here. This wedding's been a wonderful diversion for me."

"I hoped it was helping a bit. In fact, that's why..."

"What?" Ruth prompted her when she paused.

Cynthia laughed awkwardly. "Partly, that's why J.T. and I got so involved in all of this. Of course, we love Lisa, and we'd want her wedding to be nice regardless of the circumstances, but I also thought a big happy celebration was something we could all use this winter."

"You're both so generous," Ruth said gratefully. "You really are, Cynthia."

The blond woman waved a casual hand. "Generosity doesn't have all that much to do with it. We aren't paying for anything. Lester repaid a small favor to J.T. by donating the use of the country club for the reception, and we're providing the dresses and the flowers, but Tony and Lisa are paying for everything else. Tony insisted on it. He's very old-fashioned."

"They're such a nice couple, aren't they?"

"They sure are." Cynthia grinned briefly. "Although, speaking of being a grandma, I also feel a bit like the mother of the bride. It almost seems there's some kind of conspiracy around here to make me old before my time."

Ruth laughed. "I'm sure that Lisa looks on you and J.T. as surrogate parents."

"I guess she does. She's certainly become part of the household since she arrived."

"Are many of Lisa's family coming to the wedding? They live over in New Mexico, don't they?"

Cynthia's face clouded briefly. "None of them are coming," she said.

Ruth looked up in surprise. "*None* of them? Not even her parents?"

"She just has her mother now, I gather. Her stepfather was killed in a highway accident a few months ago, not long after she arrived here."

"But isn't her mother coming to the wedding?"

Cynthia shook her head, still looking troubled.

"Why not?" Ruth asked. "Is there some kind of problem? I mean, is she sick, or something?"

"I don't think so. Lisa refuses to talk about it with me. You know, it's amazing how a gentle, soft-spoken girl like that can be so stubborn when she chooses. She just says, very quietly, that her mother won't be coming, and that's all she'll ever tell me. Period. End of conversation."

Ruth settled back in her chair, still puzzled by this information. "It seems so strange, doesn't it?" she murmured. "Imagine having your daughter just a few hundred miles away and not going to her wedding. I wonder what the problem is."

"So do I," Cynthia said. "I wonder about it all the time, but I guess it's going to remain a mystery. I certainly can't get anything out of Lisa."

"Maybe I can," Ruth said slowly. "Lisa talks to me quite freely sometimes."

"I know she does. If you could find out anything about this family thing, Ruth, that would be wonderful. It's causing me so much grief, and J.T. keeps saying it's none of my business so I should just leave it alone."

"I'll ask her as soon as I get a chance."

"Very, very tactfully," Cynthia warned. "I wouldn't want her to know I'd been talking about her."

Ruth nodded. "I'll bring up the subject of the wedding, and ask her kind of casually what her mother's going to be wearing, or something like that, and see what she says."

"That would be so good," Cynthia said gratefully. "Do it as soon as you can, Ruth, and tell me what you find out. It bothers me that I'm sending these beautiful invitations and none of them are going to Lisa's family. It doesn't seem right."

"Okay." Ruth looked wistfully at the sleeping baby. "I guess we'd better get back," she said. "It must be lunchtime by now."

"I think it is. Ruth..."

"Yes?"

"I don't know if you're ready," Cynthia began awkwardly, "but we really need to talk some business one of these days. I need your signature on a lot of forms and checks, and we also have to start making some long-term financial decisions. I was wondering if you could..."

Cynthia paused tactfully, and Ruth felt herself stiffen with resistance. She and Cynthia were full legal partners in the Double C winery, with Cynthia in charge of the financial part of the business and Ruth providing the technical expertise.

When Tyler and J.T. had first announced their decision the previous summer to bring their wives into the business on a full and equal footing, Ruth had been overjoyed. Now the responsibility seemed irksome and smothering. She didn't want to think about wine making. She just wanted to think about happy, uncomplicated things, like the ribbons on Lisa's wedding baskets and the little flowered headpiece they were making for baby Jennifer....

"Ruth?"

She pulled herself together and turned to Cynthia, forcing a smile. "All right," she said. "Anytime you say, Cynthia. What do you want to discuss?"

"Well, we've got a lot of quotes on the casks and the big fermenting tanks, but I can't make a decision without some input from you."

"Maybe I can take the quotes home with me, all right?" Ruth offered, feeling another weary pull of reluctance. "I'll check the data and specifications over the next few days and let you know what I think."

Cynthia got up and hugged her before moving toward the door. "Thanks, Ruth. I'm sorry to bother you with this, but I can't hold off any longer. We really need to order some of the equipment and start getting it installed."

"I know." Ruth followed Cynthia from the room, feeling gloomy. She had the same smothering sensation she'd felt earlier in the winter, just after her baby's death, when this big ranch and even its kindly occupants had seemed too much to bear.

Everything was pressing on her, making demands that she couldn't meet. Ruth was still learning to live with her pain, and the effort occupied all of her strength. She wasn't ready to provide the things these people wanted from her.

Especially Tyler.

Ruth thought once again about their lovemaking the previous night. Tyler would probably assume that their marriage was going to continue the same as usual from now on, with all the warmth and intimacy they'd shared before her pregnancy.

Just as if nothing had ever happened...

While she was thinking about him, he appeared suddenly in the hallway, beaming at the two women. "Hi, Ruthie. Hi, Stepmama. What's for lunch?"

"Phew!" Cynthia said, wrinkling her nose. "Nothing, until you wash off a few gallons of that fragrance you're wearing, Tyler McKinney!"

"The finest Double C manure," Tyler said cheerfully. "Better get used to it. Grapevines love it, and we're in the winery business, my girl. All of us," he added, smiling at Ruth.

She smiled back automatically, then turned toward the sunroom to pick up her sweater. Cynthia followed her as Tyler strode off down the hall to the bathroom, singing a few lines of a cowboy love ballad in his pleasant baritone.

"Well, well. Isn't *he* in a good mood today?" Cynthia commented, watching his tall form disappearing around a corner. "Ruthie, what have you been doing to your husband?"

"Nothing much," Ruth said, more shortly than she intended. She took her sweater from the chair she'd been sitting in, then smiled to soften her words. "He loves planting those grapevines, that's all. He's like a little kid playing in the mud."

"So's Frankie," Lisa volunteered, lifting Jennifer onto her knee and cuddling the child fondly. "Look at her."

All eyes turned to Frankie, who lounged in the doorway, grinning at the assembled women. Tyler's assistant had already cleaned up to some extent, scrubbing her hands, face and forearms until they glowed with pinkness and good health. But her jeans were mud-stained and damp, and, like Tyler's, still faintly redolent of the potent Double C fertilizer that was being used on the new grapevines.

Jennifer wrinkled her dainty nose as Frankie moved closer. "Poo!" she muttered. "Yucky!"

Frankie laughed, her pretty face animated with mischief. "Oh, is that so, Princess?" she asked the little girl. "Well, let me tell you, this isn't a patch on the way *you* smell sometimes, kid. Just ask anyone."

Jennifer gave her a lofty glance of dismissal. "Poo," she repeated, scrambling off Lisa's knee to pick up her wooden spools.

Frankie grinned at the others in the room, then turned to Lisa with a teasing glance. "So, how's it going, Lisa? Have you changed your mind yet? It's not too late, you know."

Lisa laughed, and Ruth was startled once again by how lovely the girl was. None of them knew a whole lot about Lisa's background, although Ruth sometimes suspected that a few of the men in the family, like her husband and J.T., had more information than they let on. All she knew was that someone dangerous had somehow followed Lisa to Crystal Creek last summer, posed a threat to her and then vanished abruptly, leaving the Double C's new nanny as happy and carefree as little Jennifer.

Ruth supposed that if she pressed Tyler, she could make him reveal what he knew about Lisa and all the mysteries that had surrounded her arrival. But Ruth was reluctant to do that, even a little afraid of what she might learn. It was better to enjoy Lisa as she was now, her face glowing with happiness, her dark eyes shining, her glossy cloud of black hair littered with bits of flowers and lace and sewing scraps from the things they were constantly fitting onto her slender body.

Lisa was radiantly happy, and so much in love with her handsome young Tony that she seemed almost ethereal, like a rainbow or a mirage, something that might rise and vanish into the distance, carried off by its own intense beauty.

Ruth thought about the disturbing things Cynthia had just told her about Lisa's family. The girl was so gentle and shy, so thoughtful and concerned with the welfare of everyone around her, that Ruth couldn't imagine Lisa Croft being bitter or vindictive. It was really impossible to picture Lisa deliberately hurting someone close to her.

Especially her own mother...

But that, apparently, was the situation. Unless it was the other way around, Ruth thought suddenly, watching as Frankie knelt on the floor, teasing Jennifer with a few pieces of the bright ribbon. Jennifer soon became absorbed in the game and forgot her objection to Frankie's smell. She chortled with delight as the ribbons appeared and vanished magically in Frankie's callused hands.

Maybe Lisa's mother was a cold and selfish woman. Maybe she felt Lisa was marrying beneath her, or was envious of her daughter's good fortune. All kinds of strange things happened in families. But it was painful to think of Lisa being hurt like that, especially on the very day that meant so much to her.

"Hey, Frankie," Lynn was saying. "Quit tormenting that poor child and do me a favor, okay?"

"Sure," the girl said amiably, getting to her feet with a final smile at Jennifer. "What do you want, Lynn?"

"Try my dress on for me."

"*That* dress?" Frankie stared in horror at the wisp of silk in Lynn's hands.

"Would you, Frankie?" Lynn pleaded. "Come on, how often have I ever asked you for favors? All you have to do is go into the other room, slip it on and come back in here for a minute so we can check the darts and the waistline. Please, Frankie? Pretty please?"

Frankie hesitated, still looking dubiously at the bridesmaid's gown. "Why me?" she asked. "Can't somebody else try it on for you?"

"Nobody else is small enough to get into it. You and I are the only ones."

"So," Frankie said reasonably, "why can't *you* do it, if it's your dress?"

Lynn rubbed her stomach through the heavy fabric of her sweatshirt with an eloquent look of despair. "A month," she said. "I've got a month to get rid of all this flab, Frankie. In the meantime, I need to know if the dress fits and hangs properly."

Frankie continued to hesitate, looking more and more uncomfortable.

"Come on, Frankie," Cynthia said from across the room, bending to lift Jennifer into her arms. "Try the dress on. It won't take but a minute, and nobody will be around but us."

Frankie glanced at the women in the room, at Lynn's eager face and Cynthia's gentle smile, Ruth's encouraging nod and Virginia's look of quiet affection.

"Oh, all right," she said finally, taking the dress and holding it gingerly away from her clothes to protect the silky fabric. She grimaced, then headed with deep reluctance for the other room. "But only for a minute," she warned darkly as she paused to glare at them through the partly opened door. "You all better believe that I'm not gonna be parading through the house in this ridiculous getup."

"Careful when you pull it on over your head," Lynn called, ignoring these grim warnings. "Virginia's just got it lightly basted in a few places until we can check the fit."

"Yeah, yeah," Frankie's voice came back, muffled and annoyed. "I can feel the pins.... *Ow!* Dammit, that *hurts....*"

The women exchanged smiling glances.

"I wonder how she'll look," Virginia murmured. "You know, I don't believe I've ever once seen Frankie Switzer in a dress. Not that I can recall, anyhow."

"I think she'll be beautiful," Cynthia said softly, waiting by the door with her baby on her hip. "Frankie has such lovely coloring, and really good bones. Amanda's been trying for months to get hold of her and dress her up, but Frankie just laughs. She's not the least bit interested."

"Who's not interested?" Tyler asked, strolling back into the room, pausing near the doorway to drop an arm around his wife's shoulders. He was freshly scrubbed and had clearly tried to appease Cynthia by dashing on a few splashes of the after-shave that J.T. kept in the downstairs bathroom. He looked, Ruth thought, almost heartbreakingly handsome.

She turned away and stood quietly in his casual embrace, sharply conscious of his nearness and of her own irrational urge to escape, to break loose and run away so he couldn't touch her again.

"Frankie's trying on my bridesmaid's dress," Lynn told her brother.

"Oh. And why's that?" Tyler asked, cocking a teasing eyebrow at her.

"Because I can't get into it, you idiot, and you know it perfectly well. But Virginia has absolute confidence that by Valentine's Day, I'll be the same size as Frankie again.''

''You should come out and work with me in the vineyards like Frankie does,'' Tyler suggested, giving Ruth's shoulder another fond hug as he grinned at his sister. ''That'd sure get you back in shape in a hurry, kid.''

Lynn looked thoughtful. ''That's not such a bad idea, you know? If I could just find a baby-sitter...''

Tyler waved his hand in an expansive gesture. ''Hell, this room's full of baby-sitters. I don't think that's a problem.''

Lynn was still considering his suggestion when the door opened and Frankie stepped back into the room, looking shyly at Lynn.

''So, how is it?'' she asked. ''Is there anything you need to change? Hurry up, so I can get back into my jeans.''

Lynn got slowly to her feet, gazing in awe at the girl. Everyone else in the room stared at her as well.

Frankie Switzer was utterly transformed. Gone was the ragged, good-humored tomboy that all of them were used to seeing. In her place stood a graceful, poised young woman, her shapely figure outlined by the delicate fabric. Her shoulders were bare and gleaming above the sheath of silk that dropped all the way to the floor, just covering her bare feet. Her pale gold hair shimmered brightly in the midday light and her skin glowed with a pearl-tinted radiance. Highlighted by the smoky-blue fabric, Frankie's eyes looked enormous, and so dark that they were almost violet.

Ruth felt Tyler stiffen beside her, felt his hand grip her shoulder so tightly that it hurt. She looked up at him, startled by the intensity of his dark face and the way his eyes were blazing.

"My God," Tyler breathed in awe, staring at the slender girl. "Frankie, look at you!"

Frankie jerked her head up when she heard his voice.

"Tyler?" she whispered, her face draining of color as she stared at the group near the doorway. "I didn't ... I didn't know you were here."

Abruptly she covered her face with her hands, then turned and fled in a whirl of silk, leaving Lynn to run after her into the other room.

"Frankie?" they heard Lynn calling. "Frankie Switzer, don't you dare take that dress off yet! I didn't even get a chance to..."

"Poor Frankie," Cynthia commented, breaking the awkward little silence that had fallen in the room. "I guess she wasn't expecting quite such a big audience."

Tyler still stood with his arm around Ruth's shoulder, gazing at the door where the girl had vanished. He looked stunned, bemused and a little troubled.

"I hope I didn't embarrass the kid," he said at last, with a shaky laugh. "God, what a knockout. I had no idea she could look like that."

Ruth felt a sudden chill, as if a shadow had crossed the sun. She glanced up at him again, but Tyler's equilibrium was fully restored by now, and he seemed as composed as ever. "Well, now, if Lynn's here," he said, smiling cheerfully at the women in the room, "I guess His Lordship can't be very far away. Where are you hiding him, Cynthia?"

"He's in the dining room."

"Then I reckon I'll go have a little visit with my nephew. Coming, Ruthie?"

"He's asleep," Ruth said.

"Can't hurt to look at him," Tyler coaxed. "Come on, honey."

When Ruth didn't move, he finally crossed the floor by himself, heading for the dining room. Ruth slipped down the hall a few minutes later and saw him kneeling by the folding bed, gazing at Lynn's baby son.

Something in Tyler's dark face, in the gentle line of his mouth and the hungry tenderness of his eyes as he looked at the sleeping baby, brought a painful lump to Ruth's throat. She had to hurry away before she burst into tears.

Frankie sat at the big oak table in the kitchen, quiet and subdued as the merry lunchtime conversation flowed around her. Ruth glanced nervously at the girl across the table, still chilled by that brief moment in the other room when she'd felt her whole world sliding briefly into a shadowy place where unknown terrors lurked in the darkness.

But that was ridiculous, Ruth told herself firmly. Tyler and Frankie were like brother and sister. He treated the girl exactly the same way he treated Lynn. Besides, Frankie had to be at least fifteen years younger than Tyler. She was just a child, really.

But somehow Ruth couldn't get that image out of her mind, the way Tyler's eyes had blazed as he stared at Frankie's slim body, her bare white shoulders and dainty bosom.

As if she didn't already have enough to make her miserable, Ruth thought with a sad little grimace. Now she was having jealous fantasies about her husband, as well, and he'd never done a single thing in their entire relationship to give her any cause for jealousy.

Tyler was the most faithful husband in the world.

In fact, it was a bit of joke in local circles, the intense loyalty of the McKinney men. They might be wild and free before they committed themselves, but once they chose a partner, they were mated for life. Even old Hank Travis, despite his colorful and irreverent personality, had prided himself on being a one-woman man to the end of his days.

Tyler, next to her, seemed conscious as well of Frankie's discomfort, and determined to set his young helper at ease by treating her as if nothing untoward had happened.

"Did you all know that Frankie went to the movies last night with the druggist's son?" he announced to the table at large. "Virginia, could you pass the butter, please?"

"Is Joey home right now?" Lettie Mae asked.

Frankie nodded, keeping her eyes fixed on her plate.

"Now *that's* a handsome child," Lettie Mae commented with a sigh. "I do love a man with big broad shoulders and a nice tight little butt."

"Why, Lettie Mae!" J.T. said, pretending to be shocked as the kitchen erupted into laughter. "Such language at my table."

"Men have talked that way about women since time began," Lettie Mae said serenely. "Now we start doing it, and you men are all upset. Why do you think women like watching baseball?"

"Well, now, I don't know," J.T. said with a grin. "Why do they, Lettie Mae?"

"Because of the way those boys look from behind in their tight pants," Lettie Mae told him. "That's why. Isn't it, girls?"

"Personally," Virginia said solemnly, "I enjoy the subtle science of the game. But," she added with a faraway smile, "if they insist on wearing the tight pants besides, I likely won't complain."

"Subtle science of the game!" Lynn scoffed, gazing with longing at the stack of fresh bread slices in the middle of the table. "You're just terrible, both of you."

Tyler buttered his bread carefully. "Frankie told me this morning that women don't get excited about those muscle men in the movies. She says she's not all that fond of Rambo types."

"Aren't you, Frankie?" Cynthia asked, smiling at her. "What kind of man do you find attractive?"

Frankie shifted in her chair when the others turned to her, waiting for her answer. "Oh, I don't know," she said awkwardly. "I guess... I guess I like more sensitive guys. The ones who think with their heads, not their biceps."

"How about Joey Wall?" J.T. asked, reaching over to pat Jennifer's plump cheek. "Does he think with his biceps, Frankie? Or is he a sensitive guy?"

"You all quit teasing Frankie," Lisa said firmly, surprising everybody.

Lisa was so shy that she usually kept silent during these rowdy conversations, smiling from one face to another and enjoying the vigorous exchange but seldom contributing to it.

"I remember when I first started going out with Tony," she added softly, blushing a little when she realized they were all looking at her. "It was really embarrassing when you all teased me about him all the time because I never knew what to say. So you just leave Frankie alone."

"Thanks, Lisa," Frankie murmured with a flash of her old sparkle. "That's telling 'em."

Lisa smiled and subsided, looking flustered. She reached over just in time to catch little Jennifer, who'd begun to nod off in her high chair, clutching a curved spoon that she almost poked into her eye.

"Come on, little lady," Lisa murmured. "Nap time for you."

Ruth excused herself and followed Lisa from the room, taking the sleepy child from her as Lisa paused to gather up a blanket and teddy bear from the sunroom. Then they went up the stairs together to the nursery, Ruth still cradling Jennifer in her arms.

"She's so sweet, isn't she?" Lisa murmured. She took the baby from Ruth and laid her down in the crib, changed Jennifer's diaper expertly and washed the little girl's hands and face before covering her and tucking the teddy in next to her.

"You're so good with her," Ruth murmured. "I guess you had lot of practice with your little brothers, didn't you, Lisa?"

"I sure did," Lisa said quietly. She drew the blind, casting the room into shadow, and came back toward Ruth, who moved with her out into the hallway.

"Are your brothers pretty excited about the wedding?" Ruth asked, keeping her voice casual. "They must be old enough to enjoy it, aren't they? Isn't the youngest going to school now?"

"Seth? Yes, he just started school last fall. He's in first grade."

Lisa began to descend the stairs.

"So," Ruth persisted, following her, "are they?"

"Are they what?"

"Are your little brothers excited about the wedding?"

Lisa paused without turning around. Ruth couldn't see her face, but she noticed how the girl's slim hand tightened suddenly on the stair railing until the knuckles were white.

"My brothers won't be coming to the wedding," Lisa murmured, so low that Ruth could hardly hear her. "None of my family will be coming."

Then she fled, hurrying down the stairs and into the cheerful uproar of the kitchen. Ruth followed more slowly, feeling baffled and concerned.

CHAPTER THREE

WINTER SUNLIGHT washed over the ragged yard, and little swirls of dust stirred and lifted on the cool morning wind. Sadie Duncan straightened and rubbed her back wearily, gazing with an absent frown at the weeds growing along the wire fence, where a few white chickens scratched busily in the dirt. Then she returned to her task, scrubbing piles of clothes on an old corrugated washboard in a big metal tub.

She'd lifted the tub onto a rickety picnic table behind the house, and hauled pails of hot water out from the stove to fill it. She was already tired, and the day had barely started.

Sadie lifted a soapy arm from the washtub, shook it and ran a hand over her hair. Once her hair had been as dark and glossy as Lisa's, but now it was faded and graying, pulled carelessly back at the nape of her neck and tied with one of Seth's shoelaces. She wore blue jeans, a red plaid shirt and an old brown cardigan that hung loosely on her slim frame.

The neighbors' black dog came loping along the fence line, barking at something across the pasture. At his approach the chickens scattered in a cloud of dust, squawking hysterically as they always did.

Sadie smiled, her weary face lightening a bit, her blue eyes sparkling. Then she sighed and returned to her job, picking up a pair of Tim's jeans and frowning at a rip in the knee, which was heavily smeared with grass stains. She rubbed bar soap on the greenish mess and began to scrub the jeans energetically on the board, her tanned forearms pumping rhythmically in the sudsy water.

Sadie knew she had to get the washing machine fixed soon. She couldn't keep washing clothes by hand, not the way her boys went through jeans and T-shirts. She liked to have them neat and presentable when they went to school, even if she couldn't afford the fancy runners and jackets that the other kids wore.

She grimaced when she thought about the old washing machine, hulking stubborn and silent on the back porch that Ralph had built onto their trailer a few years ago. That was in the days before Ralph started drinking so much, when he'd occasionally do odd jobs around the place and make a little effort to fix things up.

In recent years, not much of anything would ever have gotten done unless Sadie hunted up a hammer and nails and did it herself. She'd developed some sketchy carpentering skills, mostly out of necessity, but she was utterly baffled by the workings of motors and such. All she knew was that they seemed to break down regularly, and they cost a fortune to fix. Just having the repairman out to the house made a big hole in a fifty-dollar bill, and that was before he did any work.

And Sadie didn't have a lot of fifty-dollar bills to throw around.

There was a bit of money in the bank, though. More money, actually, than Sadie Duncan had seen in quite a few years. It turned out that Ralph had maintained a small life insurance policy with the trucking firm that he drove for on a casual basis.

Sadie couldn't believe it when the company representative had come to visit last October, a few days after her husband's fatal accident, and told her there was five thousand dollars in her name. It was the only nice thing Ralph Duncan had done for her in a long time. Sometimes Sadie had the crazy feeling she should thank Ralph for all that money. But of course, that was ridiculous. Ralph was dead.

And five thousand dollars wasn't much when you were all alone in the world with bills to pay and four young boys to raise. Sadie didn't even want to touch the money, because it was all that stood between them and utter disaster.

She knew that she had to get a job, find some way to meet their expenses and tend to things like the broken washing machine. She knew, as well, that her reputation was good, even though folks hadn't thought much of her husband. Sadie Duncan wouldn't have a hard time finding work in town as a waitress, or a gas pump attendant at the local service station, something that would earn enough money to buy groceries for a houseful of growing boys.

The problem, she thought, arching her back wearily once again, was that she didn't want to take on a job right now. She wanted to keep herself free, just in case Lisa called and asked her and the boys to come to the wedding. If Sadie had a job, she might not be able to go, and nothing in the world would keep Sadie Duncan from her daughter's wedding if she was invited.

Tears sparkled briefly in Sadie's eyes when she thought about Lisa. Sadie hadn't talked to the girl since she'd left home last spring. She wouldn't even have known where her daughter was if she hadn't run into Mrs. Watson in the supermarket a few weeks ago. Mrs. Watson was the high school English teacher, and she'd always had a real soft spot for Lisa. Apparently the girl still wrote to her sometimes, because Mrs. Watson was full of excitement about Lisa's wonderful job over in Texas, the nice family she was living with and her romantic Valentine's Day wedding.

Sadie had been stunned with shock and pain, hearing for the first time from this stranger's lips about her own daughter's marriage.

"I suppose you'll be driving over, won't you, Sadie?" Mrs. Watson had asked, smiling comfortably. "My, how excited you all must be! I'll bet the little boys will really enjoy the trip."

Sadie had murmured something and escaped, rushing off to her old van so Lisa's teacher wouldn't see the tears running down her cheeks.

She knew that Lisa wasn't going to write or call. It was obvious that Lisa didn't want her mother at the wedding. Still, Sadie couldn't help looking eagerly through the mail every morning, or jumping each time the telephone rang. And she was reluctant to tie herself down to a job, just in case. . . .

A plume of dust rose and drifted off into the field beyond the yard, accompanied by the dull throb of an approaching vehicle. Sadie squinted at the road, feeling a little tug of apprehension. She hated having anybody come and catch her like this, scrubbing clothes on a washboard in the yard.

But it was only her neighbor, Walt Kelly, who'd fallen into the habit in recent weeks of picking up Sadie's mail along with his own down at the roadside and dropping it off on his way back home.

Walt was a tall, silent man in his forties, weathered and calm, with a shock of graying hair and blue eyes that were faded from years of squinting into the sun. He had a prosperous farm just up the road, where he'd been living long before Ralph and Sadie had moved into the trailer ten years ago. Folks said Walt had a wife once, a pretty woman who'd been bored by country life. She'd run off with a singer from a country band who'd performed briefly at the hotel, years and years ago.

Sadie thought about that story sometimes, wondering how any woman could leave a man as quiet and steady as Walt Kelly. Maybe Walt's young wife had been looking for more charm and excitement.

Sadie's husband, Ralph Duncan, had certainly been charming when he was younger, a handsome, laughing man who was the life of every party. But when the party started to last for weeks on end, and Ralph's mood got more and more ugly, Sadie would have settled gladly for less charm and a lot more steadiness.

Maybe all women were just contrary, she thought, watching as Walt climbed down from his truck and ambled toward her. Maybe women always wanted what they didn't have.

"'Morning, Sadie," her neighbor said, nodding at her courteously and setting a sheaf of mail on the weathered surface of the table.

"'Morning, Walt. Thanks for bringing the mail."

She glanced hungrily at the pile, searching for anything that might possibly be a wedding invitation. But even without touching her mail, Sadie could tell that there was nothing but bills and advertising flyers. "I brought Harry's bike over," Walt told her, strolling across to his truck and lifting a bicycle from the back.

Sadie glanced at him quickly. "I didn't know he took his bike to your place, Walt. I've told them not to go bothering you all the time."

"It's no bother," the tall man said calmly, leaning the bicycle carefully by the shed. "Next time, you tell Johnny to come over and I'll teach him how to fix a flat tire. By the time a feller's getting up to Johnny's age, he should be able to tend to things like that.''

Sadie nodded and looked down at the table, thinking how little her sons had been taught about any kind of manly skills. Their father hadn't ever taken much notice of them, except to whip them brutally when he was drunk or angry.

But Walt was right. Johnny was ten, and the twins, Harry and Tim, were eight. Little Seth was only six, but growing fast. There were so many things they needed to learn, and Sadie often wondered how she'd ever be able to teach them.

''I mean it, now,'' Walt said quietly. ''You send the boy over one day after school, Sadie. I'll teach him how to look after their bikes.''

''All right,'' she murmured, feeling uneasy all at once. Lately when Walt was around, Sadie often found herself painfully conscious of her shabby clothes and carelessly arranged graying hair, things she hadn't thought about for years. She didn't understand these feelings, and usually ended up wishing the man would just go away so she could be comfortable again.

''Why are you washing out here?'' he asked, leaning on his truck and watching as she rubbed a bed sheet furiously in the cooling water. ''Isn't it pretty cold out today for a job like that?''

''The washing machine's broken,'' she said. ''I haven't had time to get it fixed.''

''Maybe I can have a look at it.''

"You don't need to bother," Sadie said, more curtly than she'd intended. "I'll get it fixed soon, Walt. You already do too much for us."

"Can't hurt to look," he said mildly. "What's the matter with it? Does the motor still run?"

"Not really. When I turn it on, it fills like usual, but then nothing happens. The agitator won't turn, and it won't drain. I've tried it twice, and wound up having to empty it by hand both times."

Walt nodded thoughtfully. "Sounds like it could be a belt. Maybe broken, or slipped off the pulley. That's easy enough to fix. I could have a look at it now, and then pick up a belt in town later this morning if it's broken."

He gave her an inquiring glance. Sadie hesitated, feeling awkward.

"If it needs a new belt, would that be...would it be very expensive?" she asked, feeling her cheeks warm with embarrassment.

He shrugged. "Four, five dollars, maybe. If you had a repairman out from town, it'd likely be five dollars for the belt and fifty for the service call," he added with a smile.

Sadie continued to hesitate, wondering if he was telling her the truth about the cost of the belt. She hated to think that Walt Kelly might be feeling sorry for them, or giving charity. He already did so much for the boys, fixing their bicycles and paying them to do odd jobs around his place that he could probably tend to better on his own.

"Come on, Sadie," he urged her gently. "You need to get your washing machine fixed. You can't wash clothes by hand all winter."

She nodded in defeat and led the way into the porch, feeling uncomfortably aware of his nearness as the door slammed behind them and enclosed them in the cramped space.

At least it was tidy, Sadie thought with relief. She'd cleaned the whole house and porch earlier in the week, and the makeshift workroom was neatly organized, even though everything was plain and shabby.

She watched as Walt wrestled the bulky washing machine away from the wall and knelt to study the panel on the back.

"I'll have to go out to my truck and get a screwdriver," he muttered.

"What kind do you need?" Sadie asked, leaning over to look at the panel.

"A small Phillips. See, like this?"

Sadie frowned at the screw head that he was indicating with a callused finger. "I've got one like that right here," she said. "It's the little star-shaped one, isn't it?"

Walt grinned. "Yeah, Sadie," he murmured. "It's the little star-shaped one."

Sadie smiled back at him shyly, her cheeks flushing again, then hurried over to her toolbox to get him the screwdriver. Walt removed the panel and bent to peer in at the motor. He fished out a frayed length of black rubber.

"See?" he said, holding it up for her. "A broken belt. I'll slip a new one on here and this old thing will run like a charm."

"Oh," Sadie said with a quick flood of relief. "That's real good, Walt. That's just great! I'll get you the money for the belt."

"Never mind," he said, getting to his feet and leaning against the machine to smile at her. "I'll pick it up and you can pay me later. I could stop by again this afternoon, right after lunch. Is that all right with you?"

"That's fine," Sadie murmured, almost light-headed with happiness.

She'd have her washing machine running again before supper time, and it wasn't going to cost a fortune after all.

"Maybe I'll just leave all those dirty clothes till later," she added, smiling at him. "It's sure a whole lot easier to toss them in the machine than it is to scrub them by hand."

"I wouldn't doubt it," Walt said dryly, glancing with sympathy at her work-worn hands. Sadie stifled a childish urge to hide them behind her back, and felt relieved when he moved toward the door.

He paused in the doorway, then turned back to her. "I heard in town that Lisa's getting married next month," he said.

Sadie tensed and looked away, avoiding his eyes. "That's true," she murmured. "It's hard to believe," she added, trying to keep her voice light. "My little girl getting married. Seems like yesterday when she was a baby.''

''I guess you and the boys will be driving over to Texas, won't you?'' Walt said casually. ''Maybe you could let me have a look at the van before you leave, Sadie. That's a pretty long trip.''

Sadie was silent, fighting down a rising panic and a terrible feeling that she was about to give way to tears.

''Sadie?'' he prompted gently. ''Were you planning on driving over there to Texas?''

''I . . . I guess I won't likely be going to the wedding,'' Sadie muttered.

Even though she wasn't looking at him, she was conscious of Walt's reaction, of the way his eyes widened in disbelief and his face took on a sudden look of concern. ''You won't be going? Why not?''

Sadie shrugged awkwardly, afraid to speak for fear she wouldn't be able to hold her emotions in check. She was appalled by her sudden urge to throw herself against his broad chest and sob like a child. It had been such a long time since anybody had shown any kind of concern for her. Such a long, lonely time . . .

''Is it money, Sadie?'' he asked gently. ''Because I could . . .''

''No,'' she whispered. ''No, it's not money. I'd be able to find the money to go, somehow. But Lisa . . . she doesn't want me there, Walt. She doesn't . . . want me.''

Sadie's voice broke and she fled, hurrying into the kitchen and shutting the door behind her. She was aghast at her rudeness, running off like that and leaving a neighbor standing on the porch. But she couldn't have stayed any longer, couldn't endure being questioned, even by someone as kind and gentle as Walt Kelly.

She sat at the table with her hands tightly folded, waiting until she heard his truck pull out of the yard and head off down the lane. Sadie stayed where she was, silent and unmoving, until the hum of his motor was lost in the distance. Then she trudged outside again to gather up the clothes on the picnic table, thinking about her lost daughter as the winter sky turned gray and dark.

FRANKIE SWITZER, too, was thinking about Lisa. It was later the same day, after supper, and Frankie had showered and changed into a clean sweatshirt and jogging pants. She was in the guest house at the Double C, seated at her desk, working her way through an assignment on plant grafting. But she couldn't forget the happy crowd around the lunch table earlier in the day, and the way Lisa had intervened to deflect their teasing attention from Frankie.

That really wasn't like Lisa, Frankie mused. The Double C housemaid was so shy that she rarely spoke up at all in public, though Frankie had sometimes seen her laughing and playing freely when she was alone with the children, or with Tony. But Lisa obviously hadn't liked the idea of Frankie being bullied and she'd told them so, even though it embarrassed her to do it.

Frankie leaned back in her chair and ran a hand through her hair with an abstracted frown, then got up and wandered across the room to the window. She opened the drape and peered out into the winter evening. While she was at the window a door opened at the big house, spilling brightness onto the darkened lawn. Lisa and Tony came out, strolling down the walk with their arms around each together. They both wore jeans and bulky winter jackets, but Lisa looked small and slim at Tony's side, her dark hair shining in the glow from the big yard lights.

While Frankie watched, Tony paused on the walk, pulling Lisa into his arms and kissing her, then laughing aloud at something she said. They disappeared into the shadows by the barn where Tony always parked his van, and in a few minutes Frankie saw the taillights winking as their vehicle pulled out of the ranch and headed for town.

She let the curtain drop and moved back across the room to her desk. The books were piled up, tons of work that she needed to do before the next semester, but she couldn't seem to concentrate.

She kept thinking about that kiss, and Lisa's adoring smile as she gazed up at her tall young lover. Soon those two would be married, sharing their lives together, wrapped in an intimacy so close and warm that it was almost impossible for Frankie to imagine.

She paused by the bed and sank down onto its quilted surface, pulling a pillow into her arms and hugging it as she gazed at the ceiling with a brooding expression.

So many upsetting things had happened during the day, it was no wonder she couldn't concentrate. First Tyler had started teasing her about boyfriends, then the group at the lunch table. And always, there was Lisa and Tony and their upcoming wedding, a constant reminder of romance, of sexual love and passion.

And finally, the awful moment at noon when she'd ventured out into the room wearing that skimpy silk dress, and found Tyler looking at her...

Frankie moaned and rolled onto her stomach, drumming her feet against the mattress. She pulled the pillow up over her head and tugged it down around her ears as if to shut out all the thoughts and memories. But there was no escape, anywhere. Even in the muffled darkness she could see Tyler's blazing eyes, his look of startled masculine appreciation. The memory was almost more than she could bear.

Frankie worshiped Tyler McKinney.

She'd always found him attractive, and had developed a mild crush on him when she was about twelve years old and he was already a grown man, working on his father's big, sprawling ranch. But in recent years, her feelings had intensified to the point where she'd hesitated quite a long time before accepting this job at the Double C vineyards.

Even then, Frankie had thought she'd be safe, because Tyler's wife was fully involved in the winery business and the two of them worked side by side all the time. Frankie hadn't figured on things turning out the way they had, with Ruth taking no interest at all in the new grapevines, leaving her husband and Frankie to do all the planting by themselves.

Not that Frankie minded the work. She'd always had a lot of energy, and she loved everything to do with vine culture. But these weeks of working alone with Tyler under the winter sky, sharing an easy camaraderie, had deepened her old girlish feelings until Frankie was really frightened by the intensity of this new emotion.

She'd lie awake sometimes in the darkness of the night, dreaming about Tyler's mouth, about his hands and shoulders, the way his hair fell over his forehead or grew down on his nape. And she'd feel almost sick with yearning, appalled at herself for the things she couldn't help thinking.

Tossing the pillow aside, Frankie levered herself off the bed with a quick movement of her agile body, then walked across the room to peer out the window again. Briefly, she allowed herself to glance up at the hillside where the lights of Tyler's big new house shone in the darkness.

Frankie stared at the lights, thinking about the stories that had started up in town a couple of years ago when she was away at her freshman year of college. Her mother had told her about the teenage girl who'd followed Tyler McKinney around, even pretended to be pregnant with his baby. The McKinneys had kept their silence on the topic, clearly doing their best to protect the poor girl and her privacy, but there'd been plenty of talk just the same.

Most folks had been puzzled by the whole incident, and wondered aloud why the girl would pick someone like Tyler to be obsessed with. After all, Tyler McKinney wasn't a glamorous kind of man like his brother Cal. He was quiet, intense and hardworking, hardly the sort to set a young girl's heart fluttering.

At least, that's what people thought. But Frankie knew better.

She'd always had a lot of sympathy for that unknown girl, who'd vanished from town by the time Frankie came home in the spring. Frankie could understand, all too well, how a girl could become obsessed by Tyler McKinney. He was so handsome and appealing, with a kind of shy humor that he didn't show very much to strangers. But he was also remote and hard to reach, all wrapped up in his work, and that made him even more attractive.

And now, there was a devastating edge of sadness to him as well, a kind of melancholy that had to do with the baby he and Ruth lost. He never spoke about the baby but Frankie was conscious of it all the time, in the bleakness of Tyler's eyes and the look of strain around his mouth. It was all she could do sometimes not to take him in her arms and hold him, just to give him some comfort.

"God," she muttered, letting the curtain fall and turning back to the desk with a burst of furious energy. "What a mess I am. I can't hang around mooning like this all night. I have to do something."

She heard a brief scratching at the door and opened it to see Hagar, Ruth's cat, who'd been wandering around the ranch pretty much at loose ends in the months since old Hank's death. The cat seemed to be constantly looking for the old man, wondering why Hank didn't show up with a tin of salmon and pull his big rocking chair into position on his front porch.

The handsome orange Persian had settled comfortably into his new life at the ranch, but he'd never adapted to Ruth and Tyler's new house. He still spent most of his time down here at the main buildings, being fed by Lettie Mae or Cynthia or whoever happened to notice him. But it was Hank he really wanted.

"Poor old cat," Frankie murmured. She opened the door and let him into the guest house, bending to pat his silky back. "Poor sweet thing. It's hell, isn't it, when there's just one person you want in all the world, and you can't have him? It's really hell."

Hagar cast her a piteous yellow glance and rubbed briefly against her legs. Frankie stroked him gratefully, hoping he'd stay and keep her company. She considered building a fire in the hearth and settling down with the cat to watch television, but Hagar soon grew restless. He made a brief tour of the guest house, checking the bathroom and closets, then demanded to be let out into the night again.

Frankie stood at the door and watched him go, feeling more lonely than ever.

At last she squared her shoulders and forced herself to cheer up. There was no point in moping like this about a married man. She despised herself for her weakness. Besides, Frankie knew all too well that she was too honorable ever to be a threat to Tyler's marriage, even if she could. But she was so lonely....

Abruptly, Frankie decided to go over to the ranch house and watch the television game shows with Lettie Mae. She suspected that the Double C cook was sometimes lonely these nights, too, now that Virginia lived in town and Lisa was always out with Tony. Frankie and Lettie Mae could watch "Wheel of Fortune" together, compete with each other to solve the puzzles and abuse the contestants for being greedy and not buying vowels. Frankie brightened, feeling more cheerful now that she had a plan. She hurried to change into jeans and a less disreputable sweatshirt, then stopped in surprise when a knock sounded on the door.

Tyler, she thought, lifting her hand to her mouth. *Oh, God, what if it's Tyler?*

But, of course, it wasn't Tyler. It was Joey Wall, standing under the porch light with his hands in the pockets of his football jacket, smiling down at her.

"Hi, punkin," he said cheerfully. "Whatcha doin'?"

His voice was casual, his words teasing, but he couldn't control the sudden flame in his eyes or the tenderness of his smile.

Frankie knew that Joey Wall was crazy about her. Everybody knew it, because he'd made no secret of it since they were little kids. Back in the fourth grade Joey had enraged her by telling the other kids that he was going to marry Frankie Switzer when he grew up, and they were going to have six children and live at Disney World.

In those days they were still about the same size, and Frankie had always been fearless. She'd caught up with him on the playground after school and pummeled him until he begged for mercy.

Now, Joey was six foot four, built like a Mack truck and being scouted by a half-dozen professional football teams.

Frankie chuckled, recalling their long-ago fight in the schoolyard. He cast her an inquiring glance.

"I was just thinking about the time I beat the stuffing out of you," she told him. "Remember that, Joey?"

He grinned amiably and followed her into the guest house. "Sure, I remember. It was a terrifying experience."

Frankie smiled up at him fondly, liking the way his golden-brown hair shone in the lamplight, and his green eyes sparkled when he recalled their childhood squabbles. Joey was one of her favorite people, always had been, even when she was beating him up in the fourth grade. But he was just a brother to her, nothing more.

If only she could feel about Joey the way she felt about Tyler, life would be so much simpler, Frankie thought with a sigh.

"What?" he asked, seeing her troubled expression. "What's the matter?"

"Nothing," Frankie said, her face coloring a little. "I'm just tired, that's all. It's not easy to work all day in the cold."

"How much longer will it take?" Joey asked, pausing to examine the messy pile of textbooks and papers on the desk. "You should quit, Frankie. You're going to get way behind in your courses. This is too hard on you."

"They need me," Frankie said. "I can't quit in the middle of the job."

"The McKinneys can find somebody else to spread manure on their grapevines, kid. It doesn't have to be you."

This was a familiar argument, and one that Frankie didn't care to pursue at the moment. After all, she could hardly let Joey know her real reason for wanting to stay at the ranch longer than she'd planned. How could she tell him that she wanted to spend every minute of every day with Tyler McKinney, and that leaving this place was going to be agony for her?

"I'm staying till all the vines are planted," she said quietly. "There's no point in talking about it, Joey."

"All right," he said, capitulating instantly, as he always did when her voice took on that steely edge.

Joey seemed to know instinctively when it was unwise to push. It was one of the things that helped them to get along so well together.

"Wanna do something?" he asked.

"Like what?"

"I dunno. We could go into town and see what's happening at Zack's."

Frankie grinned. "As if anything ever happens at Zack's."

He smiled back at her. "I guess you're right. Should we drive into Austin?"

She shook her head. "We'd be too late getting home. I have to work tomorrow."

"Okay. You name it, and we'll do it."

Frankie hesitated. Part of her wanted him to go away so she could be alone with her dreamy thoughts of Tyler. But she also hated to lose Joey's sunny, undemanding company, because the loneliness would be more intense than ever after he left.

Frankie sighed again, conscious that she was being unfair to Joey Wall. She was using his friendship as a safe barrier between her and the man she couldn't have. But all the time Joey was thinking there was something more to their relationship.

"Joey..." she began.

"Yeah?" he asked, still leafing through her textbook, looking with interest at the complex charts and diagrams on tree grafting.

"Just friends. Right?"

He glanced at her with sudden intensity. "Sure, Frankie," he said after a moment's silence. "Just friends."

"Okay." She gave him a glowing smile that made him look away quickly. "Let's go over and watch the game shows with Lettie Mae," she said, reaching for her jacket. "Then we'll drive into town and have a coffee at the Longhorn."

"Sounds good."

Joey hesitated as if about to say something more, then changed his mind and followed her out into the darkness.

CHAPTER FOUR

TYLER LEANED in the doorway, watching quietly as Ruth frowned over a sheaf of papers on the desk. She sighed and pushed her hair back with a weary gesture, then glanced up when she became aware of him.

"Is something wrong?" she asked.

Tyler shook his head. "I scratched my hand on some wire. Needed a little first aid." As he spoke he held out his left hand, on which he'd just attached a clumsy gauze bandage in the downstairs bathroom. The cut had been a fairly deep one, and a pinkish stain was already seeping through the fabric wrapped at the base of his thumb.

Ruth looked absently at the injured hand, then nodded and turned back to her papers, leaving Tyler feeling chilled and miserable. A few months ago, she'd have jumped to her feet, full of concern, and demanded to look at his wound. No doubt she'd have insisted on removing the makeshift bandage and wrapping it more tightly, after making sure the cut was properly disinfected.

Now, she didn't even seem to care. There was no apparent harshness in her actions, just a listless lack of interest that was more depressing to him than open fighting.

"What are you doing, honey?" he asked, forcing himself to sound cheerful and casual as he moved into the room and stood by the desk.

"Looking over these equipment specifications Cynthia gave me. But it seems practically hopeless. I don't know what to do."

"Why?"

Tyler lowered himself to sit in the opposite chair, trying to ignore the cut in his hand, which was beginning to throb. He wondered vaguely about the danger of tetanus, with all the dampness out in the vineyard and the liquid manure they were using as fertilizer. The base of the thumb was supposed to be a risky place for a cut, wasn't it?

He wanted to ask Ruth about it, but she seemed so preoccupied and troubled that he was reluctant to broach the topic.

"I just don't know what to do," Ruth said again, pushing at the mass of papers with a tired gesture. "Cynthia's indicated the prices she feels we can afford to pay, and I don't see how we can buy decent equipment with such a limited budget. We need to raise more cash, somehow. There's no point in going into this with second-rate stuff we'll have to replace after two or three growing seasons."

Tyler frowned at the papers. "Maybe I can ask Cal for another loan," he said bitterly, feeling a resurgence of the resentment that had been nagging him ever since Cal became a major shareholder in the winery.

Life was so damned unfair.

Cal, who'd never turned his hand to much of anything except his own enjoyment, was rolling in contentment these days. He had a successful business, a ton of money, and a beautiful wife who adored him. And as if all that wasn't enough, Tyler and Cal had gone for a drink at Zack's the previous night, and Cal had told him that Serena was pregnant. Tyler remembered his brother's face, beaming with joy, although in Tyler's presence Cal had seemed almost apologetic as he passed on his good news. Tyler had been quick to congratulate his brother heartily, but some of the old feelings still rankled.

Cal, the golden boy, had always led a charmed life. Everything he wanted seemed to drop into his lap with no visible effort. Now he was even prosperous enough to help Lynn and Sam with their current financial difficulties, something Tyler would dearly have loved to do for his sister. He wished he could have been the one to offer that loan and ease the tension in Lynn's face. But Tyler, who'd worked like a dog since he was a teenager and seldom indulged himself at all, was stuck with the short end of everything.

Sometimes, Tyler thought with a weary sigh, life was purely too hard to bear.

Still, it would all be different if he and Ruth could recapture what they'd always had between them.

When Ruth loved him, nothing else mattered. She was meat and drink to Tyler, the air he breathed and the essence of his life. With Ruth beside him he could tackle anything, but when she was separated from him, either physically as she'd been last month when she went away to California, or emotionally as she'd been ever since they lost the baby, Tyler didn't seem able to function properly.

Since their lovemaking last week, she'd avoided any situation that might lead to further intimacy, and Tyler was increasingly forced to recognize that she didn't want him.

There certainly wasn't anything physically wrong with her that should inhibit her response. She'd even had a climax that night, because he could remember the gentle rhythmic contractions of her body, a sensation so richly exquisite that he still shivered when he thought of it. But she never held him or reached for him in the darkness anymore, never kissed him or gave him the slightest hint of sexual invitation.

Tyler shifted wearily in the hard leather chair, feeling a growing despair. His hunger and loneliness were mounting so high that he was afraid he might do something really stupid, something dangerous and destructive. He never actually stopped to examine the nature of this fear or put words to the churning uneasiness in his soul, but he recognized it just the same and felt powerless to deal with it.

How could a man keep being strong when he was so alone, and aching with need?

"Well, do whatever you have to," Ruth was saying. "I don't know much about the financial side of things. My father's always looked after that. I'm just going to tell Cynthia what equipment I think we ought to buy, and let the rest of you work out where the money's going to come from."

"Good for you. Go ahead and pick what we need. We'll find the money somewhere," Tyler got to his feet. "Tell you one thing," he added grimly, moving toward the door. "I'll die before I ask Cal for any more."

Ruth nodded. "Will you and Frankie be coming in here for lunch?" she asked disinterestedly.

"Likely not. Lettie Mae sent one of the kids over to tell us she's making chili this morning. Hot chili sounds real good after a long morning in the trenches."

"I suppose it does." Ruth turned to her papers again, leaving him hesitating awkwardly by the door.

"Ruthie..."

"Hmm?"

"Will you go down to the big house for lunch with us, honey?" Tyler asked. "Do you want me to stop by for you when we're leaving?"

Ruth shook her head. "I don't think so. I'll probably run over there myself in a little while, after I'm done with this stuff. I'm hoping to get a chance to talk with Lisa," she added, looking troubled again.

"What about? More wedding stuff?"

Ruth shook her head. "Cynthia told me last week that Lisa's mother isn't coming to the wedding. She's really concerned over it, but she can't get Lisa to talk about her family at all. She was hoping maybe I could find out what the problem is."

Tyler looked at his wife, shaky with yearning. She seemed so genuinely worried about Lisa's happiness. Ruth possessed amazing depths of compassion, a warm concern for others that was one of the sweetest things about her. Tyler remembered a time when all that tenderness had been centered on him, when his life had been sheltered and enriched by her love, giving him the strength to overcome anything.

But now he often felt naked and helpless as a kitten, stripped of everything that helped him to put one foot in front of the other.

"Do you love me, Ruth?" he asked suddenly.

She glanced up at him in surprise. "Of course I do," she said automatically, then looked down and toyed with one of the papers. "I'm just... I'm really tired these days, Tyler," she said, her voice low and strained. "Just give me some time, all right? Everything will be better in... in a while."

"Sure it will," Tyler said heartily. "I guess we both just need a little more time, that's all."

He made his escape, heading for the door with his heart thudding in his chest. He couldn't believe he'd taken such a risk, actually formed the words and asked her that question.

Tyler knew he'd never chance it again. She might say no, and then his whole world would come crashing down around him.

FRANKIE WAS WORKING among the trenches when he went back out to the vineyard, her body bent double, her hair whipping in the wind beneath the old baseball cap she wore.

She glanced up as he approached, her eyes full of concern in the shadow of the cap. "Is it a pretty bad cut?"

Tyler shook his head. "Just a scratch. Where's that other flat?"

"I planted them already. If it's just a scratch," Frankie persisted, "why is the bandage all red?"

Tyler looked down at his hand. "Well, it's kind of a *deep* scratch," he said, grinning faintly. "Okay?"

"Did Ruth bandage it for you? Did you get some disinfectant on it? The thumb's a pretty dangerous place for a wire cut, you know."

"Quit fussing," Tyler growled, giving her an awkward pat on the shoulder as he moved past her. Still, he had to admit that it felt good to have somebody fussing over him a little. Ruth seemed not to care at all that he'd cut his hand. She'd barely even looked at the bandage....

"With all this manure around," Frankie went on, looking increasingly worried, "maybe you should go into town and get a tetanus shot. I can easily finish the last two rows by myself before lunch. Why don't you go, Tyler?''

"Because I'm just fine, that's why." Tyler bent to heft a tray of flats from the muddy flatbed behind the tractor.

"Men!" Frankie said, rolling her eyes. "Too bad the IQ never matches the SQ."

"SQ?"

"Stubbornness Quotient."

"That's not a very respectful way to speak to your boss, kid," Tyler remonstrated. He tried to sound stern, but his mouth was twitching with amusement.

"Sorry," Frankie muttered, looking distinctly unrepentant.

Tyler chuckled and knelt beside her to lift one of the dormant stalks into position, giving her a fond glance as she dug energetically with her trowel.

It was almost impossible to believe that this ragged, muddy urchin was the same girl he'd seen last week over at the ranch house, with her bare shoulders gleaming above the wisp of blue silk.

That image haunted Tyler a lot of the time, though he tried hard to forget about it. Instinctively he sensed that there was danger in the memory of Frankie's surprising beauty. Still, in the lonely darkness of his bed, he often found himself recalling the girl's slenderness and grace, and the swelling roundness of her young breasts, and felt hot and tense with emotions he was afraid to analyze.

Clearly unaware of his stormy thoughts, Frankie leaned back on her heels and beamed at him, brushing her face with the sleeve of her denim jacket and leaving a trail of mud on her cheek.

"So this is the new hybrid that's supposed to be totally resistant to fungus disease," she said. "And the grape's flavor is apparently a big improvement over earlier stock, too."

Tyler looked at her, suddenly conscious of her nearness. The streak of mud made her eyes seem intensely blue under the shadowy peak of her cap, and her smiling lips were full and inviting. He swayed toward her with an involuntary movement, then caught himself abruptly, horrified at his reaction.

"Should be a winner," he said curtly. "Hand me that other trowel, would you, Frankie?"

She obeyed, still rooting happily through the tray of young plants. Again Tyler glanced sidelong at her delicate profile, wondering how serious she was about young Joey Wall.

The druggist's son was a handsome, likable kid, as pleasant and sweet-tempered as he was big. Joey and Frankie had been paired in people's minds ever since Tyler could remember, though it seemed to him that Joey was probably more committed to the relationship than Frankie was.

Tyler speculated about the nature of their longstanding friendship now that they were both grown up. More to the point, he wondered whether Frankie was going to bed with her old schoolmate. His mouth went dry when he thought of her slim body and Joey's burly strength, hot and naked, wrapped together in a passionate embrace. To his horror, Tyler felt a tightening in his groin, and a surge of painful sexual desire.

Desperately he cast around for something to say or do that would ease the tension before Frankie managed, with a woman's uncanny intuition, to tune in on his guilty thoughts.

"Frankie and Joey were lovers," he sang, bending to shovel dirt over the new plants. "Oh, Lordy, how they did love...."

She responded angrily, as he'd known she would, glaring up at him with furious blue eyes. "Stop that, Tyler!"

He hummed a few more bars of the song, then gave her a teasing grin before he crawled off down the length of the trench, dragging the wooden flat. Frankie followed, still outraged.

"I *hate* that stupid song," she muttered. "I've been hearing it all my life."

"I suppose you have. How long have you and Joey been going together?" Tyler shoveled away, trying to sound detached yet interested, like a friendly neighbor almost old enough to be her father.

"We're not going together."

"Could have fooled me. They say he's down there at the guest house almost every night."

Frankie glared at him again. "Is that so? And who's doing all the spying?"

"Nobody's spying on you," Tyler told her mildly. "Lettie Mae has a crush on the boy, I think. She tends to keep me posted on his comings and goings."

Frankie relented and gave him a rueful smile. "Joey and Lettie Mae are pretty good friends, all right. The woman's a rabid football fan, you know. When they're together, I can hardly get a word in edgewise."

"So," Tyler said doggedly, "are you two getting serious? Will you be the next one wearing a wedding gown, Frankie?"

He was embarrassed to persist like this, but he found that he had a sudden urgent need to know where Frankie's relationship with Joey was going, and how she really felt about him.

Frankie shrugged. "We're friends," she said, turning away, but not before Tyler saw the unhappy shadow on her face. "Nothing more. Just friends."

Something about the girl's words and her expression made him feel awkward. He watched her in silence for a moment, then cleared his throat and changed the subject, asking her some casual questions about her college studies.

Soon their usual camaraderie was fully restored. They worked together amiably in the biting wind, the strange moment of tension almost forgotten.

WHEN SHE STARTED DOWN the path toward the big ranch house, Ruth saw the two of them crouched among the rows of trenches, digging and planting, obviously deep in conversation as they worked. The scene made her inexplicably nervous, stabbing at her with a sharp dagger of worry.

Ruth forced herself to wave and smile at them when they caught sight of her, then turned and hurried off down the trail again, her hands plunged deep in her jacket pockets. As she walked, she tried to analyze the source of her discomfort.

It went back, she realized, to the moment when she'd been standing next to Tyler and seen his face as Frankie came out wearing that dress. The memory of his hungry masculine admiration still frightened Ruth, though she tried to dismiss her feelings as being silly and completely unfounded.

Still, she couldn't help thinking that she'd never seen Tyler look at another woman that way, with the frank sexual admiration that he gave to his wife in the privacy of their bedroom.

Not that much was happening in their bedroom these days, Ruth acknowledged with a sad little grimace. She knew she was being unfair to Tyler, and it made her feel even more miserable. Ruth told herself all the time that it wasn't Tyler's fault, any of her suffering. But she wasn't really sure if she believed this.

Part of her wanted desperately to accept the fact that Nate was telling the truth, and that what happened to their baby would have happened no matter what they did. But another, darker part, couldn't stop searching for someone to blame. And Tyler *had* been drinking that night, and it was that dog he'd *insisted* on baby-sitting that...

Ruth shook her head impatiently, knowing that it was irrational to blame her husband for the physical nature of the accident. In fact, she was just beginning to understand what she really held against him. It was his stubborn refusal to give way to misery, and the fact that he seemed much more prepared than she to leave the past behind them and carry on.

Ruth resented his insistence on trying to be happy and close again. She wasn't ready to stop grieving and pretend that everything was the same as it had always been. Most of all, she didn't want to make love and start another baby. She still wanted the baby they'd lost, and she couldn't help being angry with Tyler because he didn't seem to feel the same way.

And yet, Ruth knew with her conscious mind that her husband was right. It was necessary to leave the pain behind and get on with life. She just didn't know how to accomplish that goal, and she hated the way Tyler kept pushing her.

I'm not ready, Ruth thought stubbornly as she crossed the ranch yard and climbed the steps to the veranda. Why couldn't he understand that she...

How long? A cold little voice demanded at the back of her mind. *How long will it take for you to be ready? And will he still be waiting?*

Once again Ruth envisioned Tyler's face, his eyes blazing as he stared at Frankie's naked shoulders. With a determined effort she shrugged off the disturbing memory, pushed open the front door and entered the foyer, forcing herself to call out a cheerful greeting. She was answered immediately by a chorus of laughter and welcoming shouts that echoed down the hall from the sunroom, wrapping her in warmth and comfort. Everything was going to be all right, Ruth told herself firmly. Soon she'd start feeling better. Her life with Tyler would get back to normal, and her loss would stop hurting so much.

In the meantime, Tyler would just have to be patient. Ruth loved him with all her heart, but she didn't have the strength right now to look after anybody else. All she wanted was to lose herself in the busy wedding preparations, and obtain some relief from the anguish of her own thoughts.

She hung her jacket away, then hurried down the hall and into the sunroom, smiling at the busy group who sat on the flowered chairs and couches.

This impromptu work party had developed into a regular Thursday morning tradition. Ruth sometimes wondered how she'd manage when the wedding was over and the Thursday get-togethers didn't happen anymore. But, she reminded herself, that wasn't until Valentine's Day, still a whole month away. By that time she'd probably be feeling like herself again.

She smiled at little Jennifer, who sat in her usual place beside her mother's chair, playing solemnly with a big woolly elephant.

"Effunt," the little girl said, holding her toy up for Ruth's inspection. "Pants," she added, lovingly stroking the elephant's gingham overalls.

"Yes," Ruth agreed. She bent to touch the little girl's soft golden hair. "Beautiful pants, dear. Do they come off?"

"Off?" Jennifer echoed in surprise. She gave the elephant a speculative glance and began tugging at her own flowered denim overalls. "Pants *off*," she muttered, frowning in concentration.

Cynthia chuckled. "Not now, dear," she said quietly, picking up Jennifer's elephant to distract the child.

"Sorry, Cynthia," Ruth said with a smile, as she took the chair next to Lisa's. "How's it going? Have you finished hemming?"

Lisa sighed and held up a shimmering length of white silk, the bottom of her wedding gown. There were many yards of the delicate fabric, which Lisa was hemming with stitches so small and even that they were practically invisible.

"I don't think I'll ever have it finished for the wedding," she said in despair. "It takes hours and hours to do."

"Well, I'd offer to help," Ruth told her cheerfully, reaching for a pile of the smoky-blue silk flowers that Lettie Mae was trimming and arranging in white baskets, "but there's no way I could do that lovely stitching. Beside your work, Lisa, mine looks more like the hemming on gunnysacks."

"Lisa's dress is going to be an heirloom," Virginia said, squinting through her bifocals at the flounces on Jennifer's little blue gown, which were spilling over her lap and onto the floor. "All handmade, and so exquisite. Her daughters and granddaughters will probably wear it for their weddings."

"My, won't they be beautiful girls?" Lynn said, making Lisa's cheeks flame. "Lisa's so pretty, and Tony's such a handsome guy. I'll bet their kids will be knockouts."

"Do y'all know who's going to have a beautiful baby?" Lettie Mae asked. "Cal and Serena, that's who. That baby's likely to be a heartbreaker the minute it's born, just mark my words."

Cynthia glanced quickly at Ruth, then bent to scoop Jennifer onto her lap. "Speaking of heartbreakers," she said casually, "this one has an appointment with Dr. Purdy this morning, don't you, sweetheart? Daddy should be coming by any minute to pick us up."

"You know, I think I'll go with you all, Cynthia, if that's all right." Lynn got to her feet and set aside her blue silk bridesmaid's dress. "Little Hank still has that rash on his tummy, and Nate said he'd look at it right away if I brought him in."

"It's nothing but heat rash," Virginia said comfortably. "You keep the child too warm, Lynnie."

Lynn nodded. "I think you're probably right. That's what Sam says, too, but it's always so cold at night and I can't stand thinking he might wake up and feel chilly. I can't seem to fall asleep if I think he's not warm enough.''

"Remember when Tyler was a baby?" Lettie Mae said fondly. "That little child would kick off all the covers and sleep bare, even on the coldest nights. I always wondered why he didn't catch pneumonia."

"He's still like that," Ruth volunteered, desperate to get the subject off babies. "He keeps our bedroom window open even when it's practically freezing. I always tell him I need to wear a parka and mittens to bed."

Virginia chuckled and got up as well, preparing to follow the others from the room. Ruth looked at them in dismay. "Is everybody leaving? I just got here."

"I don't have my car. Tony brought me out to the ranch this morning," Virginia said. "So I guess I'd better catch the first ride going back to town, because I'm supposed to be visiting Martin and Billie Jo this afternoon. She invited me over to have a look at their house."

"J.T. and I were there last weekend. It's really beautiful," Cynthia volunteered from the door. "You wouldn't believe what a nice job that girl's done on Martin's old house."

"Martin tried for years to sell that big old place after his folks died," Virginia said. "Now I'll bet he's glad he hung on to it."

It was clear that the group would have dearly loved to settle in and discuss the whole delicious topic of Martin and Billie Jo Avery, their house renovations and the astonishing success of their marriage. But the room was already emptying rapidly. Lynn hurried out to pack her baby things, Cynthia disappeared up the stairs with Jennifer, and Virginia went to the kitchen to collect her coat and sewing bag.

Lettie Mae picked up another flower and smiled at Ruth, who still sat next to Lisa on the couch, feeling bereft. "Never you mind, honey," she said cheerfully. "They'll all be back by lunchtime, and Tyler and Frankie will be coming down, too. It won't be lonesome for very long."

Ruth smiled at her. "I know it won't, Lettie Mae. Besides, you're not going anywhere, are you?"

"I'm sure not. Except out to the kitchen," the cook added, "to toss some of Hutch's vinegar and a couple more jalapeño peppers into that pot of chili. You know Tyler. He likes it so hot it's practically on fire."

"He sure does." Ruth watched, still smiling as Lettie Mae left the room, her tread as brisk and light as a teenager's.

She turned to Lisa, who squinted thoughtfully as she tried to thread the needle she was using on her silk dress.

"Well, would you look at this? They've gone and left us all alone, Lisa."

Lisa looked up with another of her radiant smiles. "I feel really guilty sometimes that you all are going to so much trouble for my wedding. Everybody's busy, and yet they take the time to help me. It's so nice."

"Nonsense," Ruth told her. "We all love doing it. Personally, I don't know what I'd have done," she added with sudden frankness, "if I hadn't had these wedding plans to think about. It's been a real life-saver for me, Lisa."

The girl nodded, then set down her needle and reached out to grasp Ruth's hand for a moment. "I never really got a chance to tell you how sorry I am," she murmured, her eyes sparkling with tears. "About your baby, I mean."

Ruth swallowed hard and forced herself to smile, squeezing Lisa's hand gratefully. "Thank you, Lisa. It was pretty hard at first, but it's getting better now. As I said, these wedding preparations are helping a lot to keep my mind off things."

"I'm glad," Lisa said simply, picking up her needle again. Ruth studied the girl's bent head with its dark ponytail, the delicate line of her cheek and neck and the sweetness of her mouth.

"Lisa," she said gently.

"Yes?"

"Why isn't your mother coming to the wedding?"

Lisa looked up quickly, her eyes still glistening with tears. "Please, I don't...I don't want to talk about it," she whispered after an awkward silence. "Please, Ruth."

Ruth hesitated, reluctant to press when she saw how troubled and anxious Lisa seemed. "But maybe we could help somehow if you'd tell us the problem," she murmured at last. "After all, it's a once-in-a-lifetime thing, Lisa. Wouldn't you want your family to be there?"

"Lisa!" Cynthia called from upstairs. "Do you know where Jennifer's white sweater is?"

"I moved some things into the other drawer yesterday," Lisa called back, getting to her feet with obvious relief. "I'll come and show you."

She set the mounds of white silk carefully on the couch, gave Ruth an apologetic glance and hurried from the room, leaving Ruth sitting alone in the winter sunlight with her hands full of flowers.

TONY RODRIGUEZ lounged contentedly at the kitchen table in his small apartment. He leafed through a pile of advertising flyers while Lisa moved quietly around the kitchen, gathering up the dishes from the meal they'd just eaten. Tony leaned back in his chair and smiled at her, his big body looking relaxed and comfortable in jeans and a faded plaid shirt.

"You know, I'm not sure what most guys think about when they picture being married," he said. "But this is what I like. Just having you around where I can see you and talk to you, both of us busy with our own stuff. You know?"

Lisa smiled and nodded, understanding exactly what he meant. In fact, she felt much the same way. When she thought ahead to married life, that was what she wanted most of all, just to have Tony around in the evenings where she could see him and touch him whenever she wanted.

"Of course," he added with a grin, reaching out as she passed with an armful of dishes and pulling her close to him, "I understand there's other good things about marriage, too. I guess there's a few things on my mind besides your good cooking and watching TV together, sweetheart."

Lisa rested against him briefly, still smiling, though she felt a cold little chill when he spoke.

She knew, of course, what Tony was talking about. Once they were married, they'd be sharing a bed and a sexual relationship like all married people. Though they were passionately in love, they hadn't slept together yet, mostly because of Lisa's fears and reluctance. She was deeply moved by Tony's respect for her, and how much it cost him to hold himself in check when they were alone together like this, with the bed so neat and inviting in the next room.

But the events in Lisa's past still clouded their relationship, especially the dreadful months when she'd been trapped into a life on the streets of Las Vegas, and the horrors she'd endured before she escaped.

Not that Tony was anything like those Las Vegas men. He was the sweetest, kindest, most gentle and considerate person she'd ever known. Lisa knew that there was a big difference between love and sex, and that what she'd experienced in Las Vegas had nothing at all to do with the way Tony felt about her.

Still, she wondered sometimes if it would bother him to think about her past when he held her, and whether her dark memories would ever go away and leave her totally at peace with herself.

She worried, too, if she would be able to respond to Tony with the kind of love and warmth that he deserved, or if her feelings of revulsion and fear would always stand between them.

But Tony wasn't afraid. He had so much confidence in her, and in the depths of his love. He was obviously prepared to give Lisa all the time she needed, but he believed that as soon as they were married and really, fully together, the shadows in Lisa's mind would be dispelled forever.

Lisa sighed, hoping he was right. She disengaged herself gently and moved out of his embrace to pile the dishes in the sink.

"Do you like this couch?" Tony asked, holding out one of the flyers for her to look at. "That plaid's kind of nice, isn't it? And it's on sale, too."

Lisa bent over to study the pictures he was indicating.

"Which color would we get? The brown or the blue?"

"You decide, Lisa. Which would go best with that rug we picked out?"

Lisa considered, running water over the piled dishes and adding a spray of detergent. "Probably the brown," she said at last. "I think that would look really nice, Tony."

"Great," he said with satisfaction. "Maybe we'll drive into Austin on Saturday, okay? If you like it, we can bring it home with us and keep it here until we move.''

Lisa smiled at him. "It's going to be so much fun, isn't it?" she asked softly. "Having our own house, and all our own things."

"It sure is." Tony looked around at his dingy, sparsely furnished apartment. "I've never had much of anything," he said without emotion. "Not really. This place actually looks luxurious compared to the house I grew up in."

"Me, too," Lisa said, thinking about the cramped, shabby trailer house where her mother still lived with her four little brothers. She turned away, her face shadowed with distress.

At least Ralph wasn't there anymore. Lisa could hardly imagine the place without Ralph's looming, menacing presence. They'd all been so afraid of him, especially the smaller boys. It must be wonderful for her little brothers not to live with that kind of fear anymore.

Not that Lisa was likely to find out. She had no intention, ever, of setting foot inside that trailer again. She started to wash the dishes, feeling grim and tense with the pain of her memories.

"Look, it makes into a bed, too," Tony was saying happily. "That's a good feature, right? We could use a couple of extra beds."

"Why?" Lisa looked over her shoulder at him, smiling, touched by his look of boyish enthusiasm. "Are you expecting lots of company?"

"Well, we've both got big families. It's reasonable to expect that our brothers and sisters will be coming to visit from time to time, right? And we'll need a place for them to sleep."

"My brothers won't likely be coming to my house," Lisa said, more shortly than she'd intended.

Tony looked at her with the quiet, thoughtful appraisal she'd come to dread. Despite his gentleness, there was a firm quality of uncompromising honesty about Tony that made it hard to deceive him, or to persist in a wrongheaded course of action while he was watching.

She turned aside uncomfortably and began scrubbing plates with unnecessary thoroughness, conscious of his glance still resting on her.

"Ruth asked me again this morning about the wedding," Lisa said, her voice low and strained. "She wanted to know why my mother isn't coming. I wish they'd just leave me alone."

"I don't see why they should," Tony said reasonably. "The McKinneys are doing a ton of work on our behalf, Lisa, and they're being really generous, too. I think they have a right to express some opinions about the guest list."

"It's my own business," she said. "Not theirs. Whether my mother comes or not is nobody's concern but mine."

"Is that what you told Ruth?"

"Not in so many words. I said I didn't want to talk about it."

"You never want to talk about it. You won't even talk to me about it, Lisa."

She turned to look at him, gripping the dish towel in her hands. "Tony..."

"I think we need to get this out in the open, honey. Maybe we need to talk it over, just the two of us."

"I can't," she whispered. "I just can't."

"Sure you can. Come here."

He held out his arms and she moved toward him uncertainly, sinking onto his lap and nestling against his broad chest. Lisa sighed and buried her face in his shirtfront, where she could feel the quiet, steady beating of his heart.

"Now, what's the problem between you and your mother? What can I do to help?"

"Nothing," Lisa muttered, fighting back tears. "Nobody can do anything."

"Is she a mean person? Is she in jail or something? Or is she some kind of monster, who doesn't even care that you're getting married? You've never told me a single thing about her."

Lisa was silent, thinking about her mother. Sometimes she could hardly remember what she looked like, and it made her feel both relieved and a little panicky to think she was forgetting. But now, for some reason, she saw her mother vividly in her mind's eye, recalling Sadie's lined, tired face, her careless graying hair and the startling blue of her eyes, the sweetness of her voice when she sang at her work, mending a pile of torn blue jeans or washing baskets of eggs and packing them in cardboard flats to sell in town.

"No," Lisa murmured, her voice so low that Tony had to dip his head to hear. "She's not a monster."

"Okay. Would she come to the wedding if we invited her?"

Involuntarily, Lisa remembered a sunny childhood scene she hadn't thought of for years. She saw herself sitting at the table with her dolls, pouring tea into little cups, and Sadie perched opposite on a childsize chair, sipping from her cup and solemnly discussing the weather. Her mother had put on her going-to-church hat in honor of the tea party, a modish little fedora with a sweeping brown feather in the band that Lisa especially loved, and her eyes had sparkled with enjoyment....

But that was long ago, in the days when Sadie and Lisa were still alone together, before she'd married Ralph Duncan and all the nightmares started.

"Lisa?"

"Yes," Lisa said. "She'd probably come if we invited her."

"She doesn't hate you, then?"

"No. She doesn't."

"So what's the problem? Are you angry with her, honey?"

"I never want to see her again as long as I live," Lisa burst out. She tensed and tried vainly to pull herself from Tony's arms.

"That's pretty harsh. What did she do to upset you so much?"

"Nothing," Lisa said bitterly, still sitting rigid within his embrace. "That's just the problem, Tony. She didn't do anything."

"Sweetheart, help me out here, okay? I don't understand." Tony gathered her toward him, kissing her gently.

Lisa relented, leaning against his chest and shivering with memory. "Ralph—my stepfather—he was so cruel, Tony," she whispered. "He was an awful man, especially when he was drinking. Once," she went on tonelessly, staring into the distance, her eyes bleak, "when Harry was only four years old, Ralph stopped the car and hit him for making marks on the window with the wheels of a little toy truck he was playing with. Ralph broke Harry's jaw. It had to be wired shut for about a month."

"Lisa..."

"And," she went on, unable to stop the flow of memories once they'd begun, "I went in with Mama to the doctor's office, and she told him Harry's face had been hit by a baseball. She *lied*, Tony, to protect that monster."

"Maybe she had no choice," Tony said gently. "When women are married to abusive men, honey, they do whatever they can to protect their kids."

"Protect us!" Lisa echoed bitterly. "She never protected us. That kind of thing happened all the time. She didn't try to stop him, even when he was—"

"How could she have stopped him? What could your mother have done, when he was drunk and out of control? Maybe her only choice was to keep from making him even more angry."

"She could have taken us and left," Lisa said. "She could have gotten us all away from him. It didn't have to go on for so many years."

"Maybe she realizes that now. But life isn't always so clear-cut when you're in the middle of something, you know."

"I blame her for everything," Lisa went on, not even hearing him. "If it hadn't been for Ralph, I wouldn't have run away when I was so young and gone to Las Vegas. And then Ramon wouldn't have found me, and all those other things wouldn't have . . ."

Her voice broke and she started to cry, her body racked with harsh sobs.

Tony cradled her gently, patting her back and murmuring soothing words. "It's all right, honey," he whispered. "It's all over. Nothing like that is ever going to hurt you again."

After a while she calmed and sat up to wipe her eyes, then nestled gratefully into the warmth of his arms again.

"Maybe," Tony said at last, "it's time to put it all behind you, Lisa. Mrs. Watson wrote you that your stepfather's dead and gone. Why don't we invite your mother and the boys to the wedding?"

"Never," Lisa said grimly. "Ralph may be dead, but I can't forgive her for not helping us. Especially my brothers, when they were so little. She should have tried harder to protect us all those years, Tony. I don't want her at my wedding.''

''Sweetheart . . .''

''When I left home,'' Lisa went on, her voice quivering with emotion, ''I told her I never wanted to see her again. And I meant it.''

She slipped out of his arms and walked across the kitchen to the sink, fighting to keep herself under control. The memories battered at her, images of sobbing, terrified little boys, of pain and violence and disgust, of helplessness and constant dread.

''Never,'' she repeated firmly. ''Let's not talk about it anymore, Tony.'' She grabbed the dish towel and rubbed furiously at a plate while Tony watched her in troubled silence.

CHAPTER FIVE

SADIE SAT in her old rocking chair in one corner of the kitchen, with a pile of clothes on her lap. She sorted through the mound of jeans and T-shirts, pleased by their quality. One of the ladies at the church had given her the box of children's clothes on the weekend, explaining casually that the committee wasn't really sure what shape they were in, but maybe Sadie could find a use for some of them.

Sadie didn't believe that story for a minute. She suspected that the committee had gone to some effort to put this box of clothes together for the boys, and she was touched by her neighbors' generosity. There were even a couple of warm, down-filled jackets, some running shoes that were barely worn and the kind of bright neon T-shirts that her sons coveted but seldom received.

"Who gets the shoes, Mama?" Harry asked, looking with interest at the pile of clothes. "They look really awesome."

It was Saturday morning and the twins were doing homework at the kitchen table. Little Seth sat next to them, absorbed in his molding of the play-dough that Sadie made for him from flour and salt.

Sadie frowned, holding up the expensive runners. "I think they'll just fit Johnny," she said. "But not for long, the way he's growing. Then one of you will get them."

"Tim can have them," Harry said grandly. "He likes them a lot."

Sadie smiled at her son's cheerful, freckled face. "Is that so? And what makes you so generous?"

"I want the Chicago Bulls sweatshirt," Harry confessed with a grin.

Seth gave his mother a winsome, gap-toothed smile, the cowlick in his sandy hair standing straight up like a flag. "I like the Mighty Ducks," he said. "I think they're neat."

"That's because you're stupid," Tim told his little brother rudely. "You wouldn't know a good team if it bumped you on the nose, like this."

Seth shouted in outrage, his round cheeks turning scarlet with emotion. The uproar subsided abruptly when Sadie's eldest son came into the kitchen laden with bicycle equipment.

Johnny was now almost eleven, and his body was beginning to stretch upward, turning leggy and colt-like. Since Ralph's death, Johnny had been very conscious that he was the man of the house. He shouldered responsibility before he was asked, ordered his little brothers around with merciless efficiency and tugged at Sadie's heartstrings by trying hard to be manly and protective toward her.

He smiled at his mother and placed a limp inner tube and a bicycle pump on the table along with a rubber-patching kit, then carried a pail over to the sink and filled it with water.

"Look, you guys," he told the three smaller boys over his shoulder. "I'm going to teach you all how to mend a flat tire on your bikes, okay? Pretty soon you should be able to do this by yourselves."

"You don't know how," Tim said, looking at his brother with cold skepticism. "You're just pretending. Isn't he, Mama?"

"'Course I know," Johnny said indignantly. "Walt showed me last week. It's really neat, too. Seth, pay attention."

"I don't even have a bike," Seth said, pounding his play-dough flat and starting to roll a series of little round balls about the size of marbles.

"What are those?" Harry asked.

"Dinosaur eggs," Seth told him serenely. "When they hatch, they'll be real dinosaurs. They'll grow big as the house."

"Dinosaur eggs aren't that small," Tim said. "They're more like baseballs. I saw them on TV."

Seth was unruffled by the criticism. "These are s'posed to be really small. When they hatch, I'll keep the little dinosaurs in a matchbox. Then I'll feed them magic food and they'll start to grow. They'll grow and grow until they're giants."

The eight-year-old twins stared at Seth's mound of chalky spheres.

"Where will you get the magic food?" Harry asked.

Seth gave his older brother a maddening, secretive smile and continued to roll eggs. Harry punched him on the shoulder, and he shouted again.

"Stop it, boys," Sadie said mildly from her chair. "If you all can't get along, you'll go outside in the cold."

Johnny stared at the quarrelsome little boys around the table, his face white with annoyance. "Mama, I want to show them how to fix a tire. Walt said they should learn. Make them pay attention, Mama."

"You boys watch what Johnny's trying to show you," Sadie said automatically, frowning at a torn seam in one of the T-shirts. She reached for her needle and selected a spool of thread from the basket. "Johnny's right," she added. "This is something you should learn."

"I like Walt," Harry said unexpectedly. "He's neat. Yesterday he gave me—"

The boy fell abruptly silent, casting his mother a guilty look, and became suddenly very interested in his schoolbooks.

"What?" Sadie asked, dropping the shirt into her lap. "What did he give you?"

The others waited, shuffling their feet nervously and looking at the table.

"Two dollars," Harry said at last. "He gave me two dollars to buy pop and chocolate bars. But I earned it, Mama!" the boy added defensively. "I helped Walt unload some feed sacks off his truck."

"Yeah, I bet you were a big help," Tim jeered. "Prob'ly hung around and watched while he did it, that's all."

"I've told you boys," Sadie said wearily, "that I don't want you taking money from Walt. It isn't right, when he does so much for us already."

"But I just..."

"Mama," Johnny interrupted furiously, "make them be *quiet!*"

Impressed by his anger, the three smaller boys fell silent at last and watched while their brother pumped up the inner tube, then immersed it in his pail of water.

"When you do this," Johnny instructed, holding the bulky mass of black rubber under the surface and turning it slowly, "then you can see where the leak is."

"How?" Harry asked as the boys pressed closer to watch.

"Because bubbles come up. See all those little bubbles?"

"Yeah," Tim said, excited. "There's a whole bunch of bubbles, right there. See, Harry?"

"Well, that means there's air coming out because there's a hole in the rubber. So we mark it like this...." Johnny put his index finger on the spot and withdrew the tube, holding it over the pail until it stopped dripping.

"Hey, that's neat," Tim breathed. "What d' you do next, Johnny?"

"Then you have to dry the tube completely, like this, and prepare the surface to hold the patch."

Johnny frowned, his young face intent as he dried the rubber with an old rag, then reached for the small abrading tool to roughen the black surface.

A knock sounded at the door. Seth climbed down from his chair and ran to answer, bouncing happily when he saw Walt Kelly standing on the step.

Walt wore jeans as always, and an old denim jacket lined with sheepskin, the collar turned up against the biting wind. He removed his cap and stepped into the kitchen, giving Sadie a smile as he placed a bundled newspaper on the table.

"Morning, Sadie. Hello, boys. I see Johnny's teaching you all how to fix a tire."

The boys grinned at him and shouted a chorus of greetings, then turned their attention back to Johnny, who was uncapping a tube of pungent adhesive.

Sadie got up and took a coffee mug from the cupboard, conscious of Walt's presence in the kitchen, which suddenly felt crowded and overheated.

These days, for some reason, her neighbor seemed to fill a room whenever he entered it, even the big main hall of the church. Sadie always felt uncomfortably close to him when he was nearby, as if she might touch him by accident, brush against him or be drawn into some kind of embarrassing proximity. It was a strange, troubling feeling, and it made her all hot and awkward, unsure of herself or of what to say.

"Like some coffee, Walt?" she asked.

"Sure, if it's no bother."

"I just made a fresh pot and there's nobody but me to drink it," she said as he pulled a chair over and seated himself, smiling at the group of boys around the table. "Thank you. It's real nice of you to teach them things, Walt. I surely do appreciate all your help, though you do far too much for us."

He took a sip of coffee and looked with appreciation at the tin box of fresh gingersnaps Sadie took from the cupboard.

"It's nothing," he said. "I get a real kick out of those boys. By the way," he added, "I left a sack of oyster-shell supplement out by the chicken house. Thought you might be able to use it."

Sadie looked at him, startled. "But I can't...I couldn't possibly afford that supplement, Walt. It costs a fortune these days."

He waved his hand in dismissal. "Never mind about that. They gave me a couple extra sacks by mistake, and I got no use for them," he added, avoiding her eyes as he helped himself to another cookie.

Sadie set the tin book on the counter and stared at him. "You know, Walt, I don't think I believe that," she said.

Walt grinned up at her, his eyes sparkling. "You callin' me a liar, Sadie?"

She met his teasing gaze, trying not to smile. But she could feel her cheeks growing warm, and her mouth shaping into laughter in spite of herself. There was something so nice about Walt's face. Funny how she'd never noticed, all these years, that his craggy features were sweet and gentle in repose, and his eyelashes were as thick and dark as Johnny's.

But she suppressed these wayward thoughts firmly and seated herself in the rocking chair again, reaching for the shirt she'd been mending.

"Oyster-shell supplement is a wonderful thing for hens," she commented. "Specially when they're laying heavy, like mine are these days."

Walt nodded. "These sure are tasty cookies, Sadie. I don't believe I've tasted anything this good since my mother died."

All at once Sadie wanted to ask him about his parents, and his life in general. She found that she yearned to know every single thing about him. Where he grew up, and what toys he played with when he was little and what foods he liked to eat. But, of course, that was ridiculous, so she merely nodded politely and went on with her stitching.

"Help yourself," she said. "There's lots more."

At the battered old table, the tire-mending demonstration had been successfully completed. A rubber patch was in place, neatly attached to the tube, and Johnny looked at his brothers in lofty triumph. They studied the inner tube, clearly impressed.

"Let's put it in the water again," Harry suggested. "Maybe there's more holes."

Johnny shook his head. "There was only one," he said. "I checked already. Now I have to go put the tire together."

"I'm coming with you." Harry climbed down from his chair and hurried to get his jacket.

"Are you finished your homework, Harry?" Sadie asked.

He nodded. "I did most of the arithmetic last night. Tim's got about a *hundred* problems to write out yet," he added with cheerful malice, grinning at his twin, who sighed and looked wistfully toward the door.

"Can't I go with them, Mama? I'll do my arithmetic tonight instead of watching TV, okay?"

Sadie smiled. "Just work a little longer, Tim. Do one more page, and then you won't have so much to finish later."

Silence fell in the kitchen while Sadie rocked and stitched, Walt sipped his coffee, Seth rolled dinosaur eggs and Tim labored over his messy page of arithmetic.

Somehow, though, it was a peaceful silence, not at all tense or awkward. Sadie was surprised how good it felt to have Walt sitting nearby like this, not talking, just soaking up the family warmth and comfort of Saturday morning.

"Mama," Tim said, interrupting her thoughts.

"Hmm?" Sadie looked at her son with a dreamy smile.

"Mrs. Watson was in the school library yesterday when I went down to get a book about rockets."

"Was she, dear?"

Tim nodded. "She said Lisa's getting married."

Sadie's heart began to pound. She gripped the needle tightly in her fingers.

Seth looked with interest at his older brother. "Is she? When?"

"Three weeks from now. On Valentine's Day," Tim said, clearly pleased to be passing on this important news.

"I miss Lisa," Seth said, his face puckering briefly. "Why won't she ever come to see us?"

Sadie felt her stomach knotting with tension as she looked in silence from one freckled face to the other.

"Mrs. Watson asked if we were going to the wedding," Tim went on. "Are we, Mama?"

Sadie shook her head numbly. "No, Tim," she said in a toneless voice. "We likely won't be going to the wedding."

"I want to go!" Seth yelled. "I want to see Lisa's wedding! Mama, why can't we go?"

Walt got to his feet and moved over by the table. "Maybe your mama can give you a few minutes off, Tim," he said casually. "You and Seth can go have a look at something I got out there in the back of my truck. Is that okay, Sadie?"

She nodded, grateful for the reprieve. "Maybe just a few minutes," she muttered, her voice almost inaudible.

"It's for Seth," Walt called after them as they grabbed their jackets. "Tim, you help him with it, all right?"

Sadie looked out the window at the two little boys as they ran across the yard and scrambled up on Walt's pickup to peer into the back. She heard Seth's high-pitched scream of delight, and turned to Walt with an awkward smile.

"*Now* what have you gone and done, Walt Kelly?"

He grinned, looking abashed but pleased. "Sy Wilkins had a little bike down at the store last month that he took in on trade. It was in pretty bad shape, and Sy was planning to throw it away. I brought it home, got a few parts for it and fixed it up. I think it might be just about right for Seth, since he's the only one without wheels."

Beyond the window, the little boys had lifted the bicycle out of the truck and set it on the hard-packed dirt of the yard. It was bright blue with silver trim, gleaming faintly in the cold winter light. Seth gazed at it, his eyes huge, his face so pale with excitement that his freckles stood out in sharp relief.

Sadie brushed a hand over her eyes and turned away with a little helpless gesture. "Oh, Walt," she murmured. "I just don't know what to say."

"No need to say anything." Walt carried his mug to the counter and poured himself more coffee. "It's real good coffee," he said with a gentle smile.

Sadie nodded, fighting a rising tide of misery.

"Now, what's this problem between you and Lisa?" Walt asked quietly, settling himself in the chair again.

Sadie looked out the window, where Seth was approaching the blue bicycle with halting reverence.

Johnny and Harry had both appeared from inside the barn and stood grinning at their little brother.

"I didn't think he needed the training wheels," Walt commented behind her. "He can already ride Tim's bike pretty good, even though it's too big for him."

"I know. He's been dying for a bike, Walt. One night I even overheard him mentioning it in his prayers."

"Well, there you go," Walt said comfortably. "I guess prayers get answered after all, one way or another."

A silence fell between them. Sadie shifted in the chair, staring down at her work-worn hands as she gripped them tightly together in her lap. "Lisa's mad at me," she whispered at last. "Really mad. When she left home, she said she never wanted to see me again, and I think she meant it, Walt."

She glanced up at him. His blue eyes were steady, his face thoughtful. "I can't imagine anyone being mad at you, Sadie," he said softly. "I doubt that you've ever hurt anyone in your whole life."

"That's not true," Sadie protested. "That's not true at all." She turned to look out the window again, biting her lip.

Seth was kneeling by the little blue bicycle, touching the gleaming chrome on the fender while his brothers looked on. He stood slowly erect and stroked the leather saddle.

Sadie watched him in silence. Her heart was aching with love, and she felt a sudden need to confide in

Walt, to cast herself on this man's quiet sympathy and find some ease and comfort for all the pain that never went away.

"I wasn't a good mother to Lisa," she began, anxious to tell him before the boys came tumbling back into the house, all excited about the new bicycle. "Or to my boys, either."

"Well now, Sadie, I don't think I can agree to that. I've been your neighbor for a good many years, and I know what a good mother you are. No kids ever had a better mother."

Sadie shook her head, her eyes burning with tears. "You know...Ralph was real hard on the kids," she whispered. "Real hard."

Walt's pleasant face tightened. "I reckoned maybe he was."

"He wasn't so bad with Lisa because she was already eight years old when Ralph and I got married. But she was a real bright little thing. The teachers always liked Lisa and paid her a lot of attention, and I think Ralph didn't like that. He hit her sometimes, but mostly he...he took it out on the little ones."

"So those broken arms and bruises, and the time Harry's jaw was wired shut, those weren't really accidents, Sadie?"

She shook her head, drowning in misery. "Not usually. I never knew what to do," she murmured. "It was only when he was drinking, and afterward he was always so sorry. But a couple of times when I tried to leave, he got so mad I was afraid he'd..." She fell abruptly silent, looking down at her hands again.

Walt shook his head and stared at the laughing little boys beyond the window. "I wondered," he said. "Many a time. But what could I do? God, when I thought maybe he was beating on those kids, Sadie, I wanted to come over and break his legs. But I never had any proof."

"I don't think anybody could have helped. His temper was just terrible when he'd been drinking."

"Did he hit you, too?"

She nodded silently, turning her face away.

Walt sat tensely in the chair and gripped the coffee mug in his hands. "So why is Lisa mad at you?" he said finally. "It wasn't your fault."

"When Lisa got bigger and turned out so pretty, he started passing real suggestive comments," Sadie said, her cheeks growing hot with shame. "Things a man shouldn't say to his daughter. And when she talked back or ran away from him, he'd hit one of the little ones. It got so bad Lisa couldn't stand it, and she blamed me."

"Why?"

"She said I could have stopped it," Sadie whispered miserably. "She said I shouldn't have made them stand it for so many years, that I should have taken them and run away. And she's right, Walt. She's right about everything." Sadie began to cry, big, ragged gulps of anguish that made her throat burn.

"Now, Sadie, don't cry."

Walt reached over and took her hand. It was the first time he'd ever touched her in any way, and Sadie was surprised how good it felt. There was something so comforting about the touch of his big, callused hands, as if all the pain and misery were flowing out of her body into his, and he was strong enough to bear it.

She gripped his hand, struggling to compose herself, but she couldn't stop crying. Overcome by concern, Walt hitched his chair closer and put his free arm around her, cuddling her like one of the little boys. "Don't you blame yourself, Sadie," he whispered. "I can't stand to see you hurting like this. It wasn't your fault."

"Yes, it was. Lisa hates me, and she's got every right. I was weak, and I didn't protect my kids."

"Lisa doesn't have any right to hate you. Young folks can be pretty harsh judges, Sadie. They're a lot more tolerant when they get older and find that life isn't all black and white. Now, I knew Ralph Duncan," he went on, squeezing her gently, "and I have a fair idea what you were dealing with. You were trapped, Sadie, pure and simple. If you'd ever stood up to him and tried to get those little boys away, he might've killed one of you. And where could you go? You got no family nearby, do you?"

Sadie shook her head. "Just a sister in North Dakota. Nobody else. And if I'd saved bus money for all of us and gone there to Clara's, he'd just come looking for us anyway, and somebody would have got hurt.''

"I know that. Sadie, don't cry. It'll all work out. Look, Sadie.''

He hugged her again and pointed at the window, where Seth was now mounted on the bike. The little boy made a couple of wobbly, triumphant circuits around the chicken house while his brothers shouted encouragement.

Walt grinned. "I think I'll go out there and lower that seat a couple of notches,'' he said, getting to his feet with instinctive tact. "Okay, Sadie?''

She nodded appreciatively, anxious to get her face washed and her emotions back under control before the boys came rushing into the house. "Thanks, Walt,'' she whispered.

He looked down at her and touched her cheek, his hand so tender that the small caress brought a lump to her throat. "It'll be all right, Sadie,'' he murmured again. "It's all going to be just fine. You wait and see.''

Sadie nodded. His big sturdy presence was so consoling that she was almost able to believe him. She watched with a misty smile as he started out into the yard and was met with a chorus of eager shouts from the four small boys who ran and clustered around him.

For a long time Sadie stood hugging her arms and gazing at her family through the window, still treasuring the warmth and protection she'd experienced while Walt's arms were around her. She couldn't remember the last time she'd felt quite so easy and happy, and it seemed to have dropped into her world like a miracle, like a rainbow or a shooting star.

But the bitterness of her life had trained Sadie not to take much stock in miracles. She turned away after a while, her face tightening with pain, and trudged off to the bathroom to splash cold water on her face.

TYLER LEANED BACK in one of the worn leather chairs in his father's study, sipping a glass of whiskey. He swallowed and savored the fiery warmth, then held the glass against his eye, squinting through its amber depths at the room swimming in liquid gold.

"You all done playin' peekaboo over there?" J.T. asked dryly. "Ready to talk some business?"

Tyler gave his father an awkward grin and lowered the glass. "Sure, Daddy. What do you think?"

J.T. frowned, leafing through the piles of catalogs and cost projections on his desk. "Looks like the ladies have been doing their homework, I guess. Is Ruth getting a little more interested in the business again?" He cast his son an alert, thoughtful glance.

Tyler shrugged and moved restlessly in the chair. "Not so you'd notice. I mean, she goes through the motions, Daddy, but I don't think she cares much if we ever get the winery built. Not yet, anyhow. I'm not sure if she cares about anything right now."

"She seems to care about this wedding, though. All of them are pretty much up in the air over the damned thing."

The two men exchanged identical grimaces, then grinned.

"I don't see why *you're* complaining," Tyler commented gloomily, taking another sip of whiskey. "I'm the one who has to dress up in the monkey suit."

"You'll be real pretty," his father consoled him. "Cynthia tells me there's even a blue silk cummerbund with your tux. She says it's very elegant."

"Elegant!" Tyler scoffed, glaring at the tips of his boots.

"Now, about these figures," J.T. went on, fitting his reading glasses in place and studying the papers again. "If we buy the equipment Ruth wants, it looks to Cynthia like we'll have almost a hundred-thousand-dollar shortfall over our setup year. D'you reckon we can stand that?"

"I'm not sure. What does Cynthia think?"

"Well, she's worried. These banker types are always worried," J.T. added with an easy grin. "Businessmen like you and me, Tyler, we give the bankers ulcers."

Tyler tilted his chair back and rubbed a hand thoughtfully over his flat belly just above the silver belt buckle.

"Sometimes, Daddy," he confessed, "I can feel the beginnings of an ulcer myself. This is pretty scary stuff, you know."

J.T. waved his hand with grand casualness. "Hell, boy, it's only money."

"Only money," Tyler echoed, staring into the depths of his whiskey glass.

"Now, I don't suppose you want Cal getting any deeper into the business, do you?" J.T. asked with a cautious glance at his elder son.

Tyler let his chair legs drop with a thump. "I sure as hell don't! He's into this project for twenty-one percent already, Daddy. That's enough. It's *more* than enough."

"Okay," J.T. said mildly. "That's what I thought you'd say. Now, I talked it over with Cynthia, and here's what we propose. You know the section of land over next to Carolyn's property where we've been wintering the bulls?"

"Sure. What about it?"

"Well, that property's gone way up in value the past few years, what with the dude ranch and all. Scott Harris keeps talking about buying it, and he's offering a hefty price."

Tyler stared at his father in growing alarm. "Daddy...I don't want to start selling off parts of the Double C to finance the winery! Can't we can raise the money some other way?"

"We've exhausted all the other ways. Until we're up and running, we can't realistically make another stock offering, but we'll need decent equipment to get to that point. Besides, son," J.T. said mildly, "you're jumping the gun. I'm not talking about selling. Now, this is Cynthia's idea, matter of fact, and it's a damned good one."

Tyler kept his face lowered, staring at his boots again.

"Cynthia proposes that we mortgage that land to raise enough for the good equipment Ruth wants. Then we'll rent the property to Scott on a ten-year lease for his African Safari program. The rent will cover the mortgage payments, we'll still hold title to the land, and we'll have all the capital we need in a lump sum. Hell of an idea, right?"

Tyler looked up at his father, considering. "If we're renting the land to Scott, we won't have the use of it ourselves."

"We only use it during the off-season for the bulls anyhow. Scott won't be needing it over the winter so we'll write that into the lease, an understanding that we still get to winter our bulls out there, same as always. We gain everything and lose nothing."

"Yeah, sure," Tyler said with a faint grin, "until some crazy dude on a winter safari shoots one of our big ol' Brahma bulls, and mounts the head on his trophy wall."

J.T. chuckled. "Tell you what, it'd be the most expensive trophy *he* ever bagged. Think it over," he added. "I can arrange a meeting with Ruth and Cynthia tomorrow, and if everybody's in favor, we'll talk with Scott and Cody and maybe Vern, too, about getting the deal signed up."

There was a moment's silence while Tyler considered the proposition.

Finally he looked up, his eyes full of pain. "I know it sounds reasonable and all, Daddy, and I won't deny it's a relief to know that we can raise the money. But it still hurts a lot to think of mortgaging the Double C to pay for my idea. This land's never been mortgaged."

"The land isn't precious, son," J.T. said gently. "Always remember that. It's the people living on the land who are precious."

Tyler stared at his father in openmouthed shock, trying to imagine the J.T. of other years saying such a thing. There was no doubt that his father's marriage to Cynthia and the birth of little Jennifer at this point in his life had changed and softened the man in all kinds of ways.

"You know, I think I like you better this way," Tyler said, getting to his feet.

"What way?" J.T. lowered his glasses to frown over the rims at his son.

"All warm and fuzzy," Tyler said with a grin. "One of those New-Age, sensitive men. Pretty soon you'll start wearing gold neck chains and leisure suits."

"Git!" J.T. shouted in mock outrage. "Git out, you disrespectful pup!"

Tyler grinned again and lounged toward the door. "Now you sound more like Grandpa Hank," he said wistfully.

J.T. smiled back. "God, I miss him, don't you? Seems like a dozen times a day, I'm fixin' to walk over and see what he's doing, and then I recall he's not there anymore.''

"I miss him, too," Tyler said. "I miss everybody. Mama and Frank and Dottie and Jeff. Even Cal and Lynn are gone, more or less, and Virginia, too.... Nothing's the same, Daddy."

"Things change," J.T. said with a shrug. "I can't say I mind so much anymore, though," he added thoughtfully. "I'm sure enjoying my life these days."

Tyler nodded and went out, thinking about his father's contentment.

Funny how some people seemed to fall so easily into positions of comfort and fulfillment, while others searched all their lives without finding what they wanted.

Or, Tyler thought, his jaw tightening, maybe they found it and savored it for a little while, and then some cruel twist of fate snatched it away....

He left the big house and paused on the veranda, looking around at the moonlit yard. Ruth had walked over to the main ranch with him, and was supposedly still around somewhere. She and Cynthia and Nora were all busy helping with some renovation to the bungalow that Lisa and Tony would occupy after their marriage.

Tyler frowned, trying to recall what the women were doing. Painting? Wallpaper and curtains? Installing floor tiles?

He couldn't remember, and he didn't much care. To tell the truth, Tyler resented the amount of time Ruth spent on preparations for that damned wedding. He could have used a little of his wife's attention just now, some of her warmth and interest. But nothing seemed to make her laugh and sparkle anymore unless it had something to do with Lisa's wedding. Feeling discontented, he wandered out into the yard and contemplated the long walk up the hill to his own house, where a ton of business waited on his desk, too, urgently needing attention.

Maybe he should find Ruth and see if she was ready to go home. But Tyler was growing so sensitive that he couldn't even endure the small rejections anymore, the times when his wife showed so clearly that she'd rather be doing anything else than being with him.

He could remember a time, not so long ago, when all their happiness had sprung from being together, when there was nothing about Tyler's life and his thoughts that didn't interest her. Misery flooded over him, deep and chilling, accompanied by a desperate sense of loneliness.

"I love you, Ruth," he muttered aloud. Tears stung in his eyes as he unlatched the gate and stepped into the yard. "God, sweetheart, I miss you so much...."

He stopped suddenly, caught by a glow of light from the guest house that flooded rich and warm onto the dried winter grass.

Tyler stood very still, gazing at the lighted window. For some reason his hands felt clammy and his heart began to pound with an erratic beat that left him a little breathless.

It was only Frankie in there, he told himself. Just Frankie, the mud-stained tomboy he worked with every day. What could it hurt to drop in and say hi, see what the kid was doing? Maybe he could spend a few minutes helping with her homework, or something.

At least, he told himself grimly, Frankie would be glad to see him. No matter how cold Ruth was these days, Frankie's eyes always shone with a happy greeting whenever she caught sight of Tyler.

Without giving himself time to think about it further, Tyler strode off down the flagstone walk to the guest house.

CHAPTER SIX

INSIDE THE GUEST HOUSE Frankie stared intently at the television screen, lifting herself onto her toes and kicking her legs alternately in time to the pounding beat of an exercise video.

Joey Wall sagged against the fireplace with one brawny arm hooked over the mantel, gasping for breath while he watched her appreciatively. She wore black tights and a black half-leotard held up by suspender straps, topped by a brief yellow T-shirt that barely reached her midriff. Her slim ankles were concealed by bulky yellow legwarmers, and a bright yellow-and-black striped headband held her unruly golden curls in place.

"You look like a little honeybee," Joey said fondly when he was able to talk again. "Just as cute as anything."

Frankie glared at him. "Yeah? Well, *you* look like a big out-of-shape jock," she said unkindly. "Come on, Joey. Leg kicks."

Joey groaned. "Give me a break, kid. I'm dead."

"And you're supposed to be an athlete," she scoffed, puffing a little as she added circular arm swings to the leg movements. "What about all that rigorous football training?"

"That's just doing wind sprints and practising tackles and stuff. This is brutal, Frankie. I'll bet none of the guys on my team could keep up with you on a program like this."

She paused, interested. "Really? I thought you all took aerobics as part of your training."

"Not us, but I've heard that some coaches order aerobics classes to improve stamina. I reckon I can see why, after doing a few rounds with you."

Frankie relented and smiled at him, then flicked the remote to pause the video. "What a pity," she commented, "that you're such an out-of-shape guy. Especially when you look so good."

"Do I look good?" Joey asked, beaming.

"Men!" Frankie said briefly, reaching for a glass of water on the sideboard. "You're all so vain."

Still, there was no doubt, she told herself privately, that Joey looked pretty terrific in his exercise gear. He wore a pair of brief white cotton shorts and a red singlet, and his big muscular torso gleamed and rippled with muscle.

He caught her eye and Frankie looked away quickly, embarrassed to be caught in such a frank appraisal of his body. She and Joey had been friends for so long that she'd seen his body in every possible combination of clothing and circumstances. A couple of times when they were kids, she'd even hidden in the bushes and peeked while he was skinny-dipping down at the swimming hole.

But they weren't children anymore. For the first time, Frankie really understood that Joey was no longer her childhood playmate. He was fully grown, with a man's body and a man's lustful thoughts, and it wasn't right for her to tease and taunt him the way she'd always done.

"Did you talk to the coach?" she asked, turning away and fiddling with the case for the videotape. "Will he let you take some time off for the wedding?"

"I think so. The season's mostly over by then. I'll have to miss a couple of practises to drive out here, but he's usually working the second-string guys that time of year, getting them ready for next season. I should probably be able to get away, since you need an escort."

"I wish I didn't have to go," Frankie said, her face darkening as she stared at the plastic case. "I think it's all so stupid."

"What's stupid?" Joey asked. He took a towel from the arm of a nearby chair and rubbed it across his damp shoulders.

"This wedding. Would you like a big wedding and all kinds of fuss, Joey?"

"Hey, are you proposing to me?" he asked. "Because if *you* came along with all the fuss, kid, I'd do it with champagne in a hot air balloon, or while sky-diving, or on a ski slope . . . whatever you wanted."

Frankie flushed at his teasing smile. "That's not what I meant," she said curtly. "I just don't see the sense in all this stuff. Blue silk garters and bouquets and long white gowns, and all those silly archaic traditions."

"Maybe folks feel different when they're in love," Joey suggested. "Maybe they really want the whole world to witness and share their happiness. Besides," he added gently, "there's a lot of comfort in traditions, Frankie. They weave the fabric of society, you know."

Frankie kept forgetting that in addition to his athletic prowess, Joey was also a psych major with a four-grade point average. She made a brief, impatient gesture. "Whatever," she said coldly. "I'll just be glad when the damned thing's over with, and I can get back to school."

Joey's eyes brightened. "Really?"

She nodded and moved over restlessly to pop the exercise tape out of the VCR. "I'm keeping up with the assignments pretty well, but I'm still missing a lot of classes. It's good money," she added, "but I think I'd rather be in school."

She didn't add that it was getting more painful all the time to spend her days so close to Tyler McKinney. There were times when Frankie really feared that she was going to do something rash, like throw herself into the man's arms and start kissing him. And if that happened, she'd never be able to stop.

Most distressing of all, there were also times lately when Frankie was certain that she caught a gleam of response in Tyler's dark eyes, a look of intensity that both thrilled and frightened her. Tyler always kept such a courteous, brotherly manner around her. But what if that control were to slip? What if, someday, he touched her?

Frankie was genuinely afraid that one touch would start a fire neither of them could control. Part of her dreaded the thought of his embrace, but another part of her longed for him with a fierce yearning that kept her awake at night.

He's married! she thought in anguish, clutching the video in her hands. *Why does he have to be married? Oh, God, help me....*

"Will you be finished the planting by then?" Joey asked.

"We should be. The wedding's less than three weeks away now, but I think we'll be..."

A knock sounded at the door. Joey, who was closest, went over to answer it. Frankie looked on, surprised by the sudden tension in his broad shoulders as he greeted the visitor.

But his voice was casual and cheerful. "Hi, Tyler," he said, gesturing at his shorts and damp singlet. "Frankie's been torturing me with one of her exercise videos."

Tyler muttered something and stepped into the room, taking off his Stetson and turning it awkwardly in his hands. Stunned into silence, Frankie stood by the television set and hugged her arms in the skimpy outfit, barely able to look at him. Still, she was painfully conscious of Tyler's presence here in the room where she lived and slept, where her clothes hung in the closet and her books littered the desk.

Worst of all, though, was the bed.

Frankie never thought much about the bed when Joey was visiting. But now, with Tyler in the guest house, she felt that it seemed to fill the whole room, and that anybody who looked at it could see that she spent long hours tossing and turning under that brightly patterned quilt, dreaming hot, troubled dreams about this man who stood awkwardly by the door in his leather jacket.

"Tyler, would you . . . would you like a cup of coffee or something?" Frankie asked, feeling a growing desperation. "I have some cookies here that Lettie Mae gave me this afternoon. Joey and I finished our exercise session, but if you can wait a minute while I change . . ."

"That's okay. Don't bother, Frankie." Tyler waved his hand and gave her a strained smile. "I just stopped by to let you know that we're . . ." He paused, then took a deep breath and glanced at her again. "We're having a company meeting tomorrow morning about the winery equipment. I might be late getting out to the vineyard."

"That's okay," Frankie said. "I'll just keep working on the flats that are already there. There should be enough to keep me busy until you can haul up another load."

"Good," Tyler said with obvious relief. "I guess I'll head for home, then. Evening, Joey," he added, fitting his hat back on his head. "Good night, Frankie. See you tomorrow."

He smiled again briefly, nodded at both of them and let himself out the door. Frankie and Joey stood in silence, listening to his booted feet as they rang on the flagstones of the path.

Finally, Joey turned to her with a thoughtful glance. "Does Tyler drop in often to visit you?" he asked quietly.

Frankie's cheeks flamed and she turned aside to take another sip of water. "He's never come here before. Not that I can remember, anyhow. Joey, do you want some cookies?"

"The guy's falling in love with you, Frankie. Anyone can see it."

Frankie shivered with alarm. "Don't be stupid!" she said furiously. "Tyler McKinney's in love with his wife. Joey, you *know* how crazy he is about Ruth."

Still, she couldn't deny that there'd been something in Tyler's eyes as he stood in the doorway of the guest house...a kind of hungry, desperate look that Frankie was afraid to analyze. Obviously it wasn't her imagination, because Joey had seen it, too.

He moved closer, frowning with concern. "Come on, honey," he whispered. "Quit this damned job and come back to school. Let's pack your stuff and leave right away. I'll drive you to Austin in the morning."

Frankie clenched her hands into fists and forced herself to give him a bright smile. "Don't you think you're being a little dramatic, just because my boss happened to drop in and leave a message about tomorrow's work? Give me a break, Joey. I'm not some kind of fool, you know."

But she was. She was a complete fool where Tyler McKinney was concerned. Worse, she was as weak as a kitten whenever he looked at her....

"I just don't want anything to hurt you," Joey said stubbornly. "If anybody ever hurt you, Frankie, I think I'd kill him."

"Well, that's really noble of you, Sir Joseph, but I'm perfectly able to take care of myself, you know. Now, let's take turns in the shower and then go dancing. Me first," she added, forcing herself to give him a teasing grin as she ran and locked herself in the bathroom.

Frankie stood in the shower and let the streams of water pound against her body. They were hot and stinging but she still shivered when she thought of Tyler standing in the doorway of her room.

Why had he come? If he really wanted to deliver a message about the next day's schedule, he would simply have phoned, as he often did when he needed to consult with her. There was no doubt that he'd wanted to talk in person about something.

Or, perhaps, was Joey right? Had Tyler wanted something more than talk?

Frankie trembled again and switched off the water, then stepped out of the shower stall and wrapped herself in a big green towel. With forced determination, she struggled to put the whole disturbing incident out of her mind.

It was exactly what she'd said to Joey, nothing more. A casual bit of information about the coming workday, a message from her employer that he'd chosen to drop off in person on his way home. Nothing important at all, Frankie thought, brooding over her reflection in the steamy mirror.

But what if Joey hadn't been here? What if she and Tyler had found themselves all alone in the cozy guest house, with the winter wind sighing around the eaves?

"Hey, Frankie! Hurry up, or I'm coming in there!" Joey called from beyond the door.

Frankie's breath caught in her throat. She whimpered soundlessly, then dropped to her knees and began to scrabble through a lower cabinet, searching for her hair dryer.

RUTH HURRIED around the corner of the stable and headed onto the path that led to her own house, feeling unusually happy and lighthearted. She and Lisa and Cynthia, aided by Nora Slattery, had spent the evening wallpapering the kitchen in the little bungalow that Lisa and Tony would soon be moving into.

Ruth loved wallpapering, and had developed considerable expertise during the construction of their new house. She enjoyed the careful cutting and fitting, the precision of the work and the marvelous transformation as rolls of bright yellow gingham flowed onto the dingy walls of the little bungalow.

It was fun, too, working with the other women. Their conversation was cheerfully undemanding, full of laughter and gentle teasing, just the sort of thing that Ruth needed these days.

She glanced up in the direction of their house, wondering if Tyler was already home. It would be pleasant to tell him about the wallpaper, and how they planned to paint the cabinets and make curtains, too. It had been such a long time, Ruth thought wistfully, since she and Tyler had enjoyed one of the long cozy talks that had once been a mainstay of their marriage.

Maybe she'd build a fire in the hearth, put on some nice music and slip into the white negligee that Tyler had given her for Christmas. He'd been so proud of selecting it all by himself, and Ruth hadn't even worn it since she'd unwrapped it.

She felt a warm little flowering of anticipation at the thought of the coming evening, an emotion she hadn't experienced for a long time.

Ruth quickened her steps, then stopped in confusion and sudden dread, staring through a screen of tangled mesquite at the guest house. The door had just opened, throwing a long rectangle of light onto the ground outside. The light vanished as Tyler emerged and hurried off down the path.

Ruth stood silent in the darkness, one hand covering her mouth while she cowered into the screen of brush, her heart pounding crazily. Tyler passed so close to her hiding place that she could almost have reached out and touched him, but he wasn't aware of her. His handsome face was set and hard in the moonlight as he strode briskly up the path to his own house.

Ruth listened to his departing footsteps, still huddling in the bushes and struggling not to cry. But she couldn't control her whirling thoughts. Especially the vivid memory of that day a couple of weeks earlier when Frankie had tried on Lynn's dress, and Tyler had stared hungrily at her naked shoulders....

What was he doing, visiting Frankie's quarters at this hour? And why had he rushed off with such guilty haste?

Ruth's pain was gradually replaced by a bracing flood of anger, and an urge to run after him, shouting her jealousy and fury. But she held herself in check and stood quietly in the shadows of the mesquite, trying to think.

There was no reason to suspect Tyler of any wrongdoing. After all, he and Frankie worked together all day long, and they often had things to discuss related to the job. Besides, Ruth had known he'd be down at the main ranch this evening. He'd told her when they'd walked over that he wanted to talk with J.T. about financing the winery equipment.

But none of these rational thoughts did anything to ease Ruth's fear.

Worst of all was the understanding that if her husband had been driven to find comfort in another woman, Ruth had nobody to blame but herself. With grim clarity, she reviewed her own actions in the months since the accident, and the way she'd been so relentless about shutting him out and turning away from him. Time after time, Tyler had tried to be close again, to draw his wife out and start a conversation, to hold and comfort her when they lay in bed together.

But she'd turned a cold shoulder to him every time, locked in the prison of her own suffering. She wanted to be alone with her pain, and had been so confident in his love and faithfulness, counting on the fact that he'd wait until she was ready to be close to him again.

But what if he didn't?

Ruth moaned aloud and trudged up the path he'd taken a few minutes earlier, wrestling with the confused thoughts that crowded her mind. Gradually, as she walked, she found herself growing calmer, and her turbulent emotions settled into a plan of action.

She wouldn't scream at him and make accusations. For one thing, there was an excellent possibility that Tyler's visit to Frankie's room had been completely innocent, and Ruth would look like a shrewish, jealous wife if she made an issue of it.

Besides, Ruth thought sadly, she was hardly in a position to cast blame, no matter what Tyler had done, because she'd betrayed their marriage vows, too. There were other ways to cheat besides committing adultery. Her deliberate withdrawal of affection, her coldness and isolation, were also a form of cheating, because they'd deprived Tyler of the warmth and comfort that he was entitled to expect from his marriage.

With the heightened insight that followed the shock of this new revelation, Ruth saw the past months much more clearly. She realized that Tyler, too, had suffered deeply from the loss of their child, and her intense preoccupation with her own grief had left him lonely and vulnerable.

"I'm sorry, darling," she whispered aloud. "I'll make it up to you, I swear. Things will be different from now on."

And they would. They had to be different, because Ruth couldn't endure the thought of anything else. She loved him so much. Strangely, considering the circumstances, she felt her love for Tyler grow and flare into passion as she remembered how it felt to be in his arms, kissing him, warm and safe in his embrace. . . .

She reached the house and hurried inside, calling his name.

"Tyler! Are you home?"

"In here," he called from his study.

Ruth crossed the lower floor and looked in at him, pretending surprise when she saw him hanging his jacket and hat on the polished oak coat tree. "Did you just get in?"

He nodded. "I spent quite a while talking to Daddy."

Ruth waited for him to add something casual about stopping in to deliver a message to Frankie, but he didn't. He turned aside, not looking at her, and tossed a file of papers onto the desk. "Daddy wants to call a meeting tomorrow with you and Cynthia. We need to make some final decisions about buying this equipment."

"Sure," Ruth said. "We were going to finish wallpapering Lisa's house, but it can wait until later in the day."

She hugged her arms and hesitated in the doorway, uncertain what to do. In the face of his detached coolness, all the plans she'd formed on the way up to the house now seemed clumsily embarrassing, impossible to carry out. She shifted from one foot to the other, feeling awkward and miserable.

How could she build a fire, put music on and suggest a romantic interlude, when Tyler looked so cold and preoccupied?

Ruth longed to touch him, to hurry over and nestle in his arms and beg for reassurance that everything was all right. She yearned to hear him say that nothing had changed and their marriage was still safe. But he didn't seem interested in her at all. He was already seated at his desk, frowning over the papers in the folder as he fed numbers into his computer.

Ruth lingered and watched him in silence, wondering desperately if she'd already lost him.

"Tyler..." she ventured.

"Yeah?" he asked, without looking up.

"Would you... like anything? Should I bring you some hot chocolate or something?"

And what were you doing at Frankie's place? Ruth asked him silently. *Please, Tyler, talk to me! Do you still love me?*

"No thanks," he said briefly. "I just had a drink at the ranch. I'm fine, Ruth, but you might as well go on to bed if you're tired. I'll be working for a long time, I think, getting ready for this meeting."

She nodded and turned away, aching with sorrow. Slowly she climbed the stairs, ran a hot bath for herself and went to bed, but sleep was slow in coming. For a long time she lay staring at the ceiling and listened to the mournful hooting of a solitary owl in the cedar trees by the vineyard.

As soon as Ruth left his office and went upstairs, Tyler settled in and spent an hour or so trying to work. But gradually the words and numbers blurred in front of his eyes until it became impossible to concentrate. He dropped his head onto his folded arms, shoulders stiff with emotion, and stayed that way for a long time with his face buried, so lost in shame and embarrassment that he could hardly move.

What the living hell, he asked himself furiously, *do you think you're playing at?*

Blindly, he clenched his hands into fists and pounded them on the littered surface of the desk, then grew still again, his mind whirling with troubled thoughts and images.

He saw Frankie, so tiny and shapely in her exercise suit, all black and yellow like a dainty bumblebee with her golden curls glistening in the lamplight.

The more he saw of Frankie, the more Tyler realized that he had gravely underestimated the girl's attractiveness. He'd known her since she was a child, and had always thought of her as a ragged tomboy, so athletic and tough that her father, Carl Switzer, often joked at the Longhorn about how difficult it was going to be to get little Frankie safely married and settled down.

But he was only joking, Tyler realized. The Switzers would have no shortage of applicants for Frankie's hand. In fact, young Joey Wall had been following her around since they were children, and the look in his eyes when he'd faced Tyler at her doorway tonight had certainly left no doubt about his intentions.

Tyler shuddered again, his body gripped in long spasms of misery. Standing in that guest house doorway, he'd felt like an aging stag being challenged by a glossy young buck, keen and full of fire. Joey's cold, measuring gaze had reduced the whole thing to a level of sexual challenge that made Tyler feel miserably out of place.

He'd wanted to laugh it off, shake Joey's hand and give him a smiling reassurance.

"Look, pal," he could have said. "I'm not here to steal your girl. I don't want to sleep with some kid almost young enough to be my daughter, no matter how cute she is. What I want, Joey, is to sleep with my own wife, but she won't do that sort of thing anymore. You see, Joey, my wife turns away from me every time I try to touch her, and it makes me feel like all her suffering is my own damn fault. It gets hard to bear, son. Real hard . . ."

Well, then, Tyler, he asked himself grimly, continuing the dialogue in his head, *what do you want, old son? And why are you sniffing around Frankie's room late at night, if you're not interested in taking her to bed?*

He raised his head, his face ravaged and bleak, and stared at a bright chart of winery grapes on the opposite wall.

What he really wanted, Tyler decided, was just a little bit of warmth from a woman who didn't blame him for everything. Just a smile and some happy conversation with someone who liked him and made him feel safe. Safety was so important. He wanted a conversation that could run free and smooth, not threatened by shoals of rocks that lay hidden just beneath the surface, sharp enough to rip your guts out and leave you bleeding in the water.

That was what he wanted, and he was pretty sure that Frankie offered that kind of warmth and comfort. The kid was bright and funny, there was no doubt that she liked him, and they certainly shared a passionate interest in the business of making wine.

Just as he and Ruth had once shared that same interest, Tyler thought, before they...

But the memories were too painful. He pushed them aside and continued to think about Frankie, trying to be honest as he examined his motives.

If he was really only interested in friendship and grapevines, then why did he feel so damned guilty? Why had he been ashamed and nervous when he'd realized Joey was visiting down at the guest house, and found himself slipping away from them like a thief in the night? And why had it been so hard to face Ruth when she came in soon after he did?

Tyler frowned, thinking for the first time about Ruth's response to him a few minutes ago. Was it part of his general distress and confusion, or had Ruth been acting a little friendlier than usual? It seemed to Tyler that she'd expressed some interest in what he was doing, maybe even offered to fetch him hot chocolate or something. But he'd been too uneasy and embarrassed to respond, and she'd gone away.

Briefly he felt a flare of hope. Maybe the miracle was starting to happen, and Ruth was warming to him again. Maybe now she'd begin to respond, to hold him and love him again, and find herself able to share her terrible grief so they could try to rebuild their marriage.

When Tyler thought about Ruth in his arms, loving him, all the troubling images of Frankie's face and body faded instantly from his mind. He shoved aside the papers on his desk, turned on the telephone answering machine and headed across the lower floor, then took the steps two at a time to the upper level.

He paused wistfully at the entrance to the living room, thinking she might have built a fire in the hearth and be sitting in the dark with a wineglass, listening to music and waiting for him as she'd so often done in the happy days of their marriage. But the big room was dark and silent. Tyler lingered in the moonlight for a moment, then ventured down the hall to the master bedroom.

He slipped inside and looked at her slim form huddled beneath the covers. It took a moment for his eyes to adjust to the darkness before he could make out her shoulders, the tumbled darkness of her hair. He moved around the bed to study her. Even in sleep, Ruth's face was sad and pale, her brow furrowed as if she was troubled by painful dreams. She held her clenched fists tightly under her chin, and she was huddled at the extreme edge of the bed, as far to her own side as she could get.

Tyler smiled sadly.

As if she's doing her level best to make sure there's no danger of accidentally touching me in the night, he thought, his throat tight with pain. *These days, seems like she'd rather fall out of bed than risk touching me....*

And she wore the heavy flannel pyjamas that he especially hated. Tyler grimaced, thinking about the silky white peignoir set he'd bought her for Christmas. She was always so pretty in white, and he'd thought, in his innocence, that she'd be glad to have something slim and dainty to wear after all those months when her body was distorted by pregnancy.

But as soon as she opened the package and looked at its contents, Tyler knew that he'd made a bad mistake. The gift seemed to suggest that she was nothing more than a sexual object to her husband, and that it was time to assume that role again. He'd seen the distaste on her face, and felt clumsy and foolish.

These days, he thought, standing grimly by the bed and watching her sleep, it seemed as if he felt that way most of the time. Clumsy, foolish and lonesome. Once again, unbidden, a vision of Frankie flashed into his mind.

He saw her standing wide-eyed and graceful in the blue silk dress, her naked shoulders gleaming. He saw her in the skimpy exercise suit, buttocks firm and curved, stomach flat, breasts high and inviting. He saw her smiling at him among the grapevines, her small teeth white and even in a dirt-smeared face, telling him with admiration that she'd never met a man who could work so fast and skillfully. And then she placed her little cold hand on his arm for a moment, and her touch burned like fire....

"Oh, *hell!*" Tyler moaned through gritted teeth.

He stood for a moment longer watching his wife sleep, then turned and plunged out of the room and down the stairs again.

For a long time he paced the floor, wondering what to do. At last, with a weary sigh, he went into his office, switched on the lamp and settled behind the desk. He pulled a file folder across the desk, opened it and set to work.

CHAPTER SEVEN

FOR A WEEK OR TWO after the night she saw Tyler coming out of the guest house, Ruth struggled with her emotions, trying to decide what to do about her husband and her marriage.

She couldn't really blame Tyler for rejecting her first tentative advance, not after all the times she'd turned away from him during the past months. He was hurt and wary, and he had every reason to be.

On the other hand, she didn't know how to approach him again, or what to say to get their relationship back on track. Partly she still felt numb inside, like a person who's lost the function of an arm or leg and can't remember how it used to work.

There'd been a time when intimacy came so easily to her and Tyler. A glance across a room, even a quick smile had been enough to deliver a whole complex message of invitation and loving promise. Now, she felt shy and awkward when they discussed business arrangements for the winery, or even when they tried to organize a trip into town to do the grocery shopping.

But though she watched with eyes that were newly alerted to any suspicious nuance, Ruth saw nothing to worry her about Tyler's relationship with Frankie. In fact, Frankie seemed a lot more quiet and withdrawn these days, and was talking about leaving her job early to get back to her classes at the university in Austin. Ruth had reassured the girl that if necessary, she herself could take over the last of the grapevine planting. But, privately, she wasn't entirely sure of her strength. There'd been a brief time when Ruth had felt fully recovered, at least in a physical sense, from the harsh trauma of the accident and her early labor, but lately a kind of lassitude had set in that worried her. In addition, she had some aches and pains, vaguely flulike symptoms that left her feeling tired and out of sorts.

No doubt Nate Purdy would dismiss these feelings as psychosomatic, and tell her she needed to get back to work and quit fretting. Ruth pictured his silver hair and cheerful grin as he scolded, and made a sour face at this fatherly image. Sometimes, she thought, trudging down the path to the big ranch house, she wished she could just drift away to a tropical island somewhere and spend a month lying in the sun on a peaceful beach.

But she wouldn't want to be on that beach without Tyler, and Tyler couldn't be dragged away from this place by a whole herd of wild horses. Not now, when there was so much work involved in getting the winery up and running for its first real season.

Ruth sighed again and pushed open the front door of the big house, calling out a greeting. She was met only by the sound of a telephone, which suddenly began to ring in the stillness.

"Hello?" Ruth called again. "Is anybody here?"

The telephone shrilled, echoing through the silent house. "Cynthia?" Ruth said, peering into the empty sunroom. "Lisa? Oh, for goodness' sake," she muttered, and ran to pick up the phone. "McKinney residence, Ruth McKinney speaking," she said automatically.

"Mrs. McKinney? I'd like to speak to Lisa Croft, please," a deep male voice said on the other end of the line.

Ruth wasn't good at identifying voices on the phone, but she knew that this didn't sound like Tony. She gripped the receiver and peered up the wide staircase.

"Lisa?" she called. "Is anybody home?"

She waited, but there was no response.

Finally Ruth shook her head and lifted the telephone again. "I'm sorry, Lisa doesn't seem to be here. I just came into the house, and I'm not sure where everybody is. Could I take a message, and have Lisa call you back when she comes in?"

"Well, now," the man said quietly, "I'm not sure if that's such a good idea. Could you give me some idea when I might get hold of her?"

A brief warning sounded in Ruth's mind. She thought about the mystery of Lisa's past, and the unknown danger that had apparently followed the girl to Texas during the summer. Ruth still had no idea what that was all about, but there had definitely been something in the air last August, something that chilled her with fear when she recalled it.

"I think perhaps you should tell me your name," she told the caller. "I'd prefer to know who you are before I give you any information."

"This is Mrs. McKinney?"

"Yes," Ruth said. "It is."

"Well, I'm Walt Kelly. I'm a neighbor to Lisa's family here in New Mexico."

"I see," Ruth said, puzzled and wary. "To her mother, you mean?"

"That's right. And her little brothers. I live on the next farm."

"I see. Is there . . . any problem at Lisa's home, Mr. Kelly?"

"Well, that depends," the man said after a brief silence. "I mean," he added hastily, "none of the little fellows are sick, or anything. Sadie's fine, too. It's not that."

"Sadie?" Ruth asked. "That's Lisa's mother?"

"I guess she never even told you her mother's name," Walt Kelly said. He sounded sad and defeated.

For some reason, Ruth found herself beginning to like this quiet-spoken man. She drew a deep breath, then gripped the receiver again. "Mr. Kelly," she began.

"Yes, ma'am?"

"Mr. Kelly, do you know what the problem is between Lisa and her mother? It's very difficult to get her to talk about her home life."

"I reckon I do," the man said after a brief silence. "In fact, that's why I'm calling. I'm not one to poke into other folks' business, Mrs. McKinney, but I was hoping I might have a talk with Lisa and try to straighten things out. Sadie feels real bad about all this, and the little boys, they'd love to come to that wedding."

"We'd love to have them," Ruth said with sincerity. "All of them. It's just that—" She fell abruptly silent.

"Lisa doesn't want her mother to be there," the man concluded.

"Yes," Ruth agreed. "Look, Mr. Kelly," she added nervously, "I'm not sure if it's right for me to be... talking about this. I feel uncomfortable, when it's none of my business."

"Reckon it's none of mine, either, but I sure don't like to see Sadie so upset. She's a real nice person, Mrs. McKinney. Sadie Duncan, she's... well, Sadie's a good woman."

There was no mistaking the depth of emotion in the man's voice. Ruth stared at the opposite wall, trying to square this image of Lisa's mother with her earlier picture of a cold, selfish woman who wouldn't even bother to drive across the state for her daughter's wedding.

"So this problem between them...it's something to do with Lisa?" she asked finally. "I mean, Lisa is the one who's angry?"

"I'd say that's true. I was hoping it might help if I talked to her, but I guess she won't want to say anything to me, either."

Ruth heard the sound of footsteps on the veranda outside the kitchen door, along with J.T.'s deep laughter and Jennifer's high-pitched squeals of delight.

"Listen," she said hastily, reaching for the pen and notepad that Cynthia kept in a little rack by the phone. "I hear them coming now, but I'd like a chance to talk to Lisa alone before you speak with her. Could you leave me your number, Mr. Kelly, and I'll have Lisa call you back?"

The man gave her his number as well as Sadie Duncan's, then hesitated. "Mrs. McKinney?"

"Yes?" Ruth asked, smiling automatically as the whole group spilled through the kitchen doorway and into the hall. They milled around her, talking loudly about a new colt down in the stables. "Could you hold please?" she said into the receiver, then covered it with her hand.

Cynthia and Lynn were first to arrive, pushing little Hank in his baby stroller while J.T followed with Jennifer in his arms, her cheeks bright with cold.

"Horsy!" the little girl shouted, catching sight of Ruth by the phone. "Baby horsy!"

Lettie Mae came in next, grumbling about some bread dough that was overdue to be punched down. Lisa was last to appear, laughing and beautiful in her fur-trimmed parka. She paused by the closet to hang her coat up, then took Jennifer from J.T.'s arms and vanished up the stairs.

"Mr. Kelly?" Ruth murmured into the phone. "I'm sorry about the delay. What were you saying?"

"I wonder if you'd do me a favor, Mrs. McKinney?"

"Of course," Ruth promised, still looking in a distracted fashion at the noisy group, who seemed to fill the entire house. She folded the square of paper she'd written the phone numbers on, and tucked it in her pocket.

"If Lisa doesn't want to call back, would you phone me and let me know? I sure want to get this thing settled, for Sadie's peace of mind."

"I understand," Ruth said. "Yes, I'll do that. I have to go now, I'm afraid."

"Goodbye, Mrs. McKinney. I'm real grateful for your help."

"Goodbye," Ruth said. She hung up the phone, then turned to listen as Cynthia and Lynn both tried to tell her about the colt, which had apparently been born unexpectedly during the night.

"Ruth, he's such a beauty!" Lynn said, her eyes shining. "And he's got great bloodlines. He's going to make us a fortune if he's as fast as he looks."

"Fast!" J.T. scoffed, giving his daughter a fond teasing grin. "The little critter can't even stand up yet, and Lynnie says he looks fast."

Lynn smiled calmly and bent to free her son from the confines of his stroller. "You know what I mean. Poor Sam," she added thoughtfully. "A few years ago, I'll bet he had no idea how deeply he was going to be involved with racehorses."

"A few years ago, Sam Russell had no idea this little man would be in the world, either," J.T. said, lifting his grandson and cuddling him with great tenderness. J.T. felt a special affection for the tiny boy who'd arrived so soon after old Hank's death, and who bore the same name.

Little Hank stared back solemnly, his blue eyes wide and intent.

"What a boy," J.T. said with a grin. "He looks like he's about to make a real important announcement, doesn't he?"

Lynn chuckled. "You're almost right, Daddy," she said, reaching for the warmly wrapped bundle that was her son. "Actually, I think he's filling his diaper. He always looks real solemn and thoughtful while he's doing that."

J.T. sniffed in experimental fashion, then handed the baby over hastily with a comical look of distress.

Cynthia laughed and hugged her husband. "There are obviously some limits to Grandpa's affection," she observed.

"Hey, that's not fair," J.T. protested, looking hurt. "I change diapers, you know. Even messy ones."

Cynthia smiled at him fondly. "Yes, you do. But," she added, following Lynn down the hall, "not if there's a woman around, J. T. McKinney."

J.T. turned to Ruth, who still lingered by the telephone. "I reckon that's true," he admitted. "But I've come a long way, Ruthie. Haven't I?"

"Yes," she agreed, smiling at the tall rancher. "Yes, J.T., you certainly have. Maybe there's hope for all you Texas men."

For a moment they stood beaming at each other with affection. At last Ruth turned toward the stairs, feeling suddenly more optimistic than she'd been for months.

"I need to talk to Lisa for a minute," she said. "See you at lunch, J.T."

J.T. nodded and moved down the hall in the direction of his study, and peace settled over the big house once again.

JENNIFER STOOD patiently in the middle of the nursery while Lisa removed her bulky snowsuit and mittens.

"Are you wet, sweetie?" Lisa smiled at the child's plump, rosy face.

Jennifer nodded solemnly and patted the front of her denim overalls. "Wet," she repeated with satisfaction.

Lisa hung the snowsuit away, then knelt to unfasten the snaps on the little girl's overalls. "You know, honey," she said, kissing Jennifer's cheek and sniffing the chilly outdoor freshness of her skin, "you should tell me *before*, not after. Then I could put you on the potty, and we wouldn't need to bother with these old diapers."

"Potty," Jennifer said, looking glum.

Lisa chuckled. "You have to learn sometime. And you can talk so much already, Jen-Jen. It's not going to be hard for you to tell me." She lifted the little girl onto the bed and changed her sodden diaper, then fastened the overalls again.

"Hammer," Jennifer announced, scrambling off the bed.

Lisa watched for a moment, smiling as the child ran over to her toy box and began hauling out the set of bright plastic tools that Cal had brought for her on his last visit.

When Jennifer was busily occupied, sitting on the rug and pounding pegs into a table with her yellow mallet, Lisa went down the hall to wash her hands, then hurried back to the nursery. She entered the room and found Ruth kneeling on the floor beside Jennifer, helping her manipulate a chunky blue screwdriver.

Ruth smiled over her shoulder when Lisa came in. "Isn't it something, the way she loves these tools?"

Lisa sat on the low wooden bench and began to fold clothes from a laundry basket on the floor. "Poor

Cynthia! It drives her crazy. Cal keeps bringing things like dump trucks and tools, and Jenny loves them. She never plays with dolls.''

Ruth grinned. ''You'd think Cynthia would approve of that, being the progressive woman that she is.''

''You'd think so,'' Lisa agreed. ''I believe Cynthia's a little scared,'' she added. ''Of Texas, I mean.''

''Texas?''

Lisa smoothed a small T-shirt and tucked it away in a drawer. ''Things are so different here from what Cynthia's used to. I think she's scared Jennifer will grow up really tough, and ride steers or something, and they'll have nothing in common.''

Ruth nodded thoughtfully. ''Texas can be pretty scary, all right, when you're not one of the natives. But still, I don't think those influences have much to do with how a person turns out. Look how dainty and feminine Beverly is, and her family's been Texan for about a dozen generations.''

Lisa smiled. ''Beverly's a lot tougher than people give her credit for.''

''Maybe she is. Lisa...''

Lisa reached for another T-shirt and frowned at a missing button on the shoulder. ''Hmm?''

''Lisa, a man called here this morning, and asked to speak with you.''

Fear clutched at Lisa's stomach, making her feel weak and shaky. She gripped the cotton shirt in her hand, wondering desperately if this terror would ever go away. It was irrational, after all. Ramon was gone, and he'd never be coming back. That part of her life was over and done with. Tony kept promising that nobody would ever hurt her again. But she couldn't help the flood of terror that rolled over her.

She looked up to find Ruth watching her. "He said his name was Walt Kelly," Ruth told her. "A neighbor of your family's."

Lisa sagged with relief and set the T-shirt aside on her pile of mending. "Oh," she said. "I've known Walt for years. He's a nice man."

Gradually the import of Ruth's words sank in. Lisa looked up again, chilled by a new fear.

"Did Walt . . . what did he want? Is there anything wrong with my brothers?"

"He said they're fine. And your mother, too," Ruth added casually. "He wanted you to call him."

Lisa nodded mechanically, matching small pairs of woolly socks and folding them neatly together. She thought of Walt Kelly, who had always been so kind to her while she was growing up.

There'd even been a time when Lisa had constructed a whole elaborate fantasy around Walt, imagining that he was her real father and one day he'd claim her and take her to live with him. It was embarrassing, now, to remember all those girlish dreams about Walt coming to pick her up at school, escorting her to the father-daughter banquet at Girl Scouts, praising her when her report card was good. . . .

Not that anyone could blame her, Lisa thought bitterly, for trying to create a real daddy for herself. Her own father had abandoned her and Sadie, vanishing without a trace when Lisa was smaller than Jennifer. And Ralph Duncan had never been a father. In fact, he'd been a monster.

"Will you?" Ruth was asking gently.

"Pardon?"

"Will you call him?"

Lisa made a brief, impatient gesture, wishing Ruth would go away and quit tormenting her. "I don't know," she said at last. "I'm really busy, Ruth. The wedding's only a couple of weeks away and I've got a ton of things to do, and our house still isn't ready yet, and I've got to..."

"Lisa, don't you think your mother should come to the wedding? Whatever the problem is, shouldn't you try to work it out?"

Lisa's hands dropped into her lap. She looked down at them, twisting her fingers together nervously. "I can't, Ruth," she murmured. "I truly can't. Please don't make me talk about it."

Ruth came over and sat beside her, putting an arm around her shoulders and holding her tightly. "Honey," she whispered, "I just don't understand. Maybe if you'd talk about it, we could work something out. You know I care about you, Lisa. I'm sure I'll be able to understand better if you tell me."

Lisa sat quietly in the other woman's embrace, wondering how Ruth could possibly understand. What did Ruth McKinney know about cruelty and suffering? She'd grown up in a big house with a real father, surrounded by loving protection, and then she'd moved to another big house with a whole lot more love and warmth. She'd never known a day of misery in her life.

Suddenly Lisa remembered Ruth's dead baby, and the terrible suffering she and Tyler had endured, and felt ashamed. She turned to hide her face against Ruth's shoulder, struggling not to cry. Ruth held her and waited silently.

For a moment Lisa was tempted to confide in this gentle woman, to tell her all about Ralph Duncan and his swaggering cruelty, and Lisa's terrible anger against her mother for allowing it to happen.

But as soon as the impulse came, Lisa suppressed it and sat up, squaring her shoulders and turning away. Her shame made it impossible for her to tell Ruth about the past. Besides, Lisa was afraid that if she told her story, the anger might somehow vanish and leave her empty and vulnerable.

Lisa's fear of that emptiness was all tied up with her feelings about Tony, and her anxiety about the upcoming marriage and the wedding night that would follow. She was growing less confident all the time that she'd be able to endure Tony's sexual caresses, even though she adored him and spent every spare minute of the day thinking about him. And that, in a complicated way, was her mother's fault, for allowing her stepfather to drive Lisa out of the house and onto the dangerous streets of Las Vegas.

Lisa needed desperately to blame her mother for what had happened to her, because if her problems had been her own fault, then she must be a bad person and Tony would come to despise her. And the thought of Tony hating her, even being disappointed in her, was more than Lisa could bear....

"It was all her fault," Lisa murmured in anguish. "All of it."

"What was, honey?"

Lisa looked up, startled, unaware that she'd spoken aloud. "I had some problems," she said at last. "Before I came here." She got up and moved stiffly across the room, carrying the empty laundry basket toward the door. "Mostly because of some things my mother did. Or didn't do," she corrected herself, remembering Ralph shouting and hitting Johnny while they all cowered, terrified, and little Seth whimpered with fear.

"What kind of problems?"

"I don't want to talk about it," Lisa repeated dully. "Please, Ruth, leave it be."

As Ruth looked at her in helpless silence, Lettie Mae's voice sounded from below, loud and threatening.

"Ruth! Lisa! Come down here and bring that baby. I'm putting lunch on the table, and if it gets cold, you all are in big trouble."

Lisa sagged with relief and forced a smile. "Well, I guess we'd better go, then," she said. "Come on, Jennifer. You can bring your screwdriver, honey," she added hastily, when Jennifer scowled and opened her mouth to protest.

Still looking troubled, Ruth took the little girl's hand and followed Lisa out into the hallway. The two women descended the stairs in silence, both of them deep in their own thoughts.

RUTH RUBBED GARLIC in the bottom of her big wooden salad bowl, then dumped the tossed salad into it and set the bowl aside while she checked a pan of salmon steaks in the oven. They were baking nicely, delicately browned and seasoned. If Tyler was on time, they would be perfect when he arrived.

She set her vegetable steamer in a saucepan of water, ready to cook the asparagus, and stirred a pot of wild rice on the back of the stove. Everything looked delicious, and although Ruth's appetite still didn't seem completely back to normal, there was nothing wrong with Tyler's. She was sure he'd enjoy the special pains she'd gone to for this meal.

Ruth was actually having a fair amount of success in altering Tyler's eating habits. When she first arrived at the ranch, she'd been horrified by the amount of red meat and fried foods that the McKinneys ate, but things were changing down at the other house, too, since J.T.'s heart attack. Cynthia and Lettie Mae were both deeply concerned about his diet, so even J.T. was learning to eat light, though he still grumbled bitterly about "fish and rabbit food."

Ruth smiled, then tensed when she heard the door open downstairs. Her cheeks drained of color and she hurried to set out the salad plates and dressing and light the candles. She wanted everything to be perfect tonight, in the hope that she could accomplish what she wanted without a fight.

She didn't want to fight with him....

Tyler was quiet when he came in. He dropped a polite kiss on her cheek and looked in surprise at the candles and linen napkins on the dining table. "This is sure fancy," he commented, turning to glance at Ruth as he took his place at the table. "What's the occasion? Did I forget an anniversary or something?"

Ruth shook her head, still feeling nervous and awkward. "It's just...it's a really shameless attempt to manipulate you," she said, trying to smile. "I'm going to ask for something, and I wanted to soften you up first."

She took a bottle of Chablis from the sideboard and filled their glasses, then seated herself opposite him. Tyler sipped the wine, his eyes closed in appreciation. He smiled at her.

"Well, it's working," he said. "I'm putty in your hands, Ruth. What do you want?"

She hesitated, then got up to check the salmon while Tyler began to eat his salad.

"Ruth?" he called.

"I'll tell you in a minute," Ruth called back from the kitchen, lifting the rich pink steaks onto a platter and surrounding them with asparagus spears. She came back, carrying the main course and the rice, while Tyler sniffed the air appreciatively.

"Okay," he said, with a flash of his old, teasing grin. "Honest, Ruthie, I'm hooked. Whatever it is, you can have it."

Ruth took her seat again and shook out her napkin. "I want to go away for a little while," she said abruptly.

Tyler sobered and gave her a cautious glance. "What do you mean? Back to California?"

Ruth shook her head, taking a hasty sip of wine. She hated lying to Tyler, but in this case it was necessary. If she told him the truth, that she wanted to drive over to Albuquerque and visit Lisa's mother, he would be horrified. He'd tell her that none of this problem was any of her business, that she absolutely shouldn't involve herself. And he'd be right, of course. But Ruth couldn't help herself. Whenever she thought of Lisa's pale, miserable face and the genuine sadness in Walt Kelly's voice, she knew that she had to do something, whether Tyler approved or not.

"Ruth?" he asked.

"I want to drive over to Albuquerque," she said, taking a deep breath. Ruth wasn't a very good liar, and she'd decided that it would be safest for her stay as close to the truth as possible.

"*Albuquerque?* What for? What's in Albuquerque?"

"Betsy told me..."

Ruth paused in dismay, realizing for the first time that she was going to have to clear all this with Betsy, too, just in case Tyler happened to run into her cousin somewhere and mention Ruth's trip. She sighed, hating the deepening pool of lies. She'd never lied to Tyler before.

"Betsy told me an old school friend of mine is living there. I'd lost track of her over the years, and I'd love to see her again."

"Really? Anybody I'd know about?"

"Well...yes. As a matter of fact, it's Mimsy Muldoon," Ruth said, grasping at straws. "Remember her?"

"That cute little blonde who came to the ranch with you when we were kids?"

Ruth nodded, feeling more and more treacherous. "I'd really love to see her again. I called when Betsy gave me the number, and Mimsy said she'd like to have me visit, so I thought I'd drive over there for a few days."

Tyler frowned and helped himself to rice. "Didn't you say Mimsy was living in Bel Air?"

"Apparently she got divorced again," Ruth said, startled as she always was by the accuracy of Tyler's memory. Damn him, the man never forgot anything, no matter how insignificant it might be.

Sorry, Mimsy, she thought. *I have no idea where you are or what you're doing, but I hope you understand that I need to do this....*

Tyler, however, seemed less concerned about the details of Mimsy Muldoon's life than he was about the trip itself. "It's a long drive to Albuquerque," he said, frowning. "If you want to pay a visit, why don't you fly? I hate having you drive all that way."

"But I love driving," Ruth said eagerly. "You know how much I love to drive, Tyler."

He smiled, but his eyes were bleak. "Yeah, I know. You're a real California girl."

"And I thought I'd go as far as Lubbock the first night and stay with the Kennocks. You know how they've been pestering us to visit. John wants to show off his new Chardonnay."

Tyler nodded, his face softening when he thought of their wine-making friends on the high plains of Lubbock. "Maybe I should take a few days off and go with you," he said wistfully. "We haven't had a holiday for a long time, have we, Ruthie?"

Ruth felt a chill of fear. "But you...you're not finished the planting, are you, Tyler? And you'd be bored with Mimsy, you really would. She's not your type at all."

He looked at her thoughtfully for a moment, then nodded. "Yeah," he said quietly. "I guess you're right." He lowered his head and began to eat. Ruth looked at his crisp dark hair, her heart aching. "You know I'd love to go away for a holiday with you, Tyler," she murmured. "It's just that..."

"I know. It wasn't a good idea. After the planting's done, maybe we'll think about a holiday."

"Yes," Ruth said. "Let's do that."

"So, when do you want to leave for Albuquerque?"

Ruth frowned, thinking about Lisa's unhappiness and the wedding that was approaching so quickly. "Right away," she said. "Tomorrow or the day after, if I can. I want to be back home in time to get ready for the wedding."

"Okay. I'll check the weather reports and make sure the car's in good shape. Would you rather take Cynthia's car? You two could trade for a while. I'm sure she wouldn't mind."

Ruth looked up, startled. "Why?"

"Her car's heavier, probably safer to drive." Tyler gave his wife an awkward smile. "I'd feel more secure if you were driving something a little bigger."

Ruth thought it over, then shook her head. "I like my car. I'll be careful, Tyler. Nothing's going to happen to me."

He nodded and returned to his meal while Ruth glanced at him covertly, touched by his concern. She had a sudden almost unbearable urge to be close to him, to push the dinner dishes aside and nestle in his lap and kiss him. And along with the tenderness, for the first time in ages, Ruth felt a strong thrust of sexual desire.

"Tyler..."

He looked up, and Ruth was chilled by the remote, cautious expression in his eyes. Involuntarily she remembered him coming out of the guest house and hurrying away into the night. The image seared and burned in her mind, growing more painful with the passage of time.

"Nothing," Ruth said quietly, and began to eat her salmon. "Nothing at all."

CHAPTER EIGHT

THE WINTER WIND whistled across the farmyard, carrying a trace of snow that swirled out of a cold gray sky. Sadie hesitated, plunging her hands deeper into the pockets of her shabby coat and looking at Walt Kelly's house. She hadn't been over to her neighbor's for a long time, and her courage began to fail her now that she was almost at his back door.

The house was like Walt, sturdy and solid, with a fresh coat of white paint and green shutters. He certainly kept things nice, Sadie thought, looking around at the neat sheds and outbuildings. Walt Kelly was a man who looked after things.

But she could hardly stand here all morning examining his farm. At last, with a sigh of reluctance, she rang the doorbell and then waited on the step while the wind lifted and tugged at her hair.

The door opened and Walt stood there in his stocking feet, wearing jeans and a plaid flannel shirt, looking at her in surprise. He carried a coffee mug in his hand, and had a pair of reading glasses pushed up onto his forehead. Behind him in the kitchen, Sadie could see a table with an opened newspaper.

"Good morning," she said, her shyness making her sound more brusque than she felt. "Harry says he left a school library book over here yesterday. I thought I'd walk over to pick it up."

"Sadie, you didn't need to make that trip in the cold. I could have brought it around."

"I wanted to save you the bother. You go to so much trouble over us."

He smiled, his eyes full of a warmth that gave her the same fluttery, unsettled feeling she was experiencing so often these days.

"Well, come in and have a cup of coffee with me, then," he said. "You look chilled through."

"It's a cool wind," Sadie agreed, following him into the kitchen. "It feels like snow."

She stood awkwardly, looking around while he helped her remove her coat and hung it on a peg by the door.

Walt's kitchen wasn't what she'd expected, somehow. There was no bachelor-style dirt or messiness. In fact, the room was almost clinically neat, scrubbed and orderly. Still, there was something lonely and plain about Walt's house that made Sadie feel sorry for him.

The problem, she realized, was the total absence of a woman's touch. No plants on the windowsill, no pictures, except for a serviceable calendar from the farm supply store in town, no cheery decorations or splashes of color.

"Pretty plain, isn't it?" Walt said behind her, echoing her thoughts. "I'm not much of a hand for interior decoration."

Sadie turned away, feeling guilty. "It's real nice and tidy," she murmured, seating herself in the chair he offered and watching while he crossed the room to get another coffee mug from the cupboard. "Most men wouldn't keep such a tidy kitchen."

"I'm not most men, Sadie," he told her quietly, setting the mug of coffee in front of her. "Never have been."

"No," she said, smiling up at him. "I reckon you're not."

He smiled back, and their eyes met and held for a long moment while Sadie's cheeks grew uncomfortably warm. She looked down at the paper, anxious to change the subject. "There's an article in there about a new gold mine up in the San Juan Mountains," she said. "Did you read it?"

Walt nodded and seated himself in the opposite chair. "I was just looking at it. Some feller's been looking for gold for thirty years, and just struck the mother lode. Imagine that."

"Wouldn't that be exciting?" Sadie gazed out the window at the brooding sky. "Think of it, Walt. All those years with people laughing at you and calling you crazy, and then one day you pound on the wall of a cave and see that gold shining in the dark."

Walt leaned back in his chair and gave her a teasing grin. "Why, Sadie, are you a prospector at heart?

Should we sell our farms, buy a couple of pack mules and head up into the mountains to find our fortune?''

She laughed and sipped the coffee, feeling more relaxed now that he wasn't watching her with such disturbing intensity. "It's a real nice dream," she said. "But I reckon it's slow and steady that wins the race. It's just that sometimes," Sadie added gloomily, thinking about dentist's bills and angry daughters and worn-out blue jeans, "it all seems a little too slow to bear."

"Sadie..."

But whatever Walt was about to say, it was interrupted by the ringing of the telephone. He glanced at her, then got up and crossed the room to answer.

"Hello, ma'am," he said, giving Sadie a quick, guarded look that puzzled her. "I didn't expect you to get here so soon. Did you have a good trip?"

Sadie sipped her coffee and paged through the newspaper, trying not to look like an eavesdropper. But she couldn't help wondering what woman was calling Walt, and where she'd traveled from.

"You're right here in town?" he asked in surprise. "Not in Albuquerque?"

Again he waited, giving Sadie another of those cautious glances. She began to feel a stirring of uneasiness, a feeling that intensified when Walt spoke again.

"Matter of fact," he said in his quiet voice, "she's here at my place right now. Dropped in a minute ago to pick up a book one of the boys left behind. I'll ask her, all right?"

"Who is it?" Sadie asked.

"It's a lady," Walt said, covering the receiver and giving Sadie an anxious look. "She wants to talk with you, Sadie. Will you be around this morning?"

"What lady?"

"Sadie," he said gently, "it's Mrs. McKinney, from over in Texas. She wants to talk to you about Lisa."

Sadie tensed, the color draining from her face. "I don't . . . Walt, how did she . . . Is Lisa all right?"

"Lisa's just fine. Can you talk to Mrs. McKinney?"

"When?"

"Right away," Walt said patiently. "She's here in town, Sadie. She drove out from the city this morning."

Sadie's head began to spin. "I want to talk to her in my own house," she said, fighting down a rising panic. "I need time to get home."

"Sure. I'll drive you over." Walt lifted the receiver and spoke into the phone again. "Mrs. McKinney, have you got a pencil or something there? Okay, I'll give you some directions how to get to Sadie's place, and we'll meet you over there in half an hour or so. Is that all right?"

He waited a moment, then began to give instructions while Sadie gripped her mug of cooling coffee and watched him.

At last he hung up and crossed the room to put on his boots and denim jacket. He took Sadie's old coat and held it out for her, then lifted Harry's picture book from the counter and handed it over.

She took the book in silence. Not until they were outside in his truck, heading down the lane toward Sadie's trailer, did she find her voice.

"You called, didn't you, Walt? You called those people over in Texas."

"Yes," he said quietly. "I did."

Sadie swallowed hard and gripped the book tightly in her lap. "Did you talk to Lisa?"

"No, I just talked a couple of times to this lady who's coming to see you."

"And she's Mrs. McKinney? The lady Lisa that works for?"

"Well, not exactly. It seems there's a big family over there at this ranch where Lisa is. The lady who's coming here, she's married to the son of the lady Lisa works for."

"Married to the son?" Sadie's mind worked slowly. "Then she's...she's a younger person?"

"I reckon she must be. She sounds real nice, Sadie. She cares a lot about Lisa. Seems she's been wanting to talk to you about this wedding and all."

"Does Lisa know she's coming to see me?"

Walt parked by the trailer and sat for a moment, looking uncomfortable. "I don't think so," he admitted. "But Mrs. McKinney sounds real optimistic,

Sadie. She thinks if you all can get together, maybe the problems can be worked out.''

Sadie felt a wistful surge of hope, then another flood of nervousness. ''Walt,'' she whispered, giving him a pleading glance, ''would you mind staying while she's here? I'd like you to stay with me.''

He smiled and reached over to squeeze her hand. Sadie trembled at the feel of his hard, callused palm, the strength and surprising gentleness of his fingers. For a moment they sat holding hands, while she choked back a sob and tried to smile.

''You're real good to me, Walt,'' she said at last. ''Going to all this bother, just for me.''

''I care about you, Sadie,'' he said gently, giving her hand another gentle squeeze. ''I care about you a whole lot. You're the best woman I ever met. And,'' he added solemnly, ''just about the prettiest, besides.''

''Pretty!'' she scoffed, feeling hot and confused. It had been such a long time since anybody had called Sadie Duncan pretty. In fact, since anybody had given her any praise of any kind...

''Pretty,'' Walt repeated calmly. ''When you get all excited, like about that gold mine, and your eyes sparkle, you look about sixteen years old. Make me feel about sixteen, too,'' he confessed with a grin that made her heart turn over.

Sadie struggled to get herself under control. Here she was getting ready to talk to a stranger about her lost daughter, and she was holding hands with Walt

Kelly, arguing about whether or not she was pretty. It was all too bewildering to deal with.

At last, reluctantly, Sadie withdrew her hand from his and got out of the truck, still clutching Harry's book. She headed across the chilly bare yard to her back door, while Walt followed in silence.

RUTH DROVE into the farmyard and parked by the ragged fence, wondering if she'd found the right place. Walt Kelly's directions had been very specific, but it was still hard to associate this desolate trailer with Lisa's loveliness and delicacy.

Fighting down a sense of mounting panic, Ruth pocketed her keys, gathered up her handbag and wondered, not for the first time, just what she thought she was doing. She got out of the car and stood for a moment watching the chickens pecking busily in the dusty grass near the gate. The wind sobbed and moaned across the barren plains, and Ruth felt a sudden intense longing for her husband.

Oh, Tyler, she thought, picturing his dark quiet face, his capable manner and engaging smile. *Tyler, darling, I wish you were with me. I don't even know why I've come here.* But Tyler was far away, working in his vineyard with Frankie close beside him in the place where his wife should be....

Ruth sighed and trudged across the yard to the door of the trailer.

A tall man answered her knock and stood looking down at her with grave courtesy. "Mrs. McKinney," he said, standing aside to let her enter. "I'm Walt Kelly. Nice of you to come."

Ruth nodded and stepped into a living room that was shabby, but gleaming with cleanliness and order. A woman in blue jeans and an old cardigan stood nervously by the couch, trying to smile.

"Hello," the woman said in a low voice. "I'm Sadie Duncan, Lisa's mother."

"And I'm Ruth McKinney." The woman's shyness was so painful that Ruth promptly forgot all about herself, anxious to put Sadie at ease. "I would have known you were Lisa's mother," she said with a kind smile. "The two of you look so much alike."

Sadie's face brightened. She glanced at Walt, then looked back toward Ruth. "That's real nice of you to say, Mrs. McKinney," she told Ruth. "But I don't think I was ever as pretty as Lisa, and I'm way past those days now. Please sit down," she added, indicating a worn velour armchair.

Ruth sat down and watched while Walt Kelly came and seated himself next to Sadie, resting one arm along the back of the couch in a protective manner. Sadie still looked flustered, but it was clear that she welcomed his presence. She really did look a great deal like her daughter, Ruth thought. Sadie Duncan, too, must have been a beautiful girl at one time. She was weathered now, with a careless hairstyle and worn clothes, but she still had lovely blue eyes and a delicate bone structure in her face.

"Walt says . . . he tells me that Lisa works for your family," Sadie ventured.

"Yes, she does. She's a wonderful girl," Ruth said sincerely. "We all love her."

Sadie looked down in her lap. "Is she . . . is Lisa all right?" she asked at last, giving Ruth a wistful glance. "I haven't heard from her for such a long time. She was . . ." Her voice caught and she fell silent.

Walt dropped a hand onto her shoulder. Sadie moved a little closer to him, still keeping her eyes lowered.

"She's just fine," Ruth said. "She looks after a little girl named Jennifer, and she's engaged to a young veterinarian who lives in Crystal Creek."

"A veterinarian?" Sadie repeated, her face lighting with interest. "What's he like? Is he nice?"

"He's very nice. His name is Tony Rodriguez. He and Lisa are getting married on Valentine's Day, and afterward she'll keep her job and they'll live in a little cottage on the ranch. We've all been helping Lisa to fix up the house."

Sadie nodded eagerly. She was obviously so hungry for these details about her daughter's life that she forgot her reserve and smiled at Ruth. "That sounds real nice," she whispered.

"It's a pretty little house, and the ranch is a nice place," Ruth agreed. "Lisa's planning to take some college courses in Austin, too. She hopes to get a degree in Early Childhood Education, and eventually teach or operate a day care center."

"Oh," Sadie murmured blissfully, wringing her hands. "Oh, Mrs. McKinney, that's such good news. Lisa's a real smart girl," she added with a faraway smile. "She always had the highest marks in her class, just like Harry and Johnny. But she..."

Abruptly Sadie fell silent. Walt gave her shoulder another comforting little squeeze.

"What happened, Mrs. Duncan?" Ruth asked gently. "What's the problem between you and Lisa?"

Sadie trembled slightly and Walt cast Ruth a warning glance. "Mrs. McKinney," he began, clearing his throat awkwardly, "maybe it's best if—"

But Sadie shook her head abruptly. "It's all right, Walt," she said. "I want to tell her. Maybe it'll help us."

She turned back to Ruth with a look of desperate appeal, drew a deep breath and began to talk about her marriage, about her husband and his brutal treatment of her and the children, about Lisa's anger over her mother's inability to protect them.

Ruth listened, appalled. She knew, of course, that situations like this existed, but she'd never personally encountered a victim of the kind of violence that Sadie described in her halting voice. It was a world that Ruth McKinney could hardly imagine.

At last Sadie fell silent, her shoulders heaving, and burrowed against Walt's side for comfort. Walt held her gently, looking over her head at Ruth with quiet entreaty.

"I'm so sorry," Ruth whispered, twisting the straps of her handbag. "Sadie, I'm so sorry." Impulsively she got up and crossed the room to Sadie's other side, patting the woman's thin shoulder.

Sadie put her hands over her face. "Lisa's so mad at me," she said in a muffled voice. "I don't...I don't know what I can do. If I could go back and make things different somehow, God knows I'd do whatever I could. But it's too late."

"It's *not* too late," Ruth said firmly. "It's never too late to make things right. Once Lisa understands the situation a little better, and realizes how much you've suffered, she'll..."

Forgive you. Lisa will forgive you.

The words hung in the air, unspoken.

Ruth found herself thinking about Tyler's loneliness and misery in the dreary months since their baby's death. After all, her husband, like Sadie, had been waiting to be forgiven and loved again. And hadn't her behavior, in many ways, been just as harsh as Lisa's?

When she looked at it from this point of view, Ruth understood that there were a lot of things she and Tyler needed to talk about. She filed the troubling thoughts away to examine later. There would be plenty of time on the long drive home to think about Tyler and herself, and make a decision about what to do next....

"You know what I think, Sadie?" she murmured. "I think you should come to this wedding."

Sadie lifted a ravaged face. "But I can't. Lisa doesn't want me."

"I doubt that Lisa knows what she wants," Ruth said quietly. "I know what it's like, Sadie, to be angry with someone you love because you . . . you blame them for your own pain. Those are such destructive emotions. We need to move beyond them as soon as we can, for everybody's sake."

Walt nodded thoughtfully, then looked down at Sadie's graying hair with such tenderness that Ruth felt a lump in her throat. "I'd be happy to drive you and the boys over to Texas, Sadie," he said.

"Oh, Walt . . ."

"I wouldn't expect to be invited to the wedding," he added hastily, meeting Ruth's eyes. "I'd just want to make sure they get there safe."

"Of course you'll come to the wedding," Ruth told him. "I doubt that Sadie would want to be there without you."

His eyes widened with surprise and pleasure. "Well, thank you, Mrs. McKinney," he said. "That's real nice of you."

"Please, call me Ruth."

Sadie looked up, a little dazed by the speed of all this. "I don't know if . . . I don't want to ruin Lisa's wedding," she said painfully. "If we turn up there and it upsets her to see me, she might . . ."

"Lisa will know that you're coming," Ruth said. "I'm leaving now to go home, and as soon as I get there I'm going to talk to Lisa. I plan to tell her a few things from my own experience," she added with a sad little smile, "about love and forgiveness. And I'm sure that by the time you get there, she'll be ready to see all of you."

Sadie gave her a look of intense gratitude. "Mrs. McKinney..." she began.

"Ruth."

"I want to thank you, Ruth. This is such a good thing you're doing."

Ruth hugged her and stood up. "Who knows? Maybe solving everybody else's problems will help me deal with my own," she said with an attempt at lightness. "Now, if you'll both excuse me, I really should get back on the road. I've got a long drive home, and a wedding to get ready for in just a few days."

"It's on Valentine's Day?" Sadie asked, getting automatically to her feet.

"That's right."

"The boys will have to miss a few days of school, but that won't hurt. We could all..." Sadie turned to Walt, her cheeks pink with excitement, her eyes shining. She looked so young and pretty that Ruth and Walt both stared at her in astonishment. Walt cleared his throat, obviously shaken.

"We'll work it out, Sadie," he told her gently. "Would you like some coffee, Ruth?" he asked. "You should have something before you go."

"Oh, my goodness," Sadie said with a breathless laugh. "Of course you should. Where are my manners?" She turned and hurried off toward the kitchen.

"Sadie, don't go to any trouble," Ruth said, following with Walt at her side. But despite her protests, she found that she was reluctant to leave the little trailer, which looked cozy and inviting now that Sadie was so happy.

In fact, Ruth wished she could stay forever, sitting at the kitchen table with Sadie and Walt, eating homemade doughnuts and listening to their stories about the antics of Lisa's lively brothers.

Because as soon as she left she was going to be alone with her thoughts, and they were almost too painful to bear.

Ruth was hopeful that she could mend the rift in this family. But she realized that she had a great deal less confidence about her ability to save her own marriage.

TYLER FINISHED a solitary meal of canned chili on toast, then wandered through his silent house while the winter dusk deepened beyond the windows. It was Sunday night, and the loneliness pressed up close to him, so heavy that it was almost palpable.

He climbed the stairs and went into the spacious bedroom he shared with Ruth, looking around with a bleak expression. When Ruth was gone, the entire house seemed lifeless and cold, but the bedroom was the emptiest room of all.

At last he forced himself to cross the floor and open Ruth's closet. He frowned at the clothes hanging neatly on racks and folded on the shelves, trying to figure out just how much she'd taken with her. There seemed to be an ample supply of things left behind, but that didn't comfort him much. He knew that Ruth had a lot of clothes. He looked at a couple of maternity dresses hung away at the back, hidden behind her winter coats. One of them, a roomy tent dress of bright red Mexican cotton, had been practically the only thing she'd worn for those last few months of the autumn. Tyler reached out and fingered the soft fabric, then moved into the closet and gathered the dress in his arms, burying his face in it and fighting back an embarrassing flood of tears.

Tyler was certain that his wife had left him for good this time. She was supposed to be home tomorrow, but he didn't expect to see her. He was pretty sure that she wasn't in Albuquerque, and he didn't believe for a minute that Mimsy Muldoon was there, either.

Ruth was such a truthful person that it was almost impossible for her to lie with any kind of conviction. Tyler could have pressed her before she left, accused her of lying and demanded to know where she was really going and when she planned to come back. But he'd been afraid to ask. Now, he spent the long dark evenings wandering through his house like a ghost, waiting for the phone to ring.

He knew that soon she'd get where she was going, probably back to her father's home in California, and call to tell him that she wasn't coming back. She'd ask for her things to be shipped out there, and Tyler would have to obey. He'd hurt her enough already. He couldn't keep fighting to hold on to her, not when she obviously didn't want him anymore.

But he had no idea how he was ever going to live without her.

At last he released the dress, tucked it neatly back in place and left the bedroom. He paused in the hallway, then slipped into the baby's room for a minute and looked sadly at the bare walls and empty dresser. A memory sprang to his mind of their sweet little flower-faced child, with his downy fluff of hair and his dark eyelashes sweeping onto his round cheeks.

The baby had looked so peaceful in his blue hospital blanket, as if he were just sleeping and would wake at any moment. Tyler had hardly been able to grasp what Nate was telling him when the doctor said their child hadn't made it.

"Oh, God," Tyler whispered when the pain of the memory hit him. He clenched his fists and leaned his forehead against the doorframe. "Oh, *God...*"

Finally, unable to bear the silence of his empty house, he went downstairs, put on his hat and jacket and started down the path toward the ranch house, where lighted windows blazed a cheerful welcome into the starry winter night.

Tyler passed the little bungalow that Lisa and Tony planned to occupy after their wedding, now only a few days away. The two young people were inside working, clearly visible through the big living room windows that still hadn't been covered with draperies. They were painting, both of them plying rollers against the walls while they talked and laughed together.

As Tyler watched from a screen of cedar trees near the path, Tony climbed down from the ladder to refresh his paint tray and paused to sweep Lisa into his arms, then kissed her with a passionate hunger that left Tyler feeling off-balance. He turned guiltily away from their private moment and strode off into the night again, more lonely than he'd ever thought a man could be.

Suddenly he paused in the darkness and frowned, thinking about the young couple and their upcoming wedding. Hope flared briefly within him when he remembered that Ruth was supposed to be a member of the wedding party.

Ruth's dress had been fitted and ready for a couple of weeks, and she'd seemed genuinely excited about being part of the festivities. There probably wasn't time for somebody else to take her place, and no matter how upset she was, Tyler didn't think his wife would let Lisa down without notice.

But as soon as the hope surged within him, it began to fade again. All these women were so close, tied to one another with a kind of intimate bond that Tyler couldn't begin to understand. It was entirely possible that Lisa knew where Ruth was and what she was doing. Maybe the whole thing had been worked out in advance, and a replacement was already selected and waiting to take Ruth's position in the wedding party.

How could a man ever know what the women in his life were thinking or planning?

Tyler thought about going back and confronting Lisa, demanding to be told where his wife was and if she really planned to be back in time for the wedding. But he dismissed the idea, mostly because he didn't know if he could bear to hear the truth.

The ranch house loomed ahead of him, all of its lower windows shining into the night. Tyler thought wistfully about the people behind those lighted curtains, living their vigorous and happy lives. He knew what every one of them was doing on this winter evening. Lettie Mae would be in the sitting room watching television, probably accompanied by Lynn and her children, who were spending the weekend at the ranch. Cynthia and J.T. were most likely in his study at this hour, enjoying an evening drink together and talking about business and family matters while Jennifer, fresh and rosy from her bath, played on the carpet by the fireplace in one of her fuzzy sleepers.

Soon J.T. would set the books aside and take his little daughter on his knee to tell her a bedtime story, a nightly ritual that Jennifer demanded with unyielding fierceness. Then he and Cynthia would carry their child upstairs and tuck her into bed, and join the rest of the family around the television....

Tyler stood with his hand on the latch of the gate, wondering if he could endure that much family warmth right now. It was great to be part of a big, loving family, but sometimes, too, it hurt like hell when their love only served to remind him of what he'd lost.

While he hesitated, Hagar emerged from the shadows and rubbed against his legs, mewing plaintively. Tyler bent to pat the big orange cat, fondling his ears with a gentle hand.

He smiled, remembering when he'd surprised Ruth by having her cat flown out from California. That was the day Ruth had started loving him, the day when the happiest time of his life had begun.

"Hi, there, old boy," he whispered huskily. "What are you doing outside on a cold night like this?"

Hagar fixed him with an inscrutable gaze, his green eyes glowing faintly in the darkness. He suffered Tyler's caress a moment longer, then shook himself restlessly and melted into the shadows by the fence, heading in the direction of old Hank's deserted stone house.

Tyler's sadness deepened as he watched the cat's fluffy shape disappear. Both of them were outcasts, he thought, wandering through the darkness in search of a lost love. Neither of them was part of the cheery scene inside that house. They were doomed to roam forever in the shadows, seeking and yearning....

"Oh, hell," he muttered aloud, embarrassed by his melancholy. Suddenly a light fell across the ground just ahead of him. Tyler looked up, his breath catching in his throat.

Frankie had just opened the door of the guest house and stood peering out at the winter night. She wore black tights and a long white T-shirt, but the light behind her showed the outline of her shapely body through the fabric of her shirt. Her golden hair, freshly washed, shone brightly in the night.

Tyler crouched in the shadows, arrested by the sight of her narrow waist and her breasts. Even her nipples were clearly visible through the glowing cotton, and her figure was surprisingly voluptuous despite her small size. He drew a silent, ragged breath and tried to look away.

"Hagar?" she called softly, peering into the darkness. "Are you out here? I thought I heard you by the door. Come in and keep me company, sweetie. I'm so lonely tonight. Hagar?"

She waited, but there was no response from the wandering cat. At last she closed the door again, cutting off the flood of light. Tyler stood gazing fixedly at the guest house. His mouth was dry, his heart pounding in his chest.

Finally, gripped by an urge that he was powerless to resist, he turned and started walking through the shadows toward Frankie's door.

CHAPTER NINE

INSIDE THE GUEST HOUSE, Frankie contemplated the empty room. She wandered over and looked at the fire in the hearth, wondering what to do with herself for the rest of the evening.

She could go across the yard to the ranch house, but she was reluctant to butt in while Lynn was there with her kids. No matter how welcoming the McKinneys might be, the family was still entitled to some privacy, especially on the weekend.

Frankie turned restlessly to her pile of books, wishing that she could have gone home for the weekend, too. Her parents were away, up in Oklahoma for a family reunion. She'd been invited to go along, but she wasn't exactly in the mood for a lot of attention and embarrassing questions from her aunts and cousins right now.

And Joey hadn't been able to come home for the weekend, either, because he was working extra hard these days so he could take some time off for Lisa and Tony's wedding. Frankie was a little surprised to realize how much she missed him. She really had grown far too dependent on her old friend in recent months.

She paused by the window and peered into the darkness, hoping to catch a glimpse of Hagar. It was too cold for the big Persian to be wandering around in the darkness. Frankie worried about him on these February nights when the winter chill deepened and the wind howled through the cedar trees.

There was no sign of the cat near the guest house, though she was sure she'd heard him scratching at the door earlier when she was getting out of the shower. Briefly, she thought about putting her coat on and going out to search for him, then abandoned the impulse, knowing that it would be futile.

She craned her neck to peer up at Tyler's house on the hillside. Just a couple of its lights gleamed faintly in the darkness, and the place had a lonely, deserted air.

Frankie wondered what Tyler was doing tonight. Ruth was still away, and nobody seemed to know when she'd be coming back. Tyler brushed off questions about his wife, looking so tense and unhappy that Frankie's heart ached for him.

Maybe he was over at the ranch house, watching TV with Lettie Mae and the kids. Frankie felt a guilty surge of excitement.

Really, she told herself, there was no reason she couldn't change her clothes and drop in on them, just casually. After all, she went over there almost every evening, and nobody seemed to mind. Then she'd be able to be near him, maybe even sit next to him on the couch, close enough to brush against him. . . .

Breathless with anticipation, she dropped the curtain and hurried over to the closet. A knock sounded at the door, unnaturally loud in the stillness.

She went to answer it, then stood in silence with one hand lifted to her mouth. Tyler stood on the doorstep, his face shadowed beneath the brim of his hat. He looked down at her with disturbing intentness.

"Hi, Frankie," he said quietly. "Are you busy tonight?"

Frankie swallowed hard and gazed at him, mesmerized. After all her hours of dreaming and fantasizing about him, the man seemed larger than life now that he was here in person. He looked handsome and dangerous, especially when Joey wasn't around to protect her from herself....

"No," she whispered. "Not really. I was just... wondering what to do with myself, actually. Come in, Tyler."

She gave a nervous little laugh and stood aside to let him enter, then watched in silence as he took off his jacket and hat and tossed them on the dresser.

"This is sure nice and cozy," he said with a smile, crossing the room to look at the hearth. "I like a fire on a winter night, don't you?"

"I... Yes, I do," Frankie whispered. "I like a fire, too."

She felt as shy and awkward as a child. He was almost overwhelming here inside her room, with his broad shoulders and his dark, handsome face.

Frankie had spent weeks memorizing his face. She knew every line and shadow of his mouth, every hollow in his cheeks, everything there was to know about the way his hair grew around his ears and fell across his forehead. But tonight, he was like a stranger. She didn't even know how to talk to him.

"Hitting the books?" he asked, leaning casually against the mantel and looking at her with interest. Frankie shifted from one foot to the other, suddenly conscious of her clinging tights and the thin, almost transparent shirt that she usually wore to sleep in.

"Not...not tonight," she murmured. "On the weekend, I usually try to give myself a little time off."

"Good idea. Didn't Joey come home this weekend?"

Frankie shook her head, feeling a rising panic. "He couldn't get away. He has to get a Psych paper finished and do some extra workouts for the coach so he can come for the wedding."

Tyler smiled. "This damned wedding, it's turning everybody's life upside down, isn't it?"

"It sure is. Get your tux fitted yet?" she asked, forcing a smile as she tried desperately to restore their old, teasing relationship.

He smiled back, but his eyes were grim. "Yeah, I did. I went in yesterday and tried it on. But," he added, gazing moodily at the fire, "God knows who I'll have for a partner."

Frankie stared at him in growing confusion. "But isn't Ruth...won't she be your partner?"

"I don't even know if Ruth's coming home," he said, looking up at her with so much pain in his eyes that Frankie didn't know what to say. All she could think of was her need to comfort him.

"Oh, Tyler," she whispered, moving impulsively toward him. "Tyler, I'm so sorry...."

She reached out and he took her hands, then drew her into his arms, crushing her against his chest. Frankie gasped at the strength of his embrace, almost swooning in his arms. It was here at last, the moment she'd dreamed of for so long, when she lay hot and restless in her bed at night.

She could feel the hardness of his bone and muscle through her clothes, smell the fresh, outdoor fragrance of his skin and hear his heart pounding strongly against her cheek. She clung to him silently, burying her face in his shirt, trying only to warm and comfort him with her youth and energy and her passionate love.

"Oh, God," he whispered against her hair. "Frankie..."

Blindly she lifted her face. His lips found hers, moving hungrily over her mouth. He began to caress her body, fondling her buttocks in the thin tights, reaching up to cup her breasts with a tenderness and rising passion that left her breathless and shuddering with desire.

Suddenly his hands stilled and his body went rigid, but he continued to hold her. "Frankie," he whispered in her ear. "Frankie, I'm sorry. This is wrong. I love my wife, kid. I don't know what I'm doing. God, I don't know what I'm doing...."

Despite his words, Tyler's arms strengthened around her and his lips began to roam over her face and neck again, pressing into the hollow of her throat while his hands caressed her body.

Frankie was on fire with longing, so hot and melting with emotion that she could hardly remember her own name. Still, his hoarse whisper penetrated the fog in her brain.

This is wrong. I love my wife.... Even though she writhed in his arms and returned his kisses with hungry passion, Frankie couldn't push away the memory of those words. She thought of Ruth, with her gentle manner and her unfailing kindness, and recalled how much Tyler's wife had suffered in these past few months.

I've suffered, too! Frankie thought desperately. *Why should I feel sorry for her when she doesn't even want him?*

Still, she couldn't dispel the image of Ruth's quiet brown eyes, so sad and bereft since the death of her baby.

Finally, she pulled herself away from Tyler and turned aside. She leaned down, took the poker and shoved it aimlessly into the fire, prodding at the glowing logs as she kept her face averted.

"I'm sorry, Tyler," she said in a low, choked voice. "I don't know what came over me. I must... I must be missing Joey more than I thought."

"Joey?" he echoed.

Frankie forced herself to look at him. His face was flushed, his eyes dark with passion. He was still breathing hard, and he looked so handsome and utterly desirable that it was all she could do not to throw herself into his arms again.

She picked up a heavy red sweatshirt from the bed and pulled it over her tumbled curls. "I'm so much in love with the man," she lied, "that I can barely control myself when he's away. But that's hardly a valid excuse for throwing myself into your arms like a wild woman, is it?"

Tyler watched while Frankie crossed the room and seated herself at the desk, opening one of her botany textbooks in a businesslike manner. She clenched her hands briefly in her lap, hoping he couldn't see how they were shaking.

"I didn't know you and Joey were that serious," he said quietly.

"We're sort of keeping it secret," Frankie told him without turning around. "We didn't want to steal any attention from Lisa and Tony. Later, after the wedding, I guess we'll probably announce our plans."

Her voice was calm, but she could scarcely endure the thought of what she was giving up. It was so hard to keep herself out of his arms, especially now that she'd experienced the unbearable sweetness of his hands and his mouth....

"I see," Tyler said, moving across the room to pick up his jacket. He shrugged it on, then fitted his Stetson in place and hesitated by the door, turning to her with awkward formality. "Look, Frankie, I'm so sorry about what just happened," he began. "I don't..."

"Forget it," she said briefly. "Please, let's not talk about it anymore."

She couldn't bear to have him apologize. None of it was his fault, after all.

Frankie knew that she was to blame for everything. She'd drawn him into her arms by wanting him so much, and now she had to pay. But the worst thing of all was the pain and self-loathing in his eyes. She'd set out to comfort him, but she'd left him hurting worse than before.

"Like I said, I'm just missing my boyfriend so much that I hardly know what to do with myself. It wasn't your fault, Tyler. I threw myself at you, and I'm sorry. Now get out of here," she said, making a last brave attempt to keep her voice casual and sisterly. "Hurry up, before I do it again and embarrass both of us. I want to call Joey," she added, "and tell him how much I love him."

Tyler's jaw tightened, but he forced himself to smile. "That sounds like a real good idea," he said with false heartiness. "Joey's a lucky guy."

Then he was gone, closing the door quietly behind him and striding off toward his empty house. Frankie ran to the window and watched hungrily until his tall figure was swallowed up in the darkness.

At last, long after he'd vanished into the night, she stumbled over to the bed, curled up in a little ball of agony and sobbed until she thought her heart would break.

NEXT MORNING, Lisa bundled Jennifer into her nylon snowsuit, hat and mittens, and took the little girl out for a walk. She bumped the stroller across the rough crushed rock in the front yard, and down past the bungalow where she and Tony would be living in a week or so, after they came back from their honeymoon.

At the thought of her honeymoon and all that it implied, Lisa felt a tug of worry, then a growing sense of panic.

"See, Jenny?" she said brightly, leaning forward to adjust Jennifer's pink knitted hat. "See? That's my house. Mine and Tony's."

"Tony," Jennifer repeated with satisfaction, pounding her mittened hands on the bar of the stroller. "Tony come?" she asked hopefully, twisting to look up at Lisa.

Lisa shook her head, smiling at the child's look of disappointment. There was nothing complicated about Jennifer's tastes and emotions. This little girl liked men.

And no wonder, Lisa thought, when there were so many nice, handsome men in her life. Her daddy and her tall brothers, Tony and Ken and her doting Uncle Vern, to say nothing of Bubba, Warren, Sam, the sheriff...

Lisa's smile faded as she thought about her own childhood and brutal, blustering Ralph Duncan, who'd been the only adult male figure in her life. "You're a real lucky girl, Jennifer," she said quietly. "Did you know that?"

But Jennifer wasn't listening. She'd caught sight of the path leading up to Ruth and Tyler's house, and was pointing at it with an imperious hand. "Ty'er," she demanded. "See Ty'er."

"Oh, honey, that's kind of a long walk...."

"Ty'er!" Jennifer shouted, pounding her boots on the footrest.

"All right," Lisa said. "We'll go see Tyler. I need to talk to Frankie anyhow," she added sternly. "Otherwise I'd never let you push me around like this, you big bully."

But Jennifer had subsided now that she was getting her own way. She rode in queenly silence, looking at the mesquite and cactus with a benign expression as Lisa toiled up the path. Near the grove of cedar, Lisa could see Tyler digging in the tilled soil, setting out the last of the spindly grapevines. There was no sign of Frankie, who usually worked beside him.

"Hi, Tyler," Lisa called, lifting Jennifer from the stroller as Tyler stood erect, then crossed the field to greet them.

Jennifer shouted joyfully and clamored to be picked up. Tyler smiled and hoisted her into the air, then held her in the crook of his arm and listened as she babbled a stream of excited baby talk.

"Isn't she the cutest thing?" he said to Lisa, cuddling the baby and kissing her laughing face. "Look at those rosy cheeks."

"Oh, yes, she's cute," Lisa said dryly. "And I'm afraid she knows it."

"She's a real man killer, all right. God help the boys in this county when she turns seventeen."

"I wanted to talk with Frankie," Lisa said, looking around at the tractor and trailer loaded with flats of vine stock. "Where is she?"

"I think she must be feeling sick this morning," Tyler said, fussing with one of Jennifer's boot straps. "She hasn't turned up for work yet."

"Is she still down at the guest house?" Lisa asked.

"Must be. I haven't heard from her."

"Maybe we'll stop in there on our way home, then, and see if she's all right."

"Thanks, Lisa. I was getting a little worried about her."

"I want to ask her if she'll look after the guest book for the wedding," Lisa said. "We thought Beverly might want to do it, but she won't be able to get there until later in the day, so it would be nice if Frankie could take over."

Tyler looked dubious. "Frankie isn't too thrilled about all this wedding stuff, you know."

"Oh, I know," Lisa said, smiling. "But I think she'll do it for me, if I ask nicely. Actually I was hoping she and Joey could do the book together, and sort of greet people at the door as they come in. Everybody likes them so much."

"Yeah," Tyler said with another enigmatic glance across the rolling vineyards. "How's it going?" he asked suddenly, turning back to Lisa.

"The wedding, you mean?" she asked, startled. Most of the men at the Double C expressed very little interest in the upcoming festivities, dismissing all the feverish plans as "women stuff."

"Is it all running smooth? No big last-minute problems?"

"None at all." Lisa paused, then added with a laugh, "Well, I shouldn't say that. The caterers have suddenly decided they can't do a roast beef plate for early evening, and the order for the flowers had to be changed, but apart from that . . . oh, and the napkins and matchbooks are going to be—"

"Lisa! Spare me," he said eloquently, making her smile.

Tyler fell silent again, hugging Jennifer and gazing over her head with a brooding expression.

"I was wondering about Ruth," he said at last.

"What about her?"

"I'm not sure if she's going to be back in time from this holiday of hers. I know you're counting on her to be in the wedding party."

"Of course she'll be back," Lisa said in surprise. "Why wouldn't she?"

"I thought she might decide to extend her visit a little longer, past the weekend."

"Oh, I don't think so," Lisa said firmly. "Ruth would have told me if she couldn't be here for the wedding. She'd never, ever go away without letting me know."

He nodded, apparently satisfied, and set Jennifer carefully on her feet, smiling as she promptly sat down in the dirt and started playing with a couple of small pebbles by the path.

"Don't, Jenny," Lisa said automatically. "You'll get your mittens all dirty. Come on," she added, moving the baby stroller into position and settling the little girl inside. "Let's go see Frankie."

"F'ankie!" Jennifer shouted, pounding her feet again. "See F'ankie!"

Tyler patted her head and started back into the vineyard, then paused. "Lisa?"

"Yes?"

"When you see Frankie," he said, avoiding her eyes, "tell her I likely won't be working up here for the rest of the week, because I have a lot of business to attend to. Tell her I'd appreciate it if she could finish these last few plots by herself."

"Okay," Lisa said.

"And could you call me and let me know if she's not feeling well?"

"Sure," Lisa said, wondering why Frankie couldn't call herself. But Tyler was already striding away, heading toward the tractor with its load of wooden flats. She watched him for a moment, then turned the stroller and started down the trail to the guest house.

JENNIFER PUFFED in excitement and hammered on the bar of the stroller while Lisa waited at the door, wondering if Frankie had gone over to the ranch house for something. But at last the girl opened the door and peered out.

Lisa stared at Frankie's pale face and the dark blue smudges under her eyes.

"Frankie," she said in concern. "Aren't you feeling well? You look awful!"

"Well, thanks," Frankie said with a flash of her usual dry humor, though her eyes were bleak. "Same to you. Hi, Princess," she added, kneeling to greet Jennifer, who beamed and reached her mittened hands upward.

Frankie unfastened the strap and lifted the little girl into her arms, carrying her inside the guest house. "I must be coming down with something," she said over her shoulder. "I'm not feeling a hundred percent this morning."

Lisa nodded in sympathy, then looked around, dismayed. "Frankie!" she said. "You're not leaving, are you?"

The little house was in turmoil, with clothes and books stacked everywhere. A couple of suitcases and duffel bags lay open on the bed, half-filled with folded jeans and sweatshirts.

"No," Frankie said with a mirthless smile. "I'm just doing an inventory of all my belongings to see how much stuff I own. Jen-Jen want a cookie?"

"Cookie," Jennifer said. She squirmed with impatience as Lisa knelt to remove her bulky snowsuit.

Frankie rummaged in her closet, emerged with a bag of digestive cookies and handed one to Jennifer. Then she crossed the room and stared moodily at the untidy pile of clothes on the bed.

"But you can't leave," Lisa said. "The wedding's just a few days away."

"Honey," Frankie said gently, "I'm not the one getting married. You are."

"I know, but—"

"The planting's almost finished," Frankie went on, prowling restlessly around the room, looking tired and disheveled in her old sweatpants and ragged denim shirt. "And I'm getting behind in my classes. I need to start catching up."

"But Tyler said..."

Lisa paused, distressed by the way the other girl whirled to stare at her. "What?" Frankie asked tensely. "What did Tyler say?"

Lisa bent to extricate Jennifer, who had tried to crawl under the bed in search of a stuffed monkey she'd seen beneath the edge of the blankets, and was now stuck. The little girl emerged triumphant, clutching the monkey in her arms. She beamed at Lisa and settled in a corner to play with the toy, crooning happily.

"Lisa?" Frankie asked, standing rigidly in the middle of the room with a pile of books in her arms.

"Those eyes won't come loose, will they?" Lisa asked, looking dubiously at the stuffed animal.

"*Lisa!*"

"What? Oh, Tyler," Lisa said, returning to the topic. "I went up there looking for you this morning, but he said he thought you weren't feeling well. He asked me to pass a message to you. Hasn't the man ever heard of telephones, or are you two not speaking for some reason?" She smiled, trying to lighten the strange tension in the room.

Frankie dumped the books into a duffel bag and busied herself arranging them. "What was the message?"

"He asked if you could finish the last of the planting by yourself this week, because he's got to spend the next few days on business. Computer entries and stuff, I guess."

"You mean..." Frankie looked suddenly hopeful. "He's not going to be out in the vineyards at all? I can work all by myself?"

"That's what he said. Jenny, don't chew on the monkey's ears. That's Frankie's monkey, not yours," she said sternly.

"Yeah, kid," Frankie said, sounding a little more like her old self. "How'd you like it if I nibbled on *your* ears, like this? Huh?"

She dropped onto her knees and crawled over to nuzzle the baby's delicate pink ears, sending Jennifer into gales of laughter.

Both women smiled. Frankie looked awkwardly at the piles of clothes and papers. "What a mess." She sighed. "I might as well go ahead and leave, now that I've gone this far."

"But, Frankie... I wanted to ask you a favor."

"A favor?"

"For the wedding," Lisa said, feeling reticent all at once, as she always did when she asked someone for help. "I need someone to handle the guest book at the reception, and you'd be perfect. I thought you and Joey could sort of... do it together."

"Joey and I? Do what?" Frankie shook her head ruefully. "Lisa, honey, I don't have the slightest idea what you're talking about."

"It's a guest book," Lisa said patiently. "A list of all the people who came to our wedding. And there's a fancy pen, decorated with a plume from one of Mary Gibson's ostriches...."

Frankie giggled, then sobered hastily when she saw how serious Lisa was. "Sorry," she muttered. "Carry on. Ostrich plumes, right?"

"Yes. And there'll be a table at the door where you greet all the arriving guests and help them with anything they need, like where to hang their coats and put the gifts, that kind of thing. You and Joey would be a sort of welcoming party."

Frankie nodded, considering. "Joey would love doing that," she said with a wistful smile. "He's friends with everybody in three counties."

"I know," Lisa said eagerly. "And people love you, too, Frankie. I thought the two of you would be perfect at the welcoming table. Please?" she urged.

Frankie considered. "Can I wear jeans and my Harley Davidson T-shirt? The one with the hogs on it?"

"No. Certainly not."

"Oh, well," Frankie said, feigning regret. "It was worth a try. Does poor Joey need a tux?"

"Oh, no. A sport jacket and slacks would be just fine."

"Okay, I'll do it," Frankie said, taking a deep breath.

Lisa smiled and hugged her. "Thanks, Frankie. I'm sorry to make you hang around when you need to get back to school, but I'd really love for you to be at the wedding and it's only a few days...."

"That's okay. I guess I should go up to the vineyard now," Frankie said, extricating herself gently from Lisa's embrace. "You're certain Tyler's not going to be up there?"

"He was already heading into the house when we reached the bottom of the hill."

"Good. Jen-Jen, you want that monkey?"

"Frankie, you can't let her..."

"Pay no attention to mean old Lisa," Frankie told the baby. "Jenny want the monkey?"

"Munty," Jennifer said, clutching the toy to her chest with fierce possessiveness.

"Then it's yours."

Jennifer gave Frankie an enchanting smile and blew kisses off her chubby palms, one of her newest tricks.

"God, what shameful manipulation," Frankie muttered. "The woman's a master of feminine wiles already, and she's smaller than a breadbox."

Lisa laughed and gathered up her small charge, bundling her into the snowsuit while Frankie, too, dressed in warm outdoor clothes and prepared to trudge up the hill for one of her final days of work at the Double C vineyards.

RUTH ARRIVED home late on Tuesday night when the moon was high and full, spilling a wash of silvery blue over the sleeping buildings and pastures. She drove slowly around the edge of the neat haystacks and along the road that wound up to the house she shared with Tyler.

Their house was dark and silent, looming above her on the face of the cliff. Ruth wondered if Tyler was at home, and if he was alone....

She'd deliberately avoided telling him when exactly she'd be back, and she hadn't called him since she left home. He probably thought she was still in Albuquerque, partying and bar-hopping with Mimsy.

Maybe he didn't even care what she was doing. Perhaps tonight he was sleeping down in the guest house with Frankie, holding that slim young body, delighting in the girl's warmth and energy....

Ruth's face twisted. She gripped the wheel, forcing herself to stay calm, and parked in the garage, then started up the rocky path to the house.

Suddenly a shape materialized from the darkness. Ghostly and silent, it brushed against her legs, almost making her stumble and lose her footing. Ruth gasped and pressed a hand to her mouth, reminded with almost unbearable vividness of the night she'd lost her baby. The big dog had leaped out of the shadows, just like this, and tripped her on the path....

Shaking with fear, she gripped her suitcase and forced herself to peer into the darkness at her feet. "What's there?" she demanded in a breathless whisper. "What is it?"

She felt a gentle, familiar pressure on her leg. It was Hagar, his fur glistening silver and blue in the moonlight. He stood on the path in front of her, calmly dignified now that his first frenzy of greeting was past. Purring loudly, he stretched himself upward to rub his head against her knees once more.

"Hagar?" Ruth said in wonder. She knelt and reached out a trembling hand to touch his head, his ears, his skinny ribs and matted, silky hide. "Oh, sweetie . . ." Her voice broke.

Hagar pressed closer to her, rubbing himself comfortably back and forth against her arms, still purring with noisy exuberance.

"Have you come home, darling? Are you finally going to live with me again?"

The big cat licked her hand with his warm, rough tongue. Ruth could no longer hold back the tears. She stumbled toward the back door, dragging her suitcases along with her while Hagar followed, stepping calmly past the dried rosebushes at the edge of the path.

Ruth put on a small light in the kitchen and searched out the tins of cat food she'd stored in the wistful hope that her cat would return to her someday. She spooned some into a dish and set it down, then watched as Hagar ate with dainty greed, looking up at her from time to time, so complacently that he might never have left.

"Tomorrow you need to have a bath and a good brushing," Ruth told him, still dazed with happiness.

He licked his paws as if in agreement, groomed his whiskers and then looked around expectantly. Ruth ran into the back room and brought out his padded basket, settling it near the heating vent in a cozy corner of the room.

Hagar climbed into the basket without hesitation, turned around a couple of times and subsided in a fluffy orange heap, his eyes dropping shut with an air of weary homecoming.

"Oh, Hagar," Ruth whispered, watching him sleep. "Darling, you came home. You came home after all."

Her spirits lifted. She had an instinct that everything was going to turn out all right now. Somehow their problems would all be solved, and they'd find a way to be happy. She turned off the light and hurried up the stairs, hoping Tyler was home and still awake. There was so much to tell him....

But he was deeply asleep, lying on his back, his face so quiet and boyish in repose that she longed to kiss him.

"I love you, Tyler," she whispered after she climbed into bed, careful not to wake him "Sweetheart, I love you so much...."

But he didn't hear, and Ruth didn't know if it would be possible to say those words tomorrow when he was awake.

As it turned out, she had no opportunity to say anything to him. She slept late, exhausted from the long drive and the emotional tension of her visit with Lisa's mother. When she woke, the winter sunlight filtered softly through the blinds and she was alone in the bed.

Ruth looked out at the vineyard, where Frankie worked all by herself, digging busily among the rows of wooden trellises at the far side of the field, while the wind whipped at her hair and clothes. Tyler was nowhere in sight.

Ruth showered and dressed in jeans and a warm plaid shirt. She went downstairs through the silent house, hoping to find Tyler in his office. But that room, too, was neat and deserted. Finally she wandered into the kitchen, where he'd made a pot of coffee and left a note propped against the African violet in the center of the table. The note read:

Dear Ruth...
   I had to run up to Dallas for a couple of days on business. If Lisa's worried, tell her I'll be home in time for the wedding, and my tux is all fitted and ready.

Ruth held the sheet of paper, her heart aching. There were no special words of love for her, not even a welcome home.

Not that she deserved any warmth from Tyler after the way she'd treated him. But she missed him so bitterly that it was all she could do to keep from bursting into tears.

She made herself a couple of slices of toast and poured some orange juice, forcing herself to eat although her throat was tight and her stomach felt vaguely queasy. The trip to New Mexico must have drained her even more than she'd thought.

After she finished eating, Ruth put on her jacket and left the house, making a brief detour to greet Frankie, who knelt by one of the freshly dug trenches, her hands covered with mud.

"Hi, Frankie," Ruth said. "Almost finished, I see."

Frankie looked up at her, then turned away quickly to haul another flat of vines into position. "Tomorrow will be my last day," she said. "Joey's taking me back to school after the wedding."

"Well, you've done a wonderful job to finish all this," Ruth said quietly. "Nobody could have worked harder, Frankie."

The girl shook her head, looking so tense that Ruth was puzzled. "Frankie?" she asked in concern. "Are you all right?"

"I'm fine," Frankie said, avoiding her eyes. "It's real nice to see you home again, Ruth. I hope you had a good trip."

Her nervousness affected Ruth, making her feel vaguely frightened. Had something happened between Frankie and Tyler during her absence? Was that why Frankie seemed so awkward and strange?

While Ruth hesitated, trying to think of something to say, Frankie hurried away to fetch the spray nozzle hooked to a tank nearby, and began to direct a pungent stream of liquid fertilizer into the trench. Ruth watched her a moment longer, then turned and headed back down toward the ranch house.

She found Lisa alone in the sunroom, putting the finishing touches on her veil. It was a lovely, gossamer fall of lace trimmed with white satin embroidery, all of which Lisa and Virginia had done by hand.

"Hi, Ruth!" Lisa said, looking up in delight. "I'm so glad you're back. Look," she added, holding up the veil. "Isn't it beautiful?"

"It's exquisite." Ruth came into the room and seated herself on the opposite couch, smiling at the pretty, dark-haired girl. "I can't believe you and Virginia embroidered it by yourselves. I could never learn to do handwork like that."

"Of course you could. It just takes time and patience, that's all."

"I seem to be running out of both, these days," Ruth muttered, then felt guilty when she saw Lisa's quick frown of concern. "Sorry, Lisa," she said contritely. "I didn't mean to be so gloomy. I must be getting the flu or something. I hope it holds off until after the wedding."

"Frankie said the same thing yesterday, but I think she's better now."

Ruth felt another stab of pain when she thought of her husband and Frankie. "Where's everybody else?" she asked quickly, looking around.

"Cynthia took Jennifer to the doctor for her checkup, Lynn's in town shopping for shoes for the girls to wear to the wedding, Lettie Mae's in the kitchen making pralines, and Virginia couldn't come out today because it's Neale's birthday and she's making a cake for the party tonight."

"I didn't know that. Will Clint be coming down for Neale's party?"

Lisa smiled. "He'd better be. It wouldn't be much of a celebration for Neale if Clint didn't come. She said he'll drive down today and stay over for the wedding. It's going to be so much fun," Lisa added with a sigh. "Everybody's going to be here."

Ruth twisted her hands nervously together in her lap, searching for words.

"Lisa," she said gently. "There's... something I want to tell you."

"Yes? Ruth, could you hand me that spool of white silk thread, please? It's just behind you on the lamp table."

Ruth handed over the spool and drew a deep breath. "Lisa, when I went away this week, I didn't go to visit a friend in Albuquerque. That was all just a story."

Lisa looked up in surprise. "Really? Where did you go?"

"I went to see your mother."

Lisa's busy hands stilled. She gripped the spool tightly and looked up at Ruth in shocked disbelief.

"My *mother?*" she whispered.

Ruth nodded. "After Walt Kelly phoned, I started thinking about what he said. I called him back and talked to him a couple of times, and finally decided to drive over there and visit Sadie."

Lisa was still pale and stunned. Ruth looked at her in growing concern. "I would have liked to meet your brothers," she went on, trying to keep her voice casual, "but they were all at school and I couldn't wait. Walt and Sadie were both there, though. We had a nice visit."

"I can't believe ... I can't believe you went there."

"She loves you, Lisa. No matter what you think or how you feel, your mother really, really loves you."

"Did she tell you about everything? About why I..."

"Yes, she did," Ruth said gently. "She told me what your stepfather was like, and how he treated you. It was a very difficult story for her to tell, Lisa. Your mother's life must have been a living hell all those years."

"*Her* life!" Lisa said with passion. "What about ours? What about Harry with his broken jaw, and little Seth so scared he cried himself to sleep, and Tim with his arm in a cast? What about me, having to..."

She fell silent, her shoulders heaving. The soft folds of lace tumbled into her lap as she covered her eyes with her hands.

"Lisa," Ruth said, moving over to sit beside the girl and putting an arm around her shoulders. "Lisa, it wasn't your mother's fault. You know that. She never wanted any of you to be hurt."

Lisa sobbed and murmured something incoherent.

"I think you should let it go, Lisa," Ruth whispered. "I think you should put it all behind you and forget it. Your mother's life is better now. I'm pretty sure that Walt's in love with her, and I think she cares a lot for him even though she doesn't realize it yet," Ruth added with a brief smile.

"Walt?" Lisa echoed blankly, looking up through her tears. "Walt and my mother?"

Ruth nodded. "I think he's been very good to her and the boys. He's a nice man, Lisa."

"I know he is. But I never thought..." She looked down again, digging into her sewing bag for a tissue to mop her eyes.

"Lisa," Ruth went on, looking anxiously at the girl's dark cloud of hair, "I asked your mother to come to the wedding. All of them are coming, Sadie and Walt and your little brothers. I've booked rooms for them in the motel in town. They should be arriving sometime tomorrow night."

"They're coming to the *wedding?*" Lisa looked up again, her eyes wide with horror.

"Yes, they are," Ruth said, forcing herself to sound calm and matter-of-fact. "Lisa, this is a wonderful occasion, one you'll remember all your life. I'm sorry to interfere like this, but if your family weren't there, I'm sure you'd come to regret it someday. I don't want that to happen."

"But I don't know... I don't know what to say to her. I don't want to see her," Lisa said in panic.

"Give it a little time," Ruth told her quietly. "Think about it, Lisa, and try to understand just why you feel so angry. Maybe it's time to let all those feelings go and forgive your mother so you can get on with your own life."

"I can get on with my life anyway. I don't need my mother to have a good life."

"Oh, Lisa, you're wrong. The anger and resentment are so important, because I don't think it's really possible to hate and love at the same time. We can't nurse grudges for a lifetime without doing harm to ourselves. If you can't bring yourself to forgive your mother, your whole life will suffer."

"How do you know?"

"Believe me, I know," Ruth told her sadly. "I know all about it, Lisa. I'm learning how important it is to get past your own pain and forgive before you can really love again."

"I don't know what you mean."

"I mean," Ruth said quietly, "that I've been struggling with a lot of the same angry feelings you have. You see, I blamed Tyler for... for what happened to our baby."

"But it wasn't his fault, was it?"

"Of course not. When bad things happen to us, Lisa, we often look for someone to blame. In some strange way, we think it will ease the pain for us. But it only makes things worse, because it separates us from the people we really need and care about."

"But my mother..."

"Your mother loves you. She'd give her life for you and those boys, Lisa. I'm not denying that she made some mistakes. So did Tyler, but neither of them deserves the kind of punishment we've been giving them."

Lisa looked at her with unfathomable dark eyes, biting her lip.

"Lisa," Ruth murmured, "since I talked with your mother, I've been trying my best to be more fair with Tyler. I want you to promise me that you'll think about this, too. I want you to try really hard to see your mother's life from her point of view, so you can understand how she feels."

Lisa stared down at her hands in silence.

"Promise," Ruth urged the girl gently.

"All right," Lisa said in a low voice. "I promise I'll try."

She stood up hastily, gathered her veil in her arms and ran out of the room without looking back.

CHAPTER TEN

"HOW MANY ROOMS do we have at the motel, Mama?" Harry said. "Can I stay with Walt? I don't want to be in the same room with Tim."

"Well, I don't want to be with *you,* either," Tim retorted. "Mama, make him give me back my ball. He took it."

"No, he didn't. *I* took it," Johnny said fiercely to his younger brother. "And I'm not giving it back, neither. You shouldn't be throwing a ball around while Walt's driving. It's dangerous."

"Shut up!" Tim shouted in outrage. "I *wasn't* throwing it around. I was just sort of bouncing it. Mama, he's got my ball!"

Sadie glared over her shoulder at the three older boys, then turned to Walt with a look of wry apology. "I'm sorry," she murmured. "You must be sick of all this fighting. They've never been on such a long trip."

Walt drove calmly through the deepening twilight. "Don't worry, Sadie. We're almost ready to stop for the night. I think they've been real good."

Sadie felt a flood of gratitude for his kindness. She shifted on the front seat of Walt's big van, moving carefully to avoid disturbing Seth, who slept in her lap, his flushed cheek pressed against her shirtfront.

"You're so good to us, Walt," she said again. "I really, truly appreciate it."

"It's about time I had a holiday," Walt said placidly. "Can't remember the last time I got away from that old farm of mine. Hey, boys," he called over his shoulder. "What do you all want for supper?"

A chorus of shouts rose from the back, most of them seeming to agree on hamburgers, fries and milkshakes.

"That's what we had for lunch," Walt protested. "Maybe your mama would like a nicer meal, like a steak or some lobster or something. What do you think, Sadie?"

"I think," Sadie told him with a solemn twinkle, "we should all have liver and onions. That's a nice healthy meal, isn't it?"

They grinned at each other as a howl of outrage rose from the back seat, waking Seth, who sat up, round-eyed and blinking.

"Where are we?" he asked. "Are we there yet?"

"We're about fifteen miles from Lubbock," Walt told the little boy. "Maybe we should go straight to the motel and eat in the coffee shop, okay?" he added, glancing at Sadie. "That way, everybody can order whatever they want."

"That sounds real good, Walt."

"Will there be a circus at the motel?" Seth asked, rubbing his eyes.

The twins hooted in derision. "Listen to the dummy!" Tim yelled. "Seth doesn't know what a motel is."

Walt looked at the child in surprise. "Haven't you ever been to a motel, Seth?"

Seth shook his head and began to bounce with excitement.

"None of them has ever been to a motel," Sadie told Walt.

"Never?" Walt asked in disbelief.

In the back, the three boys shook their heads vigorously. "Other kids always get to go on holidays," Tim said. "But we never did."

"Well, for sure you're on one now," Walt said firmly. "And after everybody eats supper, there's going to be a little surprise."

"A surprise?" Seth started to bounce again. "What kind of surprise, Walt?"

Walt gazed calmly down the highway, a smile tugging at the corners of his mouth. "Well, now," he said in his quiet voice, "maybe I should just let you wait and find out."

But Johnny and the twins pressed closer, straining against their seat belts, demanding to know what the surprise was. Sadie, too, looked at Walt curiously. "I never heard anything about a surprise," she said.

"I thought it might be too hard to wait, if I was to tell about it early in the day," Walt said.

"What surprise?" Tim shouted, almost beside himself with excitement.

Walt chuckled. "This motel we're staying at in Lubbock, it's a pretty big place," he told the boys. "It doesn't have a circus, but it has something else that's kind of neat. Especially for boys."

"Come on, Walt," Harry pleaded. "Tell us what it is."

"It's an indoor water slide," Walt told them.

"A *water slide*," Tim breathed, enchanted. "A *real* one?"

"A superbig, triple-decker one," Walt said solemnly. "I made sure of it before I booked the rooms."

"Mama, what's a water slide?" Seth whispered, twisting to look up at his mother as a babble of excited voices rose from the back seat.

Sadie smiled down at her son, blinking tears from her eyes as she hugged him. "It's a great big slide, kind of like a plastic tube full of water," she told the little boy. "And you climb up and then slide down into a swimming pool."

"How high? Bigger than our windmill?"

Sadie glanced at Walt in silent appeal.

"Way bigger," Walt assured him. "There's a smaller slide for little guys like you to start on, and a couple of real big ones for those three daredevils in the back seat."

Johnny and the twins were talking among themselves in hushed voices, their restlessness and temper forgotten in the wonder of this revelation. Seth sat on his mother's knee, wide-eyed with astonishment.

"I want Walt to come with me on the big slide," he said after some thought. "I don't want to go alone."

"Now, Seth," Sadie began. "You can't be asking Walt to—"

"Well, of course I'll come with you," Walt said firmly. "I don't aim to miss out on this kind of fun. I bought bathing trunks for me and the boys," he told Sadie with an apologetic glance, "but we'll have to rent one if you want to slide, too. I don't know much about buying ladies' bathing suits."

"Oh, Walt..."

Seth twisted in her lap again and looked at her curiously. "Mama's crying," he reported.

"Sadie?" Walt asked in alarm.

"I'm fine," Sadie told him, dashing a hand across her eyes. "I'm just so... Walt, this is just about the nicest thing anybody's ever done for us."

"It's time you and these boys had a whole lot of nice things done for you, Sadie. Nobody ever deserved it more," he told her with sincerity.

Sadie relaxed in the soft leather seat and cuddled her small son in her arms. She looked out the window at the lights of the city spreading all around them, overcome with happiness.

HOURS LATER, the boys were still shouting and rocketing down the water slides. Sadie sat in a deck chair under a screen of potted palm trees, surrounded with wet towels and discarded clothes, watching as Walt climbed out of the pool and shook water from his hair, then bent to help Seth, who struggled out behind him.

Walt was a fine figure of a man, Sadie thought. She'd been a little surprised by his lean, muscular body in bathing trunks, his broad shoulders and fine strong legs. When he took Seth's hand and walked toward her, she was startled, as well, by a warm, melting sensation that hadn't been part of her life for years. The feeling was sexual desire, and she could hardly remember the last time it had stirred in her.

Firmly, Sadie quelled her treacherous emotions and smiled at the two as they approached. "Still going?" she asked.

"Not me," Walt said, taking a towel from the heap and wrapping it around his waist. "I'm plumb tuckered out." He sprawled in the chair next to Sadie's and extended his large bare feet.

"Come on, Walt!" Seth yelled, leaping from one foot to the other in excitement. "Come on, let's go again!"

"No way," Walt said calmly. "I'm getting too old to keep up with you wild men. I'm going to sit right here with Mama and take a little breather."

Seth hugged himself, shivering, then ran off alone to the stairs leading to the smaller slide while Walt and Sadie watched him in fond silence.

On the bigger slide, Johnny and the twins were involved in a complicated game of water tag with a group of other children, all of whom seemed to be fast friends after a few hours of rowdy play. Sadie listened to their shouts and laughter, feeling misty again.

"Look at them," she murmured to Walt. "They take to this like ducks to water, don't they? You'd never know it's the first time they've even been away from home."

"They're all nice, bright boys, Sadie. They deserve to go places and see lots of things. Matter of fact," Walt confessed, running a hand through his damp hair, "I've got a couple more little surprises planned for this trip, Sadie."

"More surprises? Walt Kelly, you're just full of surprises, aren't you?"

He gave her a smile so warm and direct that Sadie had to look away in confusion. "I hope I am, Sadie. I wouldn't want you to get bored with me."

"I'm not bored," she said softly. "Not bored at all, Walt."

There was a brief, charged silence. Walt waved at Tim, who shouted down to them from the top of the taller slide, demanding their attention before he started his descent.

"So, what are the other surprises?" Sadie asked.

"We're taking a longer trip home, and spending a few days on the road. I reckon the boys can miss a bit of school if they're having an educational experience."

"I see. And where is it we're going?"

"Carlsbad Caverns," Walt said. "They should get a real kick out of that, don't you think?"

"Oh, my," Sadie murmured, captivated. "Carlsbad Caverns. Walt, that's wonderful!"

"Have you ever been there?"

"Not once in all my life. For a while right after we were married, Ralph and I lived down at Roswell, but he never took me to see the caves. I always wanted to go down there."

"That's because you're a born gold miner," Walt teased her. "You'd like to get underground and find that ol' mother lode."

Sadie smiled. "I reckon anybody would."

"They sure would. It's a real good feeling when you find a treasure," Walt said quietly, looking into the shimmering depths of the pool.

Another of those awkward, meaningful silences fell between them. Sadie bit her lip, searching for some way to get the conversation back on a less portentous footing.

"Walt," she began, clearing her throat nervously.

"Hmm?"

"It's a real nice thought, going to the Caverns and all, but I'm not sure I can afford a trip like that. It's going to cost a lot for the motel bills, and the boys are eating so much...."

"Sadie, this holiday is my treat. I thought you understood that."

"I have no intention of letting you pay for everything. I have some money in the bank, you know. Ralph had a little life insurance policy with the trucking company. I can afford to pay our way, but I can't..."

"Look," he told her, his voice suddenly firm, "let's not talk about this anymore. You're ruining my whole day."

"Why?" she asked in surprise.

Walt looked at her gravely. "I have that big farm and no debts to speak of. My farm brings in a lot of money, and I have nobody to spend it on but myself. It's a pretty lonely kind of life.''

"Walt..."

"This trip with you and the boys," he went on, "it's the most fun I've had in years. I want to pay for it, and I don't want you to argue. Okay?''

Sadie met his eyes, then looked away quickly. "Okay," she whispered. She watched as the boys shouted and splashed in the pool nearby. "You know what? I wish we could just stay here forever," she said, her voice low and strained. "I wish we didn't have to leave in the morning and drive over to Crystal Creek."

Walt took her hand and held it gently, running his thumb over her callused fingers. "Are you scared, Sadie?"

"Terrified," she confessed, letting her hand rest in his, relaxing into the comfort of his presence. "Walt, I'm more scared of this wedding than I've ever been of anything in all my life."

"It's just another day," he told her, hitching his chair over to put a comforting arm around her. "The sun will come up nice and bright, and after a while it'll go down and the day will be over. And I reckon you'll be glad you were there."

"Oh, Walt..." Sadie's voice broke. She burrowed against him, not even aware of the other people nearby and her four little boys grinning up at them from the side of the pool.

As WALT HAD PREDICTED, the morning of the wedding dawned clear and fair, with a soft breeze carrying a promise of spring. The sun climbed into the blue arch of Texas sky, warming the rolling hills and coaxing green grass and flower buds out of cover. Across the town of Crystal Creek, throughout the whole of Claro County and all the way into Austin, people were busy getting ready for the afternoon ceremony, and the reception and dance to be held later at the country club.

Now that the long-awaited moment had arrived, Sadie's boys were almost beside themselves with excitement. Sadie and Walt hurried frantically around their separate motel rooms in Crystal Creek, trying to dress themselves while they refereed fights, slicked back unruly cowlicks and fastened shoelaces and bow ties.

In fact, many of the houses in and around Crystal Creek were unusually full of life and activity on this fine golden morning. Out at the Flying Horse Ranch, Sara and Warren Trent had arrived from Houston the night before with their two children. Sara was in the early months of pregnancy, looking radiantly happy but so pale and wan that her freckles stood out across her nose in sharp relief. Warren treated her like a piece of fragile china, causing his mother-in-law, Mary Gibson, to beam at him in fond approval while Bubba struggled to deal with the noisy demands of his grandchildren.

Next door at the Double Bar, Brock and Amanda Munroe were getting ready, too, while their dog, Alvin, sat in the bedroom and watched them with dark, mournful eyes.

Brock shoved Alvin aside gently with his foot so he could reach the closet. Alvin glared at him and retreated into the hallway with an injured look.

"Just because he came to our wedding," Brock observed, "he thinks he should be invited to every social event in the county."

"Poor baby. He'll get over it if we bring him back a treat. Brock, do you really think this color is all right on me?" Amanda frowned at the mirror as she held a wispy, flame-colored silk dress against her shapely body, clad only in a bra and panties.

Brock grinned. "Sweetheart, if you looked any better, we'd never make it to the wedding." He examined her thoughtfully for a moment, then consulted his watch. "As a matter of fact, we've got a few minutes to spare. Come here, woman." He set his new suit jacket aside and moved toward her with a purposeful look.

"Oh, *Brock,*" she protested. After a brief struggle, she began to laugh softly in his arms. Alvin watched for a moment, then sighed and trudged down the hall to the kitchen, his ears drooping as he crossed the room to nose listlessly among the dried crumbs in his feeding dish.

While Brock and Amanda were stealing a few minutes from the wedding preparations to renew their own recent vows, other households were also busy getting ready.

At the Avery mansion and the Pollocks' big old house on Main Street, both newly refurbished; in the manse and the sheriff's cottage and the veterinarian's house, at Lynn and Sam Russells' place, the Hole in the Wall Dude Ranch and the Circle T; and at Cal and Serena McKinneys' luxurious condo in Austin; all over the Hill Country, dresses were being fitted in place, ties knotted, shoes polished and gifts wrapped.

In his house near the vineyard at the Double C, Tyler stood near the window of his bedroom, glaring at the pleated silk cummerbund that went with his tuxedo. For the life of him he couldn't recall how the damned thing was supposed to be fastened, and Ruth wasn't around to give advice. As usual, she was over at the ranch house, helping Lisa get dressed and ready.

In fact, Tyler had hardly spoken with his wife since his return from Dallas late the previous evening. He still had no idea where she'd gone last week on her strange little holiday, and he was still afraid to ask.

"Maybe after all this circus is over," he said to Hagar, who drowsed in the middle of the bed, "I'll have a chance to talk to my wife for a minute or two. What do you think, pal?"

Hagar blinked and yawned hugely, then sat up and began to wash his face, licking a front paw and scrubbing it industriously across his whiskered jowls. Tyler watched, still bemused by the presence of the big orange cat.

Hagar had come back home the same night Ruth did. But unlike his mistress, he'd settled into the routine of the house as placidly as if he'd never been gone. He even showed a new tolerance for Tyler, whom he usually avoided. Tyler knew it was irrational, but he'd always felt that Hagar resented him because it had been his idea to have the cat shipped all the way from California in a cramped plastic pet carrier.

"Even *you* can get to like me if you try," Tyler told the cat sadly. "I don't see why my wife can't."

Hagar blinked again, then settled into a lazy orange ball in the morning sunlight. Tyler watched him, aching with loneliness.

What a pathetic figure he must look, talking to a cat on this fine springlike day because there was nobody else who cared about him....

He sighed and began to rummage through Ruth's jewelry box for his only pair of cuff links, which didn't seem to be anywhere in sight.

ELSEWHERE AT the Double C Ranch, preparations spilled all the way from Ken and Nora's bungalow to the guest house now occupied by Frankie to the upstairs bedroom at the big ranch house, formerly Tyler's, that had been commandeered for the bride. People ran up and down stairs delivering flowers, shouting instructions, looking for articles of clothing that had mysteriously vanished and answering the telephone, which seemed to ring constantly.

J.T. took refuge in his study, entrusted with the job of looking after Jennifer while the women were busy.

His daughter was freshly bathed, her soft blond curls brushed and shining. She wore white lace tights and a clean white cotton undershirt, but it was too early to put on her silk dress and flowered headpiece. She sat on her father's knee, playing with an ugly stuffed monkey that she'd recently acquired somewhere. The little girl had one of her red plastic wrenches in her hand and was apparently trying to remove the monkey's head.

"No, no," J.T. told his daughter, gripping her firm little body in both hands. "Don't hurt the monkey, sweetheart. Not nice to hurt the monkey."

Jennifer cast a bright glance at her father, then reached up and gave him an experimental whack on the jaw with her wrench.

"Ow!" J.T. shouted, making her giggle delightedly. She dropped the wrench and touched his lips with her hand. "Hurt mouf?" she asked.

"Poor Daddy," J.T said soulfully, fingering his jaw. "Poor, poor Daddy."

"Daddy," Jennifer echoed, scrambling upright on his knee to kiss him.

J.T. delighted in her little butterfly kisses, his heart melting. "Jenny, you won't ever get married and leave Daddy, will you?"

She ignored him, clutching the monkey to her chest and kissing it, too.

"Of course you will," J.T. said sadly, in answer to his own question. "Before I can turn around, it'll be time to take you into that church and give you away to some young buck. Sweetheart, I don't know if Daddy will be able to stand it."

"Daddy," she repeated, kissing him again.

Tears burned in his eyes. He brushed them away and smiled at his daughter. "Where's Mama?" he asked, his voice husky.

"Mama?" Jennifer said, suddenly alert. "Mama come?"

"I don't think Mama's got time to come see us right now, sugar. I think she's upstairs helping Lisa put on her wedding dress."

"D'ess," Jennifer told her father happily, pointing at the tiny wisp of silk that hung on the door. "Jenny d'ess."

"Yeah, honey, I see it." J.T hugged her. "You'll be the prettiest girl there. At least, your old daddy is sure going to think so."

"P'itty," Jennifer repeated with satisfaction. She nestled contentedly in her father's lap and began to suck her thumb.

J.T. held her and rocked slowly in the chair, listening to the bustle of activity that swirled all through his house.

"WHERE'S LETTIE MAE?" Virginia asked, running into the bedroom with an armful of flower baskets. "I need some more blue flowers and baby's breath."

"She's in the kitchen making Lisa a cup of tea," Cynthia mumbled through a mouthful of straight pins.

"No, she isn't. I just passed by there and she was nowhere in sight."

"She must be. Either that or she's in her room getting ready. Look, Virginia, this bit of lace needs to be higher, don't you think?"

Virginia moved closer and frowned at the bodice of Lisa's wedding dress, still hanging in a corner of the bedroom while Lisa herself sat at the dressing table in a satiny white slip.

"I think maybe a bit. Does it feel too low, Lisa?"

"*I* don't know," Lisa said in distracted fashion. She stared at herself in the mirror with growing desperation while Ruth plied a curling iron on her long, dark hair. "Ruth, it just doesn't look right, does it? Maybe we should pile it up or something."

"It'll be fine," Ruth soothed her. "Stop fretting, honey. There's nothing to worry about."

Their eyes met briefly in the mirror, and Ruth was shaken by Lisa's look of panic. The bride appeared to be on the verge of tears.

"It's fine," Ruth said again, bending to hug the girl. "Everything will be just fine. You're going to be the prettiest bride in the world, and Tony loves you, and everybody's going to have a wonderful time at your wedding. Quit looking so tragic."

Lisa continued to brood over her reflection. "I just *know* I'll never get through this. I'm going to stumble and fall flat on my face halfway down the aisle, and make a complete idiot of myself," she muttered.

"Oh, my. I'd better warn J.T. about that," Cynthia told her gravely. "Otherwise you'll haul him down with you and there'll be a real mess of arms and legs in that church aisle."

Lisa giggled in spite of herself at this picture, then sobered and examined her reflection again. "Look, there's a huge pimple right in the middle of my chin!" she said in horror. "It's the size of a boulder. Look at it, Ruth."

Ruth bent to study the tiny blemish. "Yep," she announced, straightening and looking over at Cynthia. "Call the whole thing off, ladies. We can't have the wedding today. The bride's got a pimple."

"That's good," Virginia said placidly, squinting as she threaded a needle. "Maybe I'll just mosey on into town and marry Tony myself, since the poor boy's going to be all dressed up and waiting at the church. Do you think he'll notice the difference, Miss C.?"

"He won't mind. He certainly wouldn't want to marry anybody with a big old pimple on her chin." Cynthia pinned the lace deftly and watched while Virginia began to stitch it in place.

"You're just impossible, all of you," Lisa complained, dabbing at her chin with a cover stick. "You have no sympathy whatever." But after their lighthearted teasing, her face had a little more color and her eyes looked somewhat less panicky.

"There," Ruth said, letting a final lock of shining hair fall into place on Lisa's shoulder. "That's done. After the dress is on, we'll brush it back and then fit the veil in place just before we leave."

"Is Jennifer ready?" Virginia asked. "I can't wait to see her in that dress."

"She's downstairs with J.T." Cynthia smiled fondly. "Knowing those two, we'll be lucky if they don't wander down to the stables while they're waiting and get themselves all dirty."

"I'll check on them," Virginia said. "I have to go downstairs anyhow, and then start getting myself all prettied up."

"Me, too," Ruth said. "I have my dress next door in Cal's room."

"You two go ahead," Cynthia told them. "I'll help Lisa get the gown on, and then Ruth can come back and do the veil and fix her hair."

"Okay. My goodness," Ruth said, glancing at her watch. "We'll have to hurry. It's only a little while until we leave for the church. I hope," she added with a worried frown, "that Tyler's going to be ready. He's supposed to be here in fifteen minutes."

"J.T. says he called a few minutes ago," Cynthia reported. "He wasn't sure how to attach the cummerbund, but he did say he'd finally managed to find his cuff links."

"Oh," Ruth said, feeling guilty. She thought of Tyler, getting ready all alone over at their house, and wondered in despair if the two of them would ever have a chance to talk out their problems. "Will Frankie be coming into town with us?" she asked, trying to keep her voice casual as she paused in the doorway.

Cynthia shook her head as she lifted the shimmering wedding gown carefully from its hanger. "She went in earlier with Ken and Nora. They didn't think we'd have room for anybody else in our cars."

Ruth nodded and made her escape, feeling relieved that she wouldn't have to encounter Frankie until after the wedding. She could never quite forget that dreadful image of her husband slipping away from the guest house and into the darkness, and Frankie's look of guilty discomfort the day Ruth returned from her trip. In fact, her concern over Frankie was one of the things that kept Ruth and Tyler on opposite sides of the dangerous chasm yawning between them.

But there was no time for those thoughts now. Later, after the wedding was over and all the excitement and activity finally subsided, then maybe they'd be able to...

"Ruth!" Virginia called from downstairs. "Does anybody know how this child's headpiece is supposed to be fastened?"

"Just a minute," Ruth called back. "I'll slip my dress on and come right down."

All thoughts of Tyler and Frankie and her troubled marriage left her mind for a while as she rushed to get into her dress. Her last glimpse of the bride before she ran downstairs was a pair of slim white shoulders and big frightened eyes as Cynthia moved across the room holding out the lacy wedding gown.

LISA SHIVERED when the delicate fabric rustled over her shoulders and settled around her body with a quiet whisper. She stood as still and obedient as a child while Cynthia fussed around her, smoothing the folds of the skirt, tucking in the bodice and straightening the sleeve seams.

"How does it look?" she whispered.

Cynthia stood back to examine the effect. "Beautiful. It looks absolutely beautiful," she said, leaning over to kiss Lisa's cheek. "There was never a lovelier bride, dear. I'm so proud of you."

"Don't say things like that," Lisa murmured, looking stricken. "You'll make me cry and smear my makeup."

"Don't you dare! We don't have time to fix it now. How does the bodice feel?"

"It's fine. I'm glad J.T. will be taking me down the aisle," Lisa said, twisting her fingers nervously in the string of pearls around her neck. "It'll be so much less scary if he's there."

Cynthia smiled. "He's that kind of man, all right. I always feel a whole lot safer when he's around."

Lisa turned slowly to look at herself in the mirror while Cynthia knelt to straighten the hem of her dress. She stared at her pale reflection, wondering if her mother and little brothers were somewhere in Crystal Creek at this very moment, preparing to go over to the church for her wedding.

Lisa drew a shaky breath. She couldn't imagine what it would be like to come face-to-face with Sadie after all these months of silence, and the terrible anger she'd felt.

Maybe, she thought hopefully, her mother had decided not to come after all. Maybe Sadie had thought it over and realized that it was too far to travel with four little boys. No matter what Ruth thought, Lisa didn't know if she had the strength to handle an encounter with her mother along with all the other tensions of this momentous day....

Ruth came hurrying back into the room, carrying the pins for the veil. Her face glowed at the sight of

Lisa in her gown. "Oh, isn't she *lovely?* Lisa, you're so beautiful. That Tony's a lucky man, isn't he?"

Cynthia and Ruth chatted together as they fitted the veil in place, clearly trying to distract Lisa and ease some of her nervousness. But Lisa was barely able to hear them. She moved in a kind of fog though the last of the preparations.

Then, somehow, she was descending the staircase to the foyer, where Tyler and J.T. waited to drive them to the church. Lisa was only dimly conscious of Tyler's admiring stare and J.T.'s whistle of approval. Her bouquet was fetched from Lettie Mae's spare refrigerator, a few last-minute adjustments were made to her dress and veil, and she was tucked into the back seat of J.T.'s Cadillac, parked at the front drive behind Cynthia's car, in which Jennifer, Virginia and Lettie Mae were already waiting.

They rode through the afternoon sunlight to the church. Lisa clutched Ruth's hand in an agony of tension, her stomach in knots.

"Is it too late to back out?" she whispered. "I think I've changed my mind."

Ruth laughed and squeezed her hand, while Tyler cast a worried glance over at them from the front seat.

"You'll be fine," Ruth whispered. "Just keep thinking of Tony and how much you love him."

Lisa realized in surprise that she'd hardly given a thought to Tony during this whole frantic day. When she pictured his dark face and laughing eyes, his big strong body and the tenderness of his hands, she began to feel a little better.

Oh, Tony, she thought, clinging to her mental image of him like a drowning woman clutching a life raft. *My darling, please help me to get through this. I'm so scared....*

But at some deep level of her mind, Lisa knew she was also miserably frightened of the night to come, when all the festivities were over, the merry crowd of well-wishers was far away, and she and Tony were finally alone in bed together at their honeymoon suite in Austin.

In bed....

She gave an involuntary little moan and nestled closer to Ruth, who held her hands tightly and whispered soft words of comfort and encouragement.

Then they were at the church, and there was no time at all for any more thought. Tyler vanished, rushing around to the side door of the church and the little room where the groom's party waited with Reverend Blake. Lisa and Ruth, escorted by J.T., mounted the stairs to the vestibule.

Lynn and Cynthia were already there, along with little Jennifer, who seemed calm and tranquil in her ruffled dress of smoky blue. Jennifer carried a basket of flowers with exaggerated care, and looked around wide-eyed at all the unusual goings-on. Soft organ music filtered through the polished wooden doors from the sanctuary, where most of Crystal Creek was assembled in silence, waiting for the bridal party to enter.

Lynn, who looked as small and dainty as ever in her shimmery blue-gray sheath, peeked through the doors at the congregation, then dropped back into her position behind Ruth.

"They're all set," she whispered. "Tony and the guys are by the altar now."

Cynthia took Jennifer's hand and led her to the door, smiling down at her daughter. Cynthia, too, looked beautiful in a trim suit of ice-blue linen, her golden hair shining.

"Ready, poppet?" she whispered to Jennifer. "You and Mama are going to walk down through all the people now, so everybody can see your pretty dress. We're going right up to the front where Tyler is."

"See Ty'er?" Jennifer asked. She freed one hand from the flower basket to stroke the glistening folds of her skirt.

"Hold the flowers tight, honey," Lynn murmured. "Don't drop your basket."

J.T. moved over by Lisa and gave her an encouraging smile, then offered his arm. Lisa took it gratefully and clung to him, trembling, while the doors swung open and triumphant chords of music swelled and throbbed on a gust of flower-scented air.

The bridal party was entering now, led by Cynthia and Jennifer. Lisa could hear a chorus of adoring murmurs that followed Jennifer's solemn progress down the aisle. Ruth and Lynn paced slowly behind, holding their bouquets, while faces turned to smile at them.

"All set? Here we go," J.T. murmured. "Nothing to it, honey," he added when he saw Lisa's terrified face. "I've done it twice myself, and never regretted it for a minute."

Lisa forced a smile and moved with him to the door. She found herself wanting to scan the crowd for her mother and brothers, but she was too frightened. All she could see was an ocean of faces, a wall of flowers, a whirling kaleidoscope of soft colors as sunlight filtered through the stained-glass windows.

She drifted slowly along the carpeted aisle, clutching J.T.'s arm until her fingers ached, conscious only of a few random impressions, like the rustle of her dress and the whispers of admiration from the congregation. The people's smiles were warm and sincere, making her feel a little less frightened as the music swirled around them and the bridal party took their places near the altar.

Then Lisa saw Tony's face, and everybody else disappeared. He stood next to Tyler and Manny, watching her with awe, delight and a tenderness so deep that it almost brought tears to her eyes.

Lisa smiled up at him, her throat tight with emotion, and moved over beside him while J.T. dropped quietly back to the front pew, where Cynthia sat with Jennifer.

Tony took Lisa's arm and drew her close, squeezing her elbow gently. "You look beautiful, sweetheart," he whispered huskily into the folds of her veil. "I love you so much."

The music swelled to a crescendo, then ebbed into silence as Reverend Blake smiled at the two of them and greeted the congregation.

"Dearly beloved," he began, "we are gathered together in the company of God and these witnesses. . . ."

Lisa listened in a dream as the lovely old words of the wedding service flowed around them. "For better or worse, for richer or poorer, in sickness and in health . . ."

She saw herself walking with Tony through all the years to come, standing next to him while the joys and sorrows of life came and went. She would bear his children and give him help and comfort, and when their time on earth was over, the two of them would wander into the sunset hand in hand.

She loved him, and she knew she'd be safe and happy with him. . . .

As her wedding service continued, Lisa could feel herself moving forward into the stream of humanity, taking her place with other women in a continuity that spanned all the ages.

Suddenly, in the midst of her vision of the future, Lisa recalled her mother's face. Her happiness was shadowed all at once by images of Sadie throughout the years, struggling to look after her children in the midst of poverty and suffering.

Lisa stared unseeingly at Reverend Blake's kindly face, stunned by the reality of her mother's life. She'd been reluctant to talk about it with Ruth, but ever since their conversation, Lisa had found herself thinking a great deal about her mother. And gradually, she'd begun to understand the sorrow and bitter disappointment of Sadie's life.

None of those rich dreams had ever come true for Sadie. She, too, had walked down a church aisle as a starry-eyed girl of eighteen, and vowed to be faithful to her man. But instead of being cherished, she'd been betrayed and abandoned. Twice.

Here at the flower-decked altar on her wedding day, Lisa tried for the first time to put herself in her mother's place, and to imagine what that dreadful marriage to Ralph Duncan must have been like for Sadie. *Mama,* Lisa thought, her heart aching, *oh, Mama, I'm sorry. I was so wrapped up in myself, I never thought about how you suffered....*

She heard Tony repeating the vows. Her own voice, soft and halting, said the words that bound her to him forever. Then he was lifting back her veil and bending to kiss her, crushing her in his arms so tightly that a wave of indulgent laughter rippled through the congregation.

They moved over and signed the register while Jessica Reynolds sang, her lovely voice soaring through the vaulted chamber. Many of the women began to sniffle, and there was a busy rummaging in pockets and handbags for tissues.

"Ladies and gentlemen," Reverend Blake said when the song ended, beaming at the assembled townspeople, "allow me to introduce your new neighbors, Mr. and Mrs. Tony Rodriguez!"

Tony hugged his wife, laughing aloud in happiness and relief. Ruth and Tyler started up the aisle together, followed by Lynn and Manny. Lisa and Tony moved into place behind them, Lisa blushing and radiant as the crowd greeted her. The men clapped Tony on the back when he passed, and many of the women reached out to touch Lisa's hands and pat her shoulders.

She felt wonderful, as if a crushing burden had been lifted from her. It was over, and nothing terrible had happened. She and Tony were really, truly married. Now there was nothing more to fear, just a happy party ahead where there would be music and dancing and all kinds of celebration. Then suddenly, amid the sea of laughing faces, Lisa saw her mother and the world came crashing to a halt. She stopped abruptly, gripping Tony's arm.

Sadie stood with Walt and her sons in a pew next to the aisle. Seth clutched his mother's hand and stared up at his sister, wide-eyed with astonishment at her beauty. Walt Kelly was beside Sadie, solid and handsome, looking like a man who'd found himself in exactly the place he wanted to be and had every intention of staying there. Johnny and the twins stood on Walt's other side, with their hair neatly slicked back and faces scrubbed and shining.

Lisa smiled at all of them, but her eyes went back to her mother, who stood tensely next to the aisle. Sadie wore her best dress, one that Lisa remembered well. It was made of faded brown jersey with an old-fashioned gored skirt, but somebody had given her a corsage of pink rosebuds that she wore proudly at her shoulder. She looked younger than Lisa remembered, less worn and troubled, though her eyes were dark with fear as she looked at her daughter.

A wave of love swept over Lisa, so powerful and dizzying that she swayed on her feet and would have stumbled without Tony's supporting hand.

"Mama," she whispered, moving closer to reach for Sadie. "Oh, *Mama!*"

Sadie's face crumpled. She took Lisa's hands, then drew her daughter into her arms, sobbing.

"Honey, you're so beautiful," she murmured through her tears. "So beautiful."

"I love you, Mama," Lisa told her softly, pressing her cheek against Sadie's. "Mama, I'm so sorry...."

"Sweetie, you can't be sorry on your wedding day. You'd just better be happy, or why did I bother coming all this way?"

Lisa stood back and looked at her mother's smiling, tear-streaked face.

"Go on, dear," Sadie told her. "They're all waiting for you. We'll see you at the reception."

"Are you... you'll be there, Mama? I mean, you'll have no problem getting out to the country club or anything? Because Tony and I could..."

"Walt's looking after us," Sadie said confidently. "He'll make sure we get there."

Lisa smiled mistily at Walt and leaned over to kiss him, then bent to kiss each of her little brothers in turn. Even Johnny and the twins endured a kiss from the bride in front of everybody, though they immediately rubbed their cheeks and shifted awkwardly on their feet.

Lisa laughed and drew Tony forward. "Mama, this is my... my husband, Tony," she murmured, her cheeks turning pink as she said those marvelous words for the very first time. "And this is my mother, and Walt, and these are my little brothers...."

Tony kissed Sadie, then shook hands with Walt and the boys while Lisa watched, smiling through her tears. She hugged Sadie one more time and moved up the aisle beside Tony, feeling so featherlight and full of joy that she wouldn't have been at all surprised to feel herself drift up into the air and start floating toward the stained-glass windows.

CHAPTER ELEVEN

THE COUNTRY CLUB was lavishly decorated for a Valentine's Day wedding. Pink and white hearts and flowers, cupids and rosebuds clustered on every wall. At the long table where the wedding party sat, a mass of fresh flowers banked the front and a fluffy pink heart was suspended overhead, hung with streamers and silver wedding bells.

Lisa sat next to Tony behind the table, which was now littered with sticky remnants of wedding cake, scattered flowers and half-empty champagne glasses. She watched the whirling crowd on the dance floor, smiling at the sight of her brother Johnny clumping doggedly around the edge with little Sandy Russell, while Harry and Tim hooted at them from the sidelines.

Seth sat with his mother and Walt at one of the round tables near the dance floor, sipping ginger ale through a straw and looking around at the noisy party. Though it was well past his bedtime, Seth didn't appear to be at all tired. He was clearly determined to enjoy the evening right down to its final moments.

While Lisa was watching them, Sadie caught her eye and waved, then blew a kiss in her daughter's direction before turning to whisper something to Walt. Sadie's cheeks were pink with happiness, and she was so attractive that a few of the local men looked at her with appreciation. But Sadie clearly had eyes for nobody but Walt.

"Your mama looks real pretty, doesn't she?" Tony said, bending close to Lisa so she could hear him above the music. "I might have known a girl like you would have a beautiful mother."

Lisa laughed, then sobered. "I've been so mean to her since I left home, Tony," she said, feeling a wave of sadness and regret. "I was just awful about... everything."

"She understands, sweetheart. She loves you. All that bad stuff, we're leaving it behind. From now on we're only thinking about happy things."

Lisa nodded. "You're right. But I wish I had a little more time to spend with her, now that things are better between us. I've barely been able to say more than a few words to her since they got here, and Mama says they're leaving tomorrow."

"I know. I was talking to them a while ago when you were dancing with Cal."

Lisa looked at him in surprise. "You were?"

"Yeah. I told them..." Tony glanced down at his wife with a smile. "I told them we were going over to El Paso at Easter time to visit my folks, and we could probably run up to Albuquerque for a few days, too, if they didn't mind the company."

Lisa felt a warm glow of gratitude. "Oh, *Tony* ..."

"I had no choice, honey. Otherwise I'd likely be taking Walt and Sadie and those kids along on my honeymoon, and I wasn't too anxious to do *that*." He gave her a meaningful grin that made her blush, then bent forward to kiss her cheek.

Lisa shifted awkwardly in her chair and looked up, startled, as Bubba Gibson two-stepped past them with his daughter, Sara, in his arms. "Hey, Tony! Quit spoonin' that girl and get out here on the dance floor," Bubba shouted genially. "Save all that lovey-dovey stuff for the honeymoon!"

"Come on, Lisa," Tony said, getting to his feet and holding her chair out. "Let's dance this one, just to keep Bubba quiet."

Lisa took his hand and walked out onto the dance floor with him, then moved into his arms as the music slowed to a dreamy ballad.

"This is only my second dance with my wife," Tony murmured in her ear. "Every other damned cowboy in this room's had a dance with the bride, and I just had to stand around and watch."

"I know," Lisa told him, nestling against him and resting her head on his shoulder. "But you're the one I'm going home with."

"Reckon I am," he whispered, tightening his arms around her. "God, I love you, honey. I love you so much, I hardly know how to tell you."

Lisa relaxed in his arms and moved dreamily in time to the music while other couples smiled and made way for them. *You're the one I'm going home with....*

She thought about the words, and all that they implied. To her amazement, Lisa realized suddenly that her fears were gone. She could picture the night to come, the moment when she and Tony would be alone in their room, and it didn't scare her at all. In fact, she was looking forward to it.

Lisa trembled in his arms, stunned by the images that warmed her mind.

Misunderstanding the trembling, Tony leaned back to look at her in concern. "You all right, honey? Getting tired? It's been a long day."

"I'm all right. I'm just so happy, Tony. I really love you."

"Lisa . . ." He tightened his arms around her again, whirling her slowly across the dance floor.

Lisa moved and swayed with him, marveling at this new rush of feeling. She'd loved Tony almost from the first time she'd ever seen him in the ranch yard at the Double C, but it had been a girlish, romantic kind of love. This emotion was different, an urgent, powerful need that left her almost breathless.

She knew this was the way a woman was supposed to feel on her wedding night. But Lisa had grown so afraid that the emotions would never come, that she'd be stiff and inhibited in his arms. Most of all she'd dreaded the thought of disappointing Tony, who deserved all the loving warmth that a wife could give him.

But she didn't worry anymore. The way she felt right now, Tony wasn't going to be disappointed in their lovemaking. They were going to be lucky, she thought with a small, private smile, if either of them got any sleep tonight....

"What?" he asked, looking down at her again. "What are you smiling about?"

"I was thinking about...about the hotel," Lisa whispered. "About us being alone together."

He drew back, startled and wary. "You were? What about it?"

"I'm thinking," she told him, "that I can hardly wait. I wish we were there right this minute."

His eyes widened. Slowly, delightedly, he smiled. "Why?" he whispered.

"Why do you think?"

"If I told you what I'm thinking," Tony said with a sigh, "you'd probably have me arrested, honey. I've been waiting a long time for this night."

"I know you have. I hope I'm going to be worth the wait, Tony."

"Oh, God, sweetheart..." He closed his arms around her and pulled her nearer to him as they circled the dance floor again.

Lisa was conscious of his arousal as her body moved against his. But his thrusting maleness didn't frighten her anymore. She felt warm and moist, almost dizzy with sexual longing as she nestled in her husband's arms.

Ruth had been right all the time, Lisa thought in wonder. The problems and tensions between her and Tony had grown out of her harsh feelings about her mother, not the traumas in Lisa's past. Ruth had obviously known what she was talking about when she told Lisa there wasn't room for love in your heart if it was full of anger.

Now that she'd managed to see things from Sadie's point of view and come to a new understanding of her mother's life, she was able to put all the old bitterness behind her. Lisa was ready at last to give herself to Tony and trust in his love, both emotionally and physically.

She was ready to be his wife. Lisa smiled and reached up to kiss his cheek, while her fingers stroked the back of his neck with a slow, tantalizing caress that made him shiver.

"CARE TO DANCE?" Walt asked, smiling at the look on Sadie's face. She sat beaming at Lisa and Tony as the bride and groom drifted around the polished dance floor gazing at each other, oblivious to everybody else in the room.

Sadie drew herself together and looked at him in alarm. "Oh, Walt," she protested. "I'm not much of a dancer."

"Well, I'm not, either. But I can still get around the floor."

"But... what about Seth?"

Walt smiled at the little boy. "He can look after himself while we're gone. Can't you, son?"

Seth nodded eagerly.

"Now, don't you get involved with that wild bunch over there," Walt cautioned, looking at the other three boys who jostled and shouted in a laughing crowd of well-dressed children that included Sam and Lynn's girls, Mary and Bubba's grandchildren and some of Tony's brothers and sisters. "You just stay here at the table and wait for Mama and me to come back, all right?"

"Okay, Walt. Can I have another soda pop?"

"You sure can. In fact, you can go over to the bar and get it now."

Seth got to his feet and made his way to the bar, looking grown-up and important in his new red sweater and dress pants.

Sadie watched him affectionately, then moved into Walt's arms. "I haven't danced for years," she said.

"Sadie, you danced a waltz with Tony just a few minutes ago. I saw you."

"Did I do all right? I was so nervous," Sadie confessed, "that I hardly knew what I was doing."

"You did fine. I was the proudest man in the room, watching my girl looking so pretty out there."

"Oh, Walt!" Sadie gave him one of those luminous smiles that always wrenched his heart.

"Sadie," he whispered when they were out on the floor together, moving to the strains of a slow country song.

"Hmm?" She gripped his hand and drew closer, unconsciously nestling against him with a trusting, childlike air that made Walt feel shaky with tenderness.

"It's Valentine's Day, Sadie."

"I know. Isn't it romantic? What a nice time for a wedding."

"That's not what I mean. It's not just Valentine's Day for Lisa and Tony. It's for you, too. Happy Valentine's Day, honey."

She smiled up at him, then stared in astonishment and confusion when he drew a small object from his pocket and offered it to her.

"Walt...what's that?"

"It's a Valentine. Maybe you should open it and look."

Sadie's throat tightened with fear, and her mouth went suddenly dry. She let Walt draw her into a shadowed alcove behind the punch table, then reached up with trepidation to take the small velvet box from his hand.

"My goodness," she murmured, her voice trembly. "What on earth..."

She flipped open the lid of the box and gasped at the diamonds flaring in their nest of white silk.

"Oh my." Sadie lifted a hand to her mouth while Walt stood watching her, silent and tense. "Walt, it's a...a ring. The most beautiful ring..."

Sadie, who had never owned anything really beautiful or costly in her life, bent forward with childlike awe to examine the lovely piece of jewelry. It was a flat gold band, wide and heavy, with three large channel-set diamonds that flared and glistened in the muted light from the dance floor.

"They told me this style would be more practical," Walt explained, "for a woman who does a lot of gardening and such. The diamonds don't stand up real high, so they won't tend to catch on things."

He might as well have been speaking a foreign language. Sadie obviously couldn't even comprehend the words, let alone make sense of their meaning. "I don't..." She paused and stole another glance at him, then looked at the ring in fascination. "I don't know what you're talking about, Walt. Whose ring is this?"

"Well, Sadie, you dummy," he said tenderly, reaching out to draw back a stray lock of hair from her face, "it's for you, honey. But only if you want me, too," he added with an awkward smile. "I'm afraid I go along with the ring. It's sort of a package deal."

His smile faded. He stood frozen, hardly able to endure the tension while Sadie looked up at his face, then back at the small velvet box in her hand. The moment thinned and stilled, quivering in the silence between them like a single note of music held for an unbearably long time.

Walt couldn't breathe, couldn't even think. Still he knew that his happiness and all the rest of his life hung in the balance while he waited for her answer.

"You're proposing to me?" she whispered at last. "You want to... to *marry* me?"

"More than anything in the world," he told her quietly. "I love you, Sadie. I guess I've loved you for ten years or more, ever since you moved into that trailer down the road. But it was hardly decent for a man to feel such things, so I tried to keep it to myself."

"I never... Walt, I never knew..." She swayed on her feet and would have stumbled if he hadn't reached out quickly to steady her.

"It's okay, Sadie," he said, miserable with embarrassment as he took the velvet box from her and slipped it back into his pocket. "I was wrong to push this on you. We can just go right on being friends, if that's all right with you, and maybe later..."

"Walt Kelly!"

He paused, a hand still in his pocket.

Sadie glared at him with flushed cheeks and eyes that shone like stars. "You just give me back that ring," she commanded. "This instant."

"Why, Sadie..." He began to smile. "This ring?"

Sadie took the box from him and opened it, delighting again in the fiery beauty of the three diamonds. "I never saw anything so pretty," she breathed. "Never in all my life."

"Want to try it on?" he asked huskily.

"Oh, Walt..."

Sadie held out her left hand and he slipped the wide gold band onto her ring finger, smiling with satisfaction at the fit.

"How did you get exactly the right size?" she asked. "It's like it was made for me."

"Reckon it was," Walt told her with a boyish grin. "There's not much I don't know about you, honey, after studying your every move for ten years."

Sadie looked proudly at the ring on her finger, then cast a glance up at him. "So if I want to keep it," she teased, "I have to take you, too?"

"I'm afraid that's the deal."

But Sadie was too deeply moved to keep up the teasing for long. Her face crumpled and tears gathered in her eyes, trickling slowly down her cheeks. "You're the kindest, best man in all the world," she told Walt, moving into his arms and hugging him. "I don't deserve a man like you, Walt. I've made such a mess of my life."

"That's not true. You've made a real success of your life, sweetheart. You've raised five great kids, pretty well single-handed, and taught them right from wrong. You've kept them fed and clothed and got them educated. You've worked hard every day of your life. And on top of all that, you've made yourself into a woman so sweet that this old farmer can't live without you."

"Walt?"

"Hmm?" He tightened his arms and rested his face against her dark hair which smelled sweetly of flowers and perfume.

"I love you, too, Walt," she told him seriously. "I think I always have, but I was like you. My feelings about you were wrong, so I never let them into my head. But lately, since you've been... Walt, sometimes it's getting real hard for me to keep my hands off you."

He laughed in delighted surprise and kissed her mouth tenderly. Then he drew her back onto the dance floor, smiling to see her pride as she rested her hand on his shoulder so the diamonds glittered in plain sight of everybody.

"Walt," she said, after a brief silence as they danced among the other couples, "I've got four kids still at home, you know. That's an awful burden to pile on a man, isn't it?''

"It's an awful burden for a woman to bear alone. I figure if we share it, we'll both have an easier time," he told her amiably.

"You're such a lovely man," Sadie murmured, tipping back her head to smile at him. Walt bent and kissed her, entirely without self-consciousness, and it felt so good that he did it again.

"You know, I think Easter would be a good time for a wedding," he commented after a dreamy silence. "Lisa and Tony are coming out for a visit, and the boys will have some time off school. What do you think?''

"I think I've died and gone to heaven," Sadie whispered against his chest.

Walt nodded, satisfied. He whirled her around a flower-decked column and settled back into the rhythm of the dance.

FRANKIE WATCHED Lisa's mother and the tall farmer moving around the floor, and thought what a nice couple they seemed to be. Tony's parents, too, looked like fun. Tony's mother was roly-poly and full of laughter. Mr. Rodriguez, who danced beautifully, was handsome and dark, with an arrogant high-bridged nose and the reckless air of a mountain bandit.

They were going to have an entertaining family, Frankie thought wistfully, with all those brothers and sisters, and such delightful parents. Lucky Lisa...

Frankie sat near the door at a little table bearing the guest book, and wondered what to do next. The dance had been in full swing for an hour or more, and the flood of new arrivals had slowed to a trickle. Pretty soon she'd have to leave this comfortable hiding place and join the crowd, pretending she was having a good time.

She glanced around cautiously, wondering where Tyler was, and then, to her surprise, realized that she didn't really care.

She didn't care!

For the first time that she could recall, Frankie hadn't memorized his every move and spent all her time watching him. She sat thunderstruck, pondering the significance of this discovery.

Apparently she was cured. Maybe the wrenching anguish of being offered his love, of actually yielding to him and tasting his kisses and then turning him away…maybe that fiery sacrifice had served as a kind of shock therapy.

At any rate, it seemed that she was really, truly, over Tyler McKinney.

The thought was almost too wonderful to comprehend. For some time now, Frankie had longed for freedom from the obsessive dreams that haunted her. There was certainly no pleasure in lusting after a married man, especially when she knew there was no possible future for that kind of love, not in a tight-knit community like Crystal Creek.

But, until now, she'd never been able to put him out of her mind for more than a few seconds, never been able to stop hungering for him.

While she was absorbed in her thoughts, Tyler came suddenly into view, crossing the room with his father. The two of them carried glasses of whiskey and were deep in conversation. Both had stripped off their suit jackets by now and J.T. in particular looked happy and relaxed, enjoying the party. Frankie bit her lip and watched Tyler cautiously, the way a person probes a newly healed injury to see how much it hurts.

He was still the handsomest man in the room, she thought, and a part of her thrilled wildly at the sight of him. But she didn't feel bereft and miserable as she watched him walk with J.T. to a table near the front, where Cynthia and Ruth were waiting. In fact, Frankie discovered to her astonishment that she was really much more concerned about Joey Wall, who should have arrived hours ago. She'd been expecting Joey ever since five o'clock, when she'd taken up her position at the reception table, but there'd been no sign of him. Frankie made a worried little grimace and paged restlessly through the guest book, trying not to think about the darkened, winding stretch of highway between Crystal Creek and Austin.

There was nothing wrong with Joey, she told herself firmly. Nothing had happened to him. Joey was the most capable person she knew. He could look after himself in any situation.

"That boy's still not here?" a voice asked at her elbow.

Frankie looked up to see Cal McKinney, whom Serena had sent to take over Joey's vacant position. He'd spent most of the early evening lounging at Frankie's side, greeting neighbors and townsfolk as they arrived. He'd begun to drift away when the newcomers thinned, but he still checked back regularly to see how Frankie was managing.

She shook herself, trying to free her mind of worried thoughts, and looked up at him with a smile. "Not yet. I'm sure he'll be here, though. Joey's usually so reliable," she added, unable to keep a little quiver from her voice. "I can't imagine what's keeping him."

"Well, he's sure missing a good party," Cal said, settling his long body into the chair next to Frankie and extending his legs comfortably. "I can't recall when I've had so much fun."

"Your life's been fun since the day you were born," Frankie told him.

Cal smiled at her. "Everybody thinks I'm such a lightweight," he complained. "I'm a real serious guy, Frankie. I've got a business, a mortgage, a wife and a baby on the way.... Why, I'm just another boring suburban yuppie. Pretty soon I'll be fat and middle-aged."

"You'll never be middle-aged," Frankie said fondly. "You're a legend, Cal. Folks around here are still going to be calling you a wild young feller when you're ninety years old."

"Just like Grandpa," he said with a faraway look. "Good old Hank. He may have got old, but he never got mellow, did he?"

"He sure wasn't boring," Frankie agreed.

The two neighbors watched the laughing crowd on the dance floor, thinking how much the old man always loved these social occasions despite all his bitter grumbling about "foolish goings-on."

"Come on, kid," Cal said after a moment, getting to his feet again and reaching for Frankie. "Come have a dance with me. You've been stuck behind this table all night, and you're looking so cute."

Frankie blushed and began to protest. "You know I'm not much of a dancer, Cal."

"Bull," he said cheerfully. "Lettie Mae keeps telling me you can do all that aerobics stuff better than Jane Fonda."

"That's not dancing."

"It sure looks like dancing when my wife does it. I never get tired of watching her. Come on, Frankie," he urged. "Leave the damn book. Anybody who hasn't signed it yet, they're too late to bother with."

Frankie gave in and moved out onto the floor with him. Cal was a wonderful dancer, and she found herself relaxing into the rhythms of the dance as they circled the floor to a lively two-step. But she still couldn't forget her nagging worries over Joey and his unexplained absence . . .

"What did you say?" Cal asked suddenly.

"He promised he'd come," Frankie repeated, surprised that she'd spoken the words aloud. "I don't think Joey's ever broken a promise to me in all the years I've known him.''

For the first time Cal recognized the depths of her concern and began to look a little worried himself.

"Do you want me to get somebody to check on him, honey? Wayne Jackson's here with the police cruiser. He could radio in and see if there's any..."

But while he was speaking, a tall figure appeared in the foyer and Frankie's heart began to pound erratically.

"There he is!" she said in delight, abandoning Cal without ceremony at the edge of the dance floor and running over to the door.

Cal grinned ruefully and shook his head, then wandered off in search of his wife while Frankie gripped Joey's arm and shook it furiously.

"Where have you *been?*" she demanded, glaring at him. "You're hours late. I've been all alone here, and I didn't know where you were, or have any idea why you..." She fell silent, shifting nervously under his admiring gaze.

"That's such a pretty dress," he said with an affectionate smile. "You look beautiful, Frankie. Just beautiful. Happy Valentine's Day, punkin.''

"Valentine's Day?" she asked blankly.

Joey looked different to her somehow, though she couldn't put her finger on the change. He was the same broad-shouldered, green-eyed boy she'd always known, but there was something about him....

"There was an accident just this side of Austin," he told her. "The car in front of me crossed the center line, sideswiped another vehicle and wound up in the ditch. I was the first one at the scene and I had to hang around for a couple of hours to give a statement to the police.''

"Was anybody hurt?'' Frankie asked, still disturbed by a strange, wild tumult of emotions that she couldn't understand.

"They took one kid to the hospital, but I don't think it was anything too serious. You should have seen how fast they were going, honey. They passed me like I was standing still, about a half mile before they crashed. A good thing, too, or I would have been in the middle of it.''

"Oh, Joey…'' She stared up at him, thinking about the accident, almost sick with relief now that her tension was over. "I was so worried about you,'' she whispered.

"Why?''

"I don't know. I guess…'' She fell silent, fiddling with the belt on her dress while Joey looked down at her in surprise.

"Frankie? What's the matter?''

"I think I…seem to be in love with you, Joey,'' she said abruptly, as astounded by her words as he was.

His eyes widened and his face drained of color as he stared at her. "What…what did you say?''

Frankie moved closer to him, trying to smile. "You know, it's not very gentlemanly to make me say it over again,'' she murmured against his shoulder. "It's your turn to say it.''

"I've been saying it since I was ten years old," Joey told her huskily. He put his arms around her and drew her into the shadowed hallway next to the coatroom. "I guess I'd just given up hope that I'd ever hear it from you. Frankie, honey..."

"I've been such a jerk." She looked up at him with tears in her eyes. "I've treated you so badly, Joey, and all the time it was you that I really loved."

Frankie heard her own voice with a kind of wondering astonishment, and realized that what she said was true. Her feelings for Joey had always been there, so close to her heart that she hadn't been able to recognize them for what they were.

The hot, bothered yearning she'd felt for Tyler McKinney had nothing to do with love. This was real love, this sweet emotion that filled her heart with happiness and a deep, deep trust that made her feel safe and cherished.

"I guess I never thought you could fall in love with your best friend," she told Joey simply as she cuddled in his arms, loving the feel of him. "I didn't think it was possible."

"Oh, it's possible, honey," Joey murmured. "I could have told you that. I've been following you around like a puppy dog all these years, waiting for you to realize it's possible. Say it again, sweetheart."

"I love you, Joey Wall," she whispered, standing on tiptoe to wrap her arms around his neck and kiss his mouth. She could feel him quivering in her arms, his big muscular body taut with emotion as they clung together.

"Oh, Lord, that feels so good," he said, sighing when she finally drew away and buried her face against his jacket front. "But if you do it one more time, Frankie, I can't be held accountable. I might just grab you and gobble you right up."

She cast him a sparkling glance. The shaky rush of emotion was beginning to calm, and Frankie was feeling cheerful and confident again, very much like her old self.

With a teasing smile, she reached up and put her arms around him once more, drawing his face down to hers and kissing him with lingering thoroughness.

RUTH SAT at the table near the dance floor, watching while the multicolored throng of dancers whirled past. Beside her, Cynthia sighed with pleasure and leaned back, running a hand wearily through her hair.

"It all went so well, didn't it, Ruth? We couldn't have hoped for a nicer day."

Ruth nodded agreement. "I'm sorry it's almost over. Lisa's dress is really beautiful, isn't it?" she said wistfully, watching the bride swirl by in her husband's arms. "And Jennifer was so good. She was amazing."

"Oh, I *know*," Cynthia said fervently. "I wasn't sure how she'd react when we walked into the church and she discovered that she was the center of attention. Fortunately the child's a real ham, just like that brother of hers." Both women smiled as Cal flashed past them with Serena in his arms, his polished riding boots twinkling across the floor.

"Do you think Virginia minded leaving early and going home to baby-sit?" Ruth asked.

"I think she was relieved. She's been so busy these past weeks, getting ready for the wedding and arranging Neale's birthday party besides. She's plumb tuckered out."

"Plumb tuckered out!" Ruth echoed with a teasing glance. "Cynthia, you're beginning to sound like a native."

"Oh, Lord. Am I?" Cynthia asked in such dismay that Ruth chuckled.

"Not really. Where's J.T.?"

"He and Tyler have disappeared again. I think they're over at the bar, talking business with Ollie Newton."

Ruth nodded, not surprised to learn that the McKinney men were taking advantage of the occasion to cement ties with the owner of another Hill Country winery. "I guess business is never far from their minds, is it?" she asked, feeling bleak.

Cynthia looked at her in concern. "Are you all right, Ruthie?" she asked gently.

"I'm fine. I just feel a little strange these days. It must be the flu or the winter blahs, something like that."

Cynthia was about to question her further when Vernon Trent appeared at the table. "Care to dance, Cynthia?" he asked.

Cynthia smiled up at him. "Carolyn sent you over here, didn't she?"

Vern nodded placidly. "She said if your husband was going to ignore you, she'd have to lend me out for a couple of dances."

"Actually, J.T.'s been unusually attentive up until now," Cynthia told him, getting to her feet with a smile. "But you can tell Carolyn I appreciate her generosity. I'd love to dance with you."

Ruth watched as they drifted away into the crowd of dancers, then sipped moodily at her tomato juice. All at once a wave of sickness washed over her, so intense that she felt in real danger of throwing up. She got to her feet in mild panic and hurried toward the foyer, genuinely afraid that she might not reach the washroom in time.

But as soon as she was safely locked in a cubicle the nausea seemed to pass, leaving her weak and shaky. Ruth's forehead was clammy, and her stomach still felt dangerously tight.

She came out into the empty washroom and looked at her white face in the mirror, shivering at the memory of that dreadful night at another dance almost two years ago, when Jodie Hiltz had cornered her in the ladies' bathroom and claimed to be pregnant with Tyler's baby.

Of course it hadn't been true, but the shock and horror of the moment still haunted Ruth occasionally. She'd been so much in love with Tyler in those days, so crazy with desire. Now they barely spoke to each other, and the image of Frankie's pretty face and youthful body seemed to hang in the air between them whenever Ruth looked at her husband.

She pushed open the heavy door and wandered back out into the foyer, still feeling mildly queasy, wondering if it was really flu, or a reaction to something she'd eaten.

Suddenly she heard the unmistakable sound of Frankie's soft laughter from behind the coatroom partition.

"Oh, I love you!" the girl was saying. "Kiss me again, quick. Once more before anybody sees, and then we'll go out there and pretend we're just friends."

Ruth froze in horror and her stomach churned again. Unable to help herself, she edged forward and peeked around the screen that hid the coatroom from view. Two people clung together in the shadows and Ruth immediately recognized Frankie's white knitted dress.

But the man who held her wasn't Tyler. It was Joey Wall, and he was smiling down at the dainty girl in his arms with such misty adoration that Ruth felt a dangerous lump in her throat.

"I love you, too, honey," he whispered, bending to kiss her. "I love you so much...."

Ruth turned away, guilty at intruding on their intimacy. She moved slowly across the carpeted foyer and sank into one of the armchairs, still stunned by what she'd just seen.

After that moment of stolen insight, there could be no doubt how Frankie and Joey felt about each other. Ruth had been dreadfully mistaken, she realized, imagining there was anything going on between Tyler and this girl. She'd done both of them an injustice.

Again she felt an urgent need to seek Tyler out and apologize for her suspicions. She wanted to hold him and cry in his arms and wipe away all the bad thoughts and loneliness of the past months. Frankie obviously wasn't a threat to her marriage. Ruth knew now that the real danger was this terrible silence that never seemed to go away. But she simply had no idea how she and Tyler could begin to ease the tension between them.

CHAPTER TWELVE

DURING THE NIGHT, as if in relief that the wedding was safely over, the sky filled with dark clouds and rain began to flow across the hills in a curtain of silver.

Early the next morning Ruth stood by the window in her nightgown, gazing at the rolling countryside with a brooding expression. She held the curtain back with her hand and looked down at the huddled ranch buildings, wrapped in a dense gray mist. Behind her, Tyler turned over sleepily in the bed, still drowsy after a late night at the wedding dance.

Suddenly Ruth was wrenched by nausea again, even more urgent than the attack of the previous evening. She ran into the bathroom and closed the door, then retched frantically until she felt weak and drained.

At last she stood erect, leaning against the sink, and splashed some cold water onto her face. When she opened the door she found Tyler standing outside, pale with alarm.

"Ruth, what is it? What's the matter? Are you sick?"

"I seem to be," she whispered, trying to give him a reassuring smile, though she knew she looked ghastly. "I must be...getting the flu or something."

"How long has..."

But while he was talking, another wave of sickness washed over her. She gave him a despairing look and vanished inside the bathroom again. When she emerged, white-faced and shaking, Tyler was already dressed and tugging at his boots.

"Come on," he said. "I'm taking you to the hospital."

"Oh, Tyler, it can't be that serious. It's probably just..."

"What?"

"I don't know," Ruth said helplessly. "Some kind of flu bug, I guess. I felt sick for a little while last night at the dance, too, but not like this."

"It started last night? Do you think it could be food poisoning?"

"You know, I thought of that at the dance when it came on so suddenly. I wonder if anybody else is sick. Maybe we should..."

"We should get you to the doctor right away," Tyler said in a voice so firm that Ruth was afraid to argue. "Come on, let's get you dressed. Can I help with anything?"

Ruth looked around vaguely. "I think my jeans are in... oh, *no!*" she muttered, running back into the bathroom.

This time when she came out, Tyler was so worried that he could hardly stand still. He'd found one of her old jogging suits in a dresser drawer and he bundled her into it hastily, tied her running shoes on her feet, then practically carried her down the stairs and out to his car.

"I feel like such an idiot," Ruth protested when they were heading for town. "Causing all this trouble over some little flu bug."

"I don't think it's flu," Tyler said grimly. "I think it's food poisoning, and the sooner Nate has a look at you, the better I'll feel."

Ruth huddled miserably in the passenger seat and stared down at her hands, too sick and weak to respond.

Still, in a bizarre way it felt good to be with him, to have his full attention concentrated on her. She could hardly remember the last time they'd been alone together like this and Tyler had been so interested in her welfare.

"What?" he asked, seeing her mouth twist in a bleak smile. "What is it, Ruth?"

"I was just thinking that it's kind of nice to be doing something together after all this time, even if what we're doing is going to the hospital."

"It's been a real busy time, hasn't it? Seems we've been communicating by notes and phone calls for months. I never really get to talk to you anymore."

Ruth was feeling too wretched to choose her words carefully. "I didn't think you wanted to talk to me," she said. "These past few months, I've felt like you'd be just as happy if I weren't even around."

He looked at her in shocked dismay. "God, Ruth! How can you say such a thing?"

She searched for an answer, but the nausea threatened to rise once more. Ruth bit her lip and stared out the window, taking deep breaths as she struggled to control her queasiness.

Tyler glanced at her, frowning. "Feeling sick again?"

She nodded.

"Well, here we are," he said in relief, pulling up at the front door of the hospital. He helped her from the car to the reception area and watched helplessly when she bolted toward the washroom as soon as they were inside the door.

She came out after a few minutes and found Tyler waiting for her, looking anxious. "I talked to Nate already," he said. "You can go straight into one of the examining rooms and get undressed. He says he'll be around as soon as he gets finished with a patient in the emergency ward."

"The same place as always? Down the hall?"

Tyler nodded. "I'll go with you."

But when they reached the examining room, Ruth found herself uncomfortable in Tyler's presence. Too many things hung between them, heavy and unspoken, making her feel smothered. "I'll be all right, Tyler," she told him. "Why don't you go up to the Longhorn for coffee and come back in an hour or so? I'll be in the waiting room."

"Are you sure? I'd rather stay with you."

"Please, Tyler. I don't want you around when I'm looking so awful," she said with a wan smile.

"Ruth..."

Nate Purdy knocked and came into the room, brisk and cheerful in his white lab coat. "What's all this?" he asked, casting a thoughtful glance at Ruth's white face and shaking hands. "A little too much celebrating last night?"

"I'm afraid so," Ruth said. "I feel awfully sick, Nate."

Nate studied her more closely, then turned to Tyler. "Give us an hour or so, would you, son? I want to give this young lady a complete examination. You come back—" he consulted his watch. "—around nine-thirty. Ask for me at the desk."

Tyler hesitated in the doorway, then nodded reluctantly and went away.

Nate smiled at Ruth, who emerged from behind the screen a few minutes later in a skimpy cotton gown. "Now then," he said comfortably.

Ruth shifted her bare feet on the cold floor tiles. "I don't know why I need a complete examination," she protested. "It's just a stomach flu, or maybe a touch of food poisoning."

"Is it now?" he said. "And since when did you start doing your own diagnostic work?"

Ruth shuddered and gulped, too weak to argue. She climbed onto the padded table and submitted herself to the indignities that followed, gritting her teeth and trying to think of other things, like the soft patter of raindrops on the window and how beautiful Lisa had looked in her wedding gown.

When he finished, Nate gave her a fatherly pat on the head and went away for a while, leaving her to get dressed. Ruth pulled on the jogging suit, tied her running shoes and sat in a chair by the desk, under a huge chart depicting the gastrointestinal system. The lurid colors made her feel sick again, and she turned away hastily.

Nate came back into the room with a couple of file folders under his arm. He seated himself at the desk, giving her a keen glance.

"How are things between you and Tyler these days?" he asked, putting his glasses on and opening one of the files.

"Not so good," Ruth confessed after an awkward silence. "We just can't seem to get past our problems. After the baby died..." Her voice caught, then steadied. "There was a lot going on," she said. "I think we had things we needed to talk about, but we couldn't seem to find a way to get started. We still can't."

"Well, in light of your medical condition," the doctor said gently, "I'm afraid you're going to have to start talking to each other again, Ruth. You're going to have to deal with this together."

"Why?" She looked up at him quickly, drymouthed with sudden fear. "What's the matter with me? Nate, what is it?"

"It's a pretty serious condition, I'm afraid," he said, writing something on the file. But when he looked up his eyes were bright with laughter, making Ruth feel more confused then ever.

"What condition?" she whispered.

"You're pregnant, Ruth."

Her mouth dropped open. She stared blankly at the doctor. "I... can't be," she said at last. "I can't possibly be pregnant."

"Why not?"

"Because Tyler and I haven't been... sleeping together. In fact, I haven't had sex at all since... since last fall. Months and months ago."

"Ah." Nate looked down at the file, his mouth twitching. "This baby... it's what you'd call an immaculate conception, then?"

"I'm serious, Nate! You've made some kind of mistake."

"There's no mistake," he told her gently. "I reckon you're about five or six weeks pregnant. You probably conceived sometime in early January."

"But I told you, we haven't—" Ruth fell abruptly silent, recalling that cold winter night when Tyler had made love to her in his sleep.

Nate grinned, watching her face. "A light dawns," he observed dryly.

"It was just one time," she murmured. "Right after New Year's. Tyler was... almost asleep the whole time. He didn't even know what he was doing."

"He must have known something," Nate said with a grin. "He surely left his mark."

"Pregnant," Ruth breathed, sitting up straighter in her chair as the full wonder of it began to dawn. But along with her joy she felt a cold touch of fear. "Nate, will it be all right this time? I don't remember being sick like this before."

He leaned back and gave her a comfortable smile. "The old wives' tales say a sick pregnancy is a healthy pregnancy, and they're usually right. The more a baby draws from you at the beginning, the healthier and stronger he seems to be, according to local wisdom. I can give you something for the nausea if you need it," he added, "but it'll likely settle down by itself in a few weeks."

"A *baby*," Ruth said, brushing at the tears that rolled down her cheeks. "I never dreamed..."

Nate sobered and gave her an intent glance. "Ruthie, I'll have a talk with Tyler later on, too, but I want the two of you to know that there's not a thing in the world for you to worry about. Your baby's condition was a purely accidental thing. There's no reason to believe it'll ever happen to the two of you again, or that you won't have a whole houseful of healthy kids in a few years."

"And I'm... all right? I didn't know a thing about this, all these weeks!" Ruth said with sudden panic. "I should have been watching what I ate, and being careful...."

"All that can start now. You haven't done anything that's going to hurt this little one. Both Mama and baby are healthy as can be, looking just great. Even if you don't feel so great right now."

"Oh, *Nate*..." She laughed aloud, suppressing an urge to fling herself across the desk and kiss the smiling doctor. "I still can't believe... When will the baby be born?"

He consulted a chart in his desk drawer. "Early January, you said?"

"I think it must have been..." Ruth frowned, trying to remember.

"We can get the exact dates later," Nate said with casual wave of his hand. "For now, I figure we can put your due date in late September or early October. You'll be pregnant all through those hot summer months, Ruth. Just like Cynthia was, come to think of it."

"I don't mind! I'll love every minute of it. I'm not a New Englander like Cynthia, you know. California girls are used to the heat."

Ruth laughed breathlessly, so happy that she hardly knew what she was saying. She thought of Cynthia, unfailingly kind and helpful, and J.T.'s quiet strength, and the rest of the family members, all of whom would be overjoyed at this news.

But most of all, she thought of Tyler....

"What time is it?" she asked the doctor abruptly.

"A little before nine," he said, consulting his watch.

"I can't wait till nine-thirty for Tyler to get back," Ruth said, bouncing with excitement. "I think I'll go up to the Longhorn and find him, if that's all right. You don't need me anymore?"

"Not for another month," Nate said cheerfully. "You can set up an appointment schedule at the desk on your way out."

"Yes, I will. Oh, thank you! Thank you so much," Ruth said, giving him an impulsive hug as they both stood up to leave. And to think she'd harbored uncharitable thoughts about this man in the past. He was wonderful! Why hadn't she noticed before?

"Not feeling sick anymore?" he asked.

"Now that I know what's causing it," she told him with a radiant smile, "even the sickness feels wonderful."

"God bless you, Ruthie," Nate said with sudden emotion. "All of you. Take good care of this little McKinney," he added, patting her stomach, "and that husband of yours, too."

"I'll try," Ruth said, giving him another glowing smile as they paused together at the door. "I'll really try."

TYLER SAT in a booth at the Longhorn with Wayne Jackson and Bubba Gibson, discussing beef prices, federal grazing fees in New Mexico and the upcoming baseball season. The three of them looked up to greet Manny Hernandez, who strolled into the coffee shop brushing raindrops from his denim jacket.

"Room for one more?" he asked, sliding into the booth opposite Tyler.

"How come you got time for coffee?" Bubba demanded. "Thought you'd be real busy these days, with that young helper of yours away on his honeymoon."

"Come on, Bubba. Even busy men get to stop for coffee once a day, don't they?" Manny said. "How about you, Tyler? We don't usually see you in town this early in the morning."

"Ruth's feeling a little sick," Tyler said, trying not to show how worried he felt. "She woke up this morning with a bad upset stomach, so I brought her in to see Nate. Has anybody heard about some kind of food poisoning going around?"

The three men shook their heads.

"Likely she's just hung over," Bubba said placidly, munching on a doughnut. "All those McKinney women are real heavy drinkers."

The others chuckled and began to tease Kasey when she came by to refill their cups.

"Jessica sure sang pretty at that wedding," Bubba said to Wayne with a sigh when the waitress departed. "You should have seen my womenfolk crying their eyes out."

"I saw you brush away a tear or two, Bubba," Wayne said with a grin. "And don't you try to deny it. I was sitting right behind you."

"That's just because it's a sad thing to see another young feller bite the dust," Bubba said defensively. "Struck down in the prime of his life," he added with a soulful look.

"Yeah, *right,*" Manny scoffed, sipping his coffee. "We all know how terrific you'd get along without Mary, you old coyote."

"That's different," Bubba argued. "I got the best wife in the world. Most guys aren't near as lucky."

"Reckon all of us have been pretty lucky," Wayne said quietly.

The other three nodded agreement, then turned the conversation to a rowdy discussion of honeymoons, a topic about which Bubba had a seemingly endless stock of funny stories.

Tyler relaxed a little, forgetting his anxiety over Ruth for a while as he listened to the cheerful banter. It still amazed him sometimes to see Bubba joking and chatting with Wayne and Manny, the two men who'd been instrumental in sending him to prison just a year or so earlier. But in Crystal Creek, friendship outlived other passing things, like the problems and conflicts that sprang up occasionally between neighbors.

It was a good place to live, Tyler thought. A man was lucky to have a life like his. If only...

He watched with an absent smile as the others finished their doughnuts, spent a few minutes wrangling amiably over the bill and then went their separate ways. He sat alone in the booth with a final cup of coffee, looking out at the quiet street, rain-washed and empty in the morning light.

The shower had ended and some wan sunlight began to filter through the clouds to the east, glistening on the damp pavement and rugged cut-stone walls of the old buildings.

"More coffee?" the waitress asked, pausing by the booth with a big coffeepot. "Come on. You can handle one more cup."

"No thanks, Kasey," Tyler said. "Time for me to push off, I guess."

"Say hi to Ruth for me, okay? Tell her and Cynthia that everybody thinks it was a beautiful wedding."

"Thanks. I'll do that."

He tossed a couple of bills onto the table, fitted his hat in place and stepped outside, breathing deeply of the fresh morning air. Tyler glanced at his watch and looked down the street at the hospital. He'd promised Ruth he'd be there at nine-thirty, but there was more than half an hour to wait.

Finally he turned and walked up the street in the opposite direction, toward the church. He hesitated briefly, opened the gate into the churchyard and moved slowly across the damp grass to the cemetery, where many former residents of Crystal Creek were buried, including his own grandparents and great-grandparents. Tyler always liked the sense of continuity that he got from reading the faded headstones of early settlers. But today he didn't pause at any of the crumbling old markers.

He walked through the McKinney family plot to a small grave with a gleaming white marble headstone. A sleeping lamb was carved into the marble above a simple inscription. "John Donald McKinney, beloved infant son of Tyler and Ruth...."

Tears burned in Tyler's eyes. He brushed at them with the back of his hand and stood looking down at the little grave. A cool breeze sprang up, tugging at his hair and clothes.

"Hi, son," he whispered. "It's a real nice day today. Looks like it's going to be sunny and warm later."

He paused a moment, choked with emotion, then went on. "The new grapevines are taking hold and starting to grow, and we've..."

His voice caught and he fell silent, shifting awkwardly on his feet. As clearly as if it were yesterday, Tyler recalled the face of his newborn son, so pale and beautiful, eyes closed as if in sleep. Whenever he thought about the baby, his arms ached with the longing to hold him. They'd named their son after both grandfathers, and planned to call him J.D....

There wasn't a day in his life that Tyler didn't think about the little boy, wonder how much he'd have grown by now and what he'd be doing if he'd lived. The pain seemed as fresh and terrible as ever, and nothing helped to ease his mind except constant, body-numbing work. He knew it would be better for him to talk about the baby, to share his grief with somebody.

But it was Ruth's comfort that he needed, and they never talked anymore.

At the thought of Ruth he felt another tug of worry, recalling how shaken she'd been when he left her at the hospital. If anything happened to Ruth, he couldn't go on living. There was only so much a man was able to bear.

The wind freshened and began to sigh around the corners of the old stone church. Tyler stood quietly in the morning light by his son's grave, waiting for it to be time to meet his wife at the hospital.

RUTH HURRIED up the street to the Longhorn, her heart singing with happiness and a soaring, incredulous wonder. She saw her blurred reflection in a store window and paused on the sidewalk to touch her body cautiously. It was so hard to believe that this miracle could have occurred weeks ago, and she'd been so completely unaware of it.

She'd only been inside the hospital for less than an hour, but in that time everything had been transformed. The sun was beginning to shine, raying soft fingers of light through the clouds and warming the sodden earth. The world seemed brighter, fresher, full of hope and beauty. Even her occasional attacks of nausea didn't seem nearly as severe now that she welcomed them with such happiness.

Ruth pushed open the door to the Longhorn and discovered that the morning crowd had all but vanished. Kasey was taking advantage of the lull to stock a glass-fronted pastry cabinet with fresh-baked apple pies and fruit cobblers.

"Hi, Kasey," Ruth said. "Has Tyler been in here this morning?"

"Hi there, Ruth. Nice to see you. He just left a few minutes ago," Kasey said. "Ooh, doesn't this look yummy?" she added, holding up a plump chocolate eclair oozing mounds of whipped cream. Ruth's stomach churned and she looked away hastily, biting her lip.

"Do you happen to know where he went? He was supposed to meet me at nine-thirty but I finished my appointment early."

Kasey gave her a thoughtful glance, her face softening. "If Tyler's got a few minutes to spare," she said quietly, "reckon you might find him over at the church."

"The church?" Ruth echoed, looking blankly at the young woman's sympathetic face.

"He usually likes to go up there for a little while when he's in town."

Ruth wanted to ask why, but she was too embarrassed. After all, a woman shouldn't have to glean information about her own husband from the waitresses in the local coffee shop. Ruth was beginning to realize how far apart she and Tyler had grown, when other people seemed to know more about his habits than she did.

"Thanks, Kasey," she said quietly. "I'll walk over and see if he's there."

She went up the street and let herself into the churchyard, then stopped by the gate, stunned to see Tyler's tall figure standing in the family plot next to their son's grave. Ruth often came to the cemetery by herself, but she and Tyler had never been here together since the day of the funeral.

She walked across the wet grass and came up beside him so quietly that he flinched and gave her a startled look, then turned away hastily.

Ruth glanced in surprise at his averted face, certain that she'd seen tears in his eyes. She slipped her hand into his and stood silently next to him, looking down at the headstone.

"He was so beautiful," Tyler said in a low, strangled voice, as if the words were being wrung from him. "Ruth, he was...such a beautiful baby."

"Did you see him?" she asked. "You never told me that."

He nodded, unable now to hide the tears that streamed down his cheeks. "They let me look at him just after he was born. He was...like a little flower, Ruth. He looked a lot like you. He was the prettiest thing I've ever seen. I always wanted to tell you, but we..."

Tyler's voice broke. He turned away, his shoulders heaving.

"Oh, darling," Ruth whispered, putting her arms around him. "Tyler, darling, I never knew."

"I can't stop thinking about him, Ruth. Every day I think about him. I imagine going into his room to pick him up in the morning, and how he'd look, and..."

"I know, sweetheart," Ruth murmured, holding him while he cried. "I do the same thing. Every day."

"Will it ever stop hurting?" he asked. "Will it always feel like this? I can't stand it anymore, Ruth. First we lost the baby, and now I feel like I'm losing you. I don't know how I can bear it."

"You're not losing me, Tyler." She drew away to look up at him. "I'm not going anywhere."

"Do you still love me, Ruth?"

"Oh, yes," she whispered. "I love you more than anything in the world. I'm so sorry for the way I've been acting these past few months."

"Ruthie..."

"I thought I was the only one who was hurting," Ruth said, looking down at the little headstone. "I didn't think about your pain because you never let it show. I've been so cruel to you, darling."

Tyler pulled her close to him again, crushing her in his arms. "Lord, it's good to hear you say this," he said. "It's so good to hear that you love me after all. I've been terrified, Ruth. And these past couple of months, I was so lonesome I almost went crazy. In fact I did some real crazy things, and I'm so sorry."

"Well, there's no reason for you to apologize. You don't have to be afraid or alone anymore, either. Things are going to be different from now on, Tyler."

In her rush of emotion, Ruth had almost forgotten the news she had to tell him. Now she drew away and looked past his shoulder at the glowing clouds, feeling breathless and weak with happiness.

"Tyler . . ." she began.

At the same moment he met her eyes with a look of panic. "Ruthie, I forgot to ask you what Nate said! Are you all right, honey? Is he worried about you?"

"Well, he's sort of worried," Ruth began solemnly, gazing down at her feet so Tyler wouldn't see the smile that tugged at her mouth. "He says it's a pretty serious condition."

"What!" Tyler asked, sounding terrified. He reached out and took her shoulders, pulling her around to face him. "Ruth, what is it? What did Nate say?"

"He figures it's all your fault," Ruth said, giving him a sober glance. "My condition is entirely your fault, Tyler. Nate said you'd better be prepared to take some responsibility for it."

Tyler watched her in growing confusion. "*My* fault? Ruthie, I'm sorry if I..."

"Wait till you hear what you did," she said, smiling through her tears. "I'm *pregnant*, Tyler. That's the only thing the matter with me. I have morning sickness!"

His jaw dropped, and a slow flush crept over his face. "But how...you can't be," he muttered. "We haven't even..."

"That's what I told Nate. He didn't believe it for a minute."

"But it's true! How can you possibly be pregnant when we haven't slept together for months?"

Ruth smiled up at him, waiting. After a moment his eyes widened with shock.

"That one time?" he breathed. "The time I was mostly asleep?"

"Nate says that at least part of you must have been wide-awake."

"God, Ruthie..." Tyler stared at her, a look of incredulous joy beginning to dawn on his face. "That was...what? Early January?"

"About six weeks ago. I'm six weeks pregnant, Nate says. That's just about the right time for morning sickness to hit."

"He's not worried about the sickness?" Tyler asked with sudden concern. "You didn't feel this bad the last time, did you, honey?"

"Not like this. But Nate says it's a healthy sign, nothing to worry about. Besides," Ruth added, "now that I know what's causing it, the nausea doesn't bother me so much anymore. It just sort of comes and goes, and in between I feel wonderful."

"Oh, *Ruth*..." Tyler took her in his arms and held her close, so gripped with emotion that Ruth could feel his whole body trembling. She tightened her arms around him, cradling him tenderly.

"Sweetheart," she murmured.

"Hmm?"

"Nate says there's nothing at all to worry about, dear. He says there's no reason this baby won't be perfectly healthy in every way. He wants you... both of us... to know that we shouldn't go around being afraid history might repeat itself."

"I can hardly believe it," Tyler said huskily, his lips moving against her hair. "I mean, the way a man's life can change completely in half an hour. I'm the happiest guy in the world right now, Ruthie. I feel as rich as a king. Lord," he added, "it's so good to hold you like this again!"

"Let's make each other a promise," she told him solemnly. "No matter what happens from now on, let's promise we'll never, ever stop holding each other and talking to each other. It's the only way to get through life, Tyler. I can't manage without you."

He grinned down at her, beginning to look joyous, full of his old buoyant confidence, and years younger than he'd seemed lately.

"You're so handsome," Ruth murmured, feeling weak with love and a warm rush of yearning. "Let's go home and go back to bed for a while. After all," she added primly, "I'm sick, right? I really should be in bed, and you should be there looking after me."

Tyler hugged her delightedly, laughing aloud. Then he sobered and turned to look down at the small grave. "Maybe we can come here together next month," he said hesitantly, "and plant some flowers, if that's all right with you, honey? I'd like to see some flowers growing here in the spring."

"I would, too," Ruth whispered with a catch in her throat. "I'd really love that, Tyler."

"Ruthie . . . do you think he knows?"

Ruth understood at once. "Yes, I think he does," she said gently. "I think he'll always know, and be glad whenever we're happy."

Tyler nodded, satisfied. He stood a moment longer by the little headstone with its gentle sleeping lamb. Then he turned, put his arm around his wife and walked slowly out of the churchyard and into the sunlight.